JOANNA GODDEN MARRIED

AND OTHER STORIES

JOANNA GODDEN MARRIED *and Other Stories by* Sheila Kaye-Smith

Short Story Index Reprint Series

 BOOKS FOR LIBRARIES PRESS
FREEPORT, NEW YORK

INTERNATIONAL STANDARD BOOK NUMBER:
0-8369-3949-2

LIBRARY OF CONGRESS CATALOG CARD NUMBER:
77-163035

PRINTED IN THE UNITED STATES OF AMERICA

78611

Contents

JOANNA GODDEN MARRIED

Joanna Godden Married

AT THE end of a June day a woman sat at the window of a house in West Street, Chichester. Beneath her the traffic of the Portsmouth Road flowed like a river—cars and carts and bicycles, and the various members of two conflicting tribes of country omnibuses, all jumbled in an apparent meaninglessness, and raked over with the dusty gold of the sunset.

Joanna Godden looked down on them without seeing them—their dazzle meant no more to her eyes than their racket to her ears. Both had grown accustomed now. Her thoughts were busy, though they had not wandered farther away than the two letters that lay on her lap. Suddenly she looked back into the blind-shaded room and called very loudly:

"Martha!"

[3]

There was an inarticulate response from a distant part of the house. The minutes went by and, as nothing more definite followed, Joanna went to the door and flung it open.

"Martha," she shouted. "Where are you? Come here."

"I'm coming all in good time."

Footsteps creaked on the stairs, and a moment later Martha Relph came in, vested in her cooking apron as a hint of a short visit.

"I'm sorry if you're busy," said Joanna, "but I'm unaccountable dull and sick of myself all alone. I'd have come down to you, but I wanted to show you this letter, and you've got your boy in the kitchen."

"Reckon I have—and where else should he be, poor lad, at the end of a long day's work?"

"I'm not finding fault—though heaven knows that boy . . . however, I won't say it. But it only shows me it's time I was up and off."

"Now, you shouldn't ought to speak like that. You know you're welcome here."

"Keeping your custom away just when it's starting holiday time and you might have your house full."

"Come to that, I'd sooner have your money regular than other people's now and again."

"But I can't stay here forever—I'd die of the gapes in a town, with nothing going on and nothing to do; and if I stay much longer I'll lose you your season. No, Martha Relph, you've been a real good friend to me, as I'll always remember, but things have begun to show me that it's time I started by myself again. Besides, I've heard from That Woman."

"Her at Sidlesham?"

"Yes, it's her letter I want to show you. She seems unaccountable anxious to get rid of the place—a bit too anxious for my thinking."

"Reckon a lone widow woman don't want to be bothered with a farm. It ain't everyone who's like yourself."

"Well, read what she says."

She handed Martha one of the letters, written

[5]

on flimsy paper in a hand both formal and straggling.

CROWN DIPS,
NEAR SIDLESHAM.

DEAR MADAM,

I received your welcome letter quite safe, and am writing to say that I am seeking to dispose of my farm, "Crown Dips," being left a widow by my dear husband who departed this life seven weeks ago and used to manage same. There is twenty acres, all grass, and a hundred head of fowl, Sussex and Orpingtons. Also three cows, one being in calf, two pigs, also sheds, coops, tools, etc., as well as one nicely built barn besides the house which is double-fronted and commodious, four bedrooms, three sitting rooms with kitchen etc. Everything in excellent repair and going well. I can show you the returns and think it would be a good thing, madam, if you could come over and see it all, which is very easily reached from Chichester. Kindly let me hear when to expect you at your earliest possible convenience.

Yours truly,

SARAH WICKEN.

"Well, what do you think of it?" asked Joanna.

"I dunno. I dunno what to think."

"It sounds worth looking at. That would be the best thing—to go over and see it."

"Maybe."

"You don't seem to like it."

"Well, you know, I've always said you shouldn't ought to settle in these parts—you should go to the shires."

"And I've always said I never will. I was born and bred in Sussex, and in Sussex I'll die, or in Kent at farthest. I'll never go venturing into foreign parts at my time of life. I'd die if I was to go and live in the shires."

"Seemingly you'd die in a good many places —first it's in a town, then it's in the shires. You'd much better get away from these parts, where folks' tongues are bound to start wagging soon. I've managed to keep 'em quiet so far, but I don't mind telling you it's been all my doing, and directly you get off by yourself I don't trust you not to spoil my work and make yourself the gossip of the county."

"Well, you'd never expect me to tell lies."

"I'd never expect you to do nothing so sensible—that's why I want you to stay with me, or to go where folks don't know you!"

"They don't know me on Manhood Marsh."

"Pooh—it's only the opposite end to Romney. They'll soon find out all about you."

"They won't. You know quite well, Martha, that East Sussex don't have any dealings with West Sussex, and so it's always been. I own it ud have been foolish of me to have gone into Kent, leastways into the Kentish Marsh and the parts near by, but over here I'm as cut off as if I was in the shires—all the Downs between me and the eastern marsh, and a day's journey in four different trains to cross 'em. After all, no one's started any talk about you."

"That's true, but then I came here with my legal husband, and no one was to know how close the marriage was to the birth. Besides, who was to bother about poor little Martha Tilden, who got herself into trouble when she had a place as chicken girl on Ansdore Farm? It's another matter when it comes to the mis-

tress of Great and Little Ansdore, Miss Joanna
Godden, who's been the talk of the three
marshes for a dunnamany years. Reckon when
you put up Ansdore for sale and flitted they
nearly broke their jaws at the Woolpack. You
yourself told me as Vine of Birdskitchen was
took to his Maker owing to an apoplexy he got
in the bar."

"The Woolpack ain't such a famous place
that we need trouble ourselves in these parts
over what it says." . . .

At that moment a shout came up from the
basement, a shout of manly outrage and disgust.

"Hi! mother! Are you going to keep me
waiting all night for my supper? Reckon you
two never stop jawing when you get together."

Joanna's lips tightened, and the already high
color in her cheeks took a richer dye, as Martha
turned obediently towards the door.

"It's a crime the way you let that boy of yours
order you about. I'd never stand it a single
minute if it was me."

Martha turned on the threshold.

"I'm not sure as you won't have to."

"What do you mean?"

"Well, it's all along of me being a poor widow this ten year. You can't bring up a son without a father."

II

JOANNA first looked angry, then meditative. She rose with big arms lifted for stretching, and the letters in her lap slid to the floor.

"A-a-ah," she sighed, then stooped to pick them up.

She had settled about Mrs. Wicken: she would write at once and fix the day after tomorrow for her visit. Ellen's letter had not been dealt with yet. Not that it required any dealing beyond being torn up . . . but she would read it again first.

The sunset was gone from the room, which had taken on dim bluish colors in the twilight. The light of an early street lamp was like some big yellow fruit among the purple shadows of the street. Joanna leaned her head against the window-frame as she read Ellen's letter.

13, Torrance Square,
S. W. 7

My Dear Joanna,

I should have answered your letter before but
I've been abroad, and it didn't reach me till I came
back only a few days ago. I'm very glad to hear
that your son was born safely and that you've made
a good recovery, but I'm afraid I can't go back on
what I said when I last saw you. If I was to be
godmother it might create an awkward situation for
both of us later on. No doubt you will think me
hard-hearted and unnatural, but I have my husband
to consider, and you must remember that you deliberately chose to put me out of your life. My decision has nothing to do with the morals of the case,
but merely with its social and practical side. If you
yourself had considered this, I should not have had
to do so. I'm very sorry, and I shall never forget
all I owe you, but you must remember that I also
owe a great deal to Tip, and where there is any
conflict between your interests and his, I'm afraid
you don't stand a chance.

Yours in regret,

Ellen Ernley.

"I don't believe her—I don't believe he's
like that. It's all an excuse for her own. . . .
Oh, my little Ellen!"

Crushing the letter in her hand, she hid her face for a moment in the unsympathetic folds of the Nottingham-lace curtain. Oh, how it wounded still, this ancient love! How cruel it was that this her oldest, homeliest tenderness must be sacrificed to others that had come later and more devastatingly. The latest love was only just born, and yet before it all loves must be offered up. Ellen—Ellen—her own sister, whom she had loved from childhood, brought up and cared for as her child—Ellen, who had been first—the first of all—long before this little Martin to whom she must be sacrificed— before the little clerk who was Martin's father, though not Joanna's husband, even before that other Martin, both dear and dim in memory, who was mystically the father of all the love and sorrow in her life. . . . Ellen was an older love than any of these, and yet they had in their sequence driven her out of Joanna's world, leaving her sister groping and crying after her.

For some months after the crash she had been uncertain as to which fragment of her shattered earth called most terribly to her heart. Sometimes she felt it was her farm—the greatness of Great and Little Ansdore, three hundred acres of Sussex marsh that she had loved and served so many years—now broken and sold, transformed by a black alchemy of shame into a bank-roll which was "filthy lucre" indeed. At other times her heaviest burden was the loss of her fair and gallant name upon the marsh. . . . The day she had left Ansdore her ears had burned as she thought of the tongues that would wag that evening in the Woolpack and in every public house from Dymchurch to Rye; and since then there had been nothing but humiliation—her refuge with Martha Relph, whom fifteen years ago she had turned away for what was now her own guilt, the lies she had been forced to tell to maintain that refuge, and to maintain the respectability which Martha had won by tardy marriage through Joanna's grace . . . it had all been terrible, sometimes it had seemed to her as if that was what had hurt most of all.

At other times the pain had been not for herself but for the silent helpless victim of her life's wreck. When her child was born would she be able to save it from its share of her dishonor? Would she not probably fail, even in spite of the deceits that she practiced in such disgust? And then, the child's father . . . had she no regrets for him? No times when she wept in longing and bitterness for that three months' passion? She had never faltered in her determination not to see him again—the one letter that she had received from him after the break she had firmly torn up unread; but she could not help thinking of him and crying over him in that pity which was the ghost of love, hoping she had not hurt him badly by her going, sometimes reproaching herself for the way she had dealt with him, not in the end, but in the beginning. Oh, she had behaved badly to poor Bertie Hill—she had pursued him, snatched him, caught him because she had forgotten the good ways in which she had been brought up, and the man she loved long ago.

All these thoughts had been her penance during the months she had stayed hidden with Martha Relph in Chichester, while she waited for her child. But they had not been constant —they had taken turns with one another, as it were, to torment her, and they had alternated with moments of mad hope and soft joy, when she thought of her baby—her baby not as shame or as stumbling block or embarrassment, but simply as her darling. In those moments the past lost its reproach. Bertie Hill was merely her child's father, an impersonal force of nature to which she owed her joy, and Martin was re-established in her memory's shrine, as the child's mystical father but for whom she would never have loved Bert and, therefore, never have had her present expectation.

But there was a wound which never ceased aching, a regret which alternated with no hope, but merely throbbed at the back of all her happier thoughts. It was the wound of her love for Ellen—the little sister for whom she had slaved and sacrificed, for whom she had lied as

she could never lie for herself in the days when
Ellen had defied morality and the Ten Commandments and the good opinion of Romney
Marsh. It was all owing to Joanna and her
battles on her behalf that she had been able to
come back to Ansdore and re-establish herself
in local reputation and finally marry a man who
was a gentleman both by birth and deed. And
when Joanna's own trouble had come, and she
had turned to Ellen for help as Ellen had
turned to her, Ellen had not stood by her. She
had reproached her, bargained with her. She
had said, "Either you marry the father of the
child that's coming or you never see me again."
She had been angry because Joanna had refused
to spoil her own and the baby's life by marrying
a man who did not love her and whom she did
not love. She had spoken of decency and respectability as if she herself had not once flouted
them and as if they were not much dearer to
Joanna than to herself, and renounced only at
the cost of her life's tranquillity.

Her love gathered anger as she thought of

Ellen thus, and a sob broke from her into the
silence of the room. She had hoped that Ellen
would have relented at the birth of the child,
that she would have been placated by her sister's request to stand godmother—a great honor
in Joanna's eyes. But it was no good—Ellen
would not forgive her. She was angry with
her, not because she had done wrong, but because she had been found out and had refused
to take what Ellen considered the only decent
course to hide her shame. Little Martin's
birth would, according to Ellen's ideas, only
make things worse instead of better.

Joanna's ideas were not the same as Ellen's.
She turned from the window to a second door,
leading into the bedroom. Here all was darkness, for the baby had been put to sleep and
the curtains drawn more than an hour ago. She
groped her way to the cot at the foot of her
bed. She could not see the child, and did not
touch him for fear of his waking, but she was
aware of a fluttering breath and a dim sweetness
of powdered skin.

"Never mind, my duckie," she whispered, "never mind, my precious lamb. She says she won't be your godmother, but we'll get Martha, who's more of a Christian woman anyway— goes to church and says her prayers, which Ellen don't, I reckon. The only reason she was angry with me was that you were coming, poor sweet. She didn't deny as she had done the same as me, but 'I never landed myself with a child,' says she, as if that was all the sin there was in it. And wanting me to marry Bert when—but I won't speak ill of your father before you."

III

THE farmstead of Crown Dips was in the parish of Sidlesham only according to the letter of parish law. For all practical purposes it belonged to the less adequate village of East Wittering, one of the half-dozen strung like beads on the string of the unfrequented road that loops round from Birdham to Sidlesham Common. Reeded acres of sheep-dotted, roadless marsh separated it from Sidlesham station on the toy railway that runs down the Manhood Peninsular to Manhood's End.

Between the cluster of red and black farm buildings and the sand dunes of the shore lay only a paddock of buttercups and coarse grass, and three reeded pools, or dips, from which the farm took its name. It looked both gay and lonely on the afternoon that Joanna Godden and Martha Relph came tramping with dusty, aching feet from Sidlesham station. The little red house, with its white-rimmed windows like staring eyes, and the flutter of cloud-flecked sunshine blowing over it, seemed almost to dance a greeting and at the same time to proclaim that it knew no neighbor but the sea.

"It won't never do for you here," said Martha.

"Why not?" asked Joanna briskly, snuffing up the marsh air like a war-horse.

"There ain't another place within miles."

"Well, I'm used to that. I like it."

"You won't like it with no one but yourself about. It was another thing at Ansdore when you had all your farm people round you; but here—"

"I'll have a maid and man, which ull be quite enough. I tell you I don't like living all crowded up with folk. I'd die if I had to live any longer in a place like Chichester—'I beg your pardon' all the way along the pavement, and more like a hen than a human being when you cross the road."

"Well, wait till you see what this place is like inside," said Martha, pushing open the drive gate.

The two women were in striking contrast as they walked up to the house together—Joanna tall and striding beside Martha's dumpling figure, Joanna's warmly colored face and eager blue eye above Martha's pale full moon and brooding gaze. In one point only were they alike, and that was the color of their dress. Both were dressed in black, Martha in ten-year-old compliment to the deceased Thomas Relph, Joanna in obedience to some undefined but compelling instinct, to some inward urgency linked with the words "I will go softly all my years, in the bitterness of my soul." Not that there was much of "going softly" about her black, indeed it had more swagger than many a woman's colors. Black to her mind was mourning, and mourning was plumes, whether on hearse or head. Therefore, on Joanna's head nodded two fine black plumes, which, with her swaying jet earrings and swinging jet necklace, produced an effect of flaunt and aggression rather than of atonement.

Mrs. Wicken, who opened the house door, eyed the effect severely. She also was in black —new black, cheap black, in contrast to Martha's, which was old, and Joanna's, which was costly. The three women were like three crows on the doorstep of the farm.

"Good morning, ma'am—Good morning, ma'am—Good morning, ma'am."

They eyed one another suspiciously—Mrs. Wicken wondered which was Mrs. Godden, and how much she would give for Crown Dips, Joanna wondered how much Mrs. Wicken would ask, and in what relation it would stand to the farm's real value, and Martha wondered to what extent Joanna would make a fool of herself over the place, which in her eyes was nothing but a hole and unworthy of human habitation.

One piece of folly she determined to prevent.

"This is Mrs. Godden," she said hastily, before Joanna could blunder with a "Miss." "I've just come along with her to see the place, having some knowledge of these things."

Joanna opened her mouth loudly to deny the latter part of the statement, but a ferocious nudge from Martha reminded her of the effect such a denial would have on the enemy, and she gulped angrily instead.

"Well, you'd better come and look at it now," said Mrs. Wicken, "unless you'd like a cup of tea first."

"Thank you, ma'am. I think we'd better start at once."

"Then will you kindly step this way."

"After you, ma'am."

"Oh, no, after you."

"You'd better go first, ma'am, since you know the place."

Thus, with much outward politeness and inward distrust the inspection started. Mrs. Wicken showed first a neat house, rather over-symmetrical in its placing of doors and stairs, but spacious, and solidly built, with two good sitting rooms and an ample kitchen, four bedrooms above, and a couple of attics. Joanna's ambitious eye noticed that there was many an opening for "improvements." She could make a good little place of this, with a veranda thrown out beyond the drawing-room, and perhaps a couple more rooms built on. She could never live in a place without scope for development, and now all her future was in the house. It was part of the change that had come that she thought of the farm only as part of the house. She did not want to develop the farm—to tear fresh acres out of the green wideness of the Marsh and fling them under her plow. She had done all that at Ansdore—done it all, and smashed it all. She could not do it again. With what had come to her from the sale of Ansdore she would re-establish herself, not as a farmer, but as a housewife, mistress of many rooms and much furniture. If she tore anything from the Marsh it would be a green lawn or a flower garden.

Her thoughts ran ahead of her eyes throughout the expedition. She did not see Crown Dips

IV

O N THE journey home she leaned back in the little train, her eyes closed in a comfort which was entirely spiritual. She was spiritually at ease, though her body ached with her dusty tramping and the unrestful seat of the train. Her spirit was at rest because she had found again a country that she knew—a country of grass and watercourse, of winding hard white roads, of buttercups and hawthorn hedges, of nibbling cows and sheep, all bounded by. the sea. Even the miniature railway, jolting along its ridiculous track, had its double on that other marsh which flowed over the borders of Sussex and Kent into the spit of Dungeness, just as this melted together the borders of Sus-sex and Hampshire at the base of Manhood's End.

She would be happy here; there would be no

strangeness for her either of street or hedgerow, no hills or undulations to make an unaccustomed view. For Joanna the dear had always been the familiar—old faces, old places. The first she could not hope to see again, but the second she could restore. Manhood might be smaller and saltier than Romney, but it would be what she had always known—the Marsh, in its flatness and greenness and mildness, its seagirt pasturage, a land alien from the rest of Sussex, apart from weald and down. It was the Marsh that she wanted; she would be happier on a marsh in the shires—supposing that the shires grew anything so gracious—than on some wealden hill twenty miles from where she was born.

Her contentment was so great that she had only good humor for Martha's scolding. They were alone in their carriage, and Martha scolded hard all the way to Chichester.

"Reckon you must be mad, Miss Godden, to do a thing like this. That farm ain't worth more than fifteen hundred—she would have

asked eighteen and been thankful to get sixteen
—and you go and offer two thousand without
even troubling to find out what she'll take."

"The farm's worth more'n two thousand to
me."

"I don't see that. You'll have to spend another five hundred before it's fit to live in."

"Well, I can run to that. I did well out of
Ansdore, and the best way to spend the money
seems to build another Ansdore for myself and
the boy."

"That place ull never be Ansdore. Why,
there's only twenty acres, and you'll never get
more—she said that herself."

"She doesn't know. Besides I don't want
more. I don't want land. I'm too old to start
all that over again. I want just enough land
to pay for improvements to the house. I'm
going to have a fine house, Martha—bathroom,
hot and cold water, same as I had at Ansdore,
a nice paddock and flower garden, and a parlormaid a lot better than Mene Tekel ever
was."

"What I can't understand is why you couldn't buy a place that was better to start with. For the money you're paying you could get a house with them things already there."

"But I don't want them already there. I want to put them there. I want to make the place grow. Besides, I'd have got nothing like that on the Marsh—the agents said so. They said there was nothing to be had on Manhood, and if I'd never lit on that woman's advertisement, I might be settling now in some tedious place inland."

"Well, you'd be a lot better inland—I told you you'd best go to the shires."

"Oh, have done do, Martha, with your shires. What you don't understand is that I'd sooner pay two thousand pounds for a thing I want than sixteen hundred for a thing I don't."

"But you could have got the thing you wanted for sixteen hundred. That's where I'm blaming you. It's only your vanity that makes you throw your money about. Your idea was to scare that Mrs. Wicken and make her tell all

the neighbors what a rich and fine and magnificent woman you are."

Joanna smiled. What Martha had said was
quite pleasantly true. She had offered more
money than she felt Mrs. Wicken would ask,
and certainly more than the farm was worth in
its present state, because she wanted to enter
the neighborhood with a flourish. At the price
of a few hundred pounds she had left Mrs.
Wicken gaping at her lavishness, and in course
of time would arrive to find the neighbors gaping too. Best of all, she herself felt once more
rich and fine and magnificent, such as she had
never felt since love had stripped her of Ansdore and sentenced her to a soft and bitter
going that she had forgotten in this glorious
hour.

V

JOANNA'S preparations for her removal took longer than Mrs. Wicken's. The latter had only to pack her trunk and order a van to take her sticks, and jolt away one still morning when the sun was driving the fog off the sea, cheerful in the hope of certain comfort for her husband's loss, since it meant her return from the exile into which he had taken her. Joanna, on the other hand, had to buy new furniture, because in a recklessness that she now regretted she had sold everything at Ansdore. She sought to reproduce as far as possible the Ansdore style of comfort—the horsehair, the mahogany, strangely mixed with the black and olive fabrics that Ellen had introduced during the last years.

Horsehair proved unprocurable, so far had the furniture trade deteriorated in the sixty

years that had gone by since Thomas Godden
bought his to set up housekeeping. Joanna had
to fall back on tapestry, studded and strewn with
the black cushions Ellen had loved. But her
dining-room suite was mahogany, and her bed-
steads were brass, and her windows were white
with the scrawliest patterns of Nottingham lace,
wherein lace roses were as the ghosts of the
red and blue and brown roses that rioted on
her carpets.

To Martha's disgust she had also papered
and painted all the walls—as a part of her in-
coming flourish, since only about half the rooms
needed redecoration. But Joanna felt depressed
by Mrs. Wicken's blue-gray stripes, and bunches
of blue sweet peas tied with mauve and gray
ribbons. She had never cared for blues and
grays, and felt she could not settle among them.
So instead she had more roses, red and yellow
and brown and golden; the house became a
bower of roses, paper roses, lace roses, carpet
roses, and tapestry roses—the riot of Joanna's
barbaric loves, unsatisfied in her life, unac-

[34]

knowledged in her heart, projected instead
upon the walls, the floor, the furniture of her
house.

Outside the house she did not do so much—
there was less opportunity for splendor, and she
had lost heart for the merely utilitarian. Her
chief improvement and only extravagance was
to enlarge the cowhouse for the stabling of four
more cows. She must have half a dozen, at
least, she said, if she was to do any good. She
did not fancy chickens as a means of livelihood,
being discouraged by experience rather than
enticed by adventurous arithmetic. But milk
was always profitable if you could get a private
round and ignore the middleman. This she
proposed to do, and in time her dairy business
would grow—she saw herself supplying hotels
in Portsmouth and Southampton at last.

She had sold Ansdore at a good price, to one
or two buyers, since no single adventurer would
undertake what she had undertaken singly for
so long. A part of the land beside the Brodnyx
road had gone in building lots, and the two

well-built houses of Great and Little Ansdore, with the manorial rights of one and the wide lands of the other had brought her enough money to face a more difficult future than any before her now. She could afford to buy Crown Dips at a price that would make her famous, to set it in order both within and without, and still have enough to settle and support the uncertain years.

So during the last days of June the Selsey Bill railway took Joanna many times to and fro between Chichester and Sidlesham. She was harassed by the needs of young Martin—his meal times were disorganized by such travel, and she was constitutionally unable to trust anyone else with his precious care. The same constitution forbade her to trust anyone with the care of Crown Dips—the builders and decorators would scamp and dawdle without supervision, and Mrs. Wicken's man, who had charge of the stock during the interregnum, would be sure to steal the milk and let the fowls die. Therefore, since she herself had made the house uninhabitable, she took a room for herself and Martin at the Falcon Inn—a little brick box of a pub on the Wittering road, staring with hard, bright windows out to sea, and offering a doubtful glass of ale to shepherds and wagoners and straying holiday-makers.

Joanna was not at all comfortable at the Falcon Inn, nor was the inn at all comfortable with Joanna, but her stay enabled her to combine the care of her two most precious treasures, Martin and Crown Dips, and hurry the latter into habitable grace. It also enabled her to make the acquaintance of Mr. and Mrs. Root.

The Roots were a middle-aged couple who lived in a small cottage near the inn, and worked on Owledge, the farm between the Falcon and Crown Dips. Root was carter, and Mrs. Root was chicken woman, but she had also some knowledge of dairy work. Though not yet old, the fact that they had lived all their lives in the district, in the remoteness of Manhood's End, had put them among the old people rather than among the young folk who wore bowler

hats and silk stockings and traveled adventur-
ously into Chichester on Saturday nights for the
Pictures. Mr. and Mrs. Root had always lived
within five miles of where they lived now, they
had never been on the Selsey Bill railway, preferring on the rare occasions when they went
into Chichester to travel by carrier's cart. They
had never been to the Pictures, in which they
dimly discerned the hand of Satan, whose constant interference with local affairs they believed
in as firmly as they believed in the Bible. They
spoke the old Sussex speech, broad and slurry
and full of strange old words, and uncorrupted
of the "bloodies" and "not halfs" of modern
education. They picked and distilled herbs for
food and medicine—they made dandelion and
nettle tea, and cowslip wine, and simples and
balsams with purslane and mugwort and suc-
cory.

Joanna esteemed them for no separate one of
these things, but the total quality was eminently
dear to her. Mr. and Mrs. Root stood to her
for the old days and the old ways, for homeli-

ness and memory—they were in the long line
of servants that she had employed both indoors
and out at Ansdore. Moreover, they provided
a very stimulating foil to her modernity, her
go-ahead methods, and brave experiment.

Most of all, her inquiries and observation
showed her that Root was as excellent in his
work with the cows as his wife in her work
with the chickens. They were the instinctive
workers of the old school, toiling in a sort of
communion with the beasts they tended. They
were the ideal couple for the outdoor work of
Crown Dips, and before she had known them
a week Joanna was coveting Mr. and Mrs. Root
as desperately as Ahab coveted Naboth's vine-
yard, or King David the wife of Uriah the Hit-
tite.

Her maneuvers to acquire them, though
scarcely more scrupulous, were less catastrophic.
They consisted chiefly in offering Mr. and Mrs.
Root half as much again as Mr. Boorman of
Owledge paid them. It is true that they would
have to walk a considerable way to their work,

but that was a common hardship, and amply atoned for by the promise of breakfast and supper in the day's gift of meals. No strong ties bound them to Owledge, which had lately changed hands and ways, and they had all their type's strong love of money as distinct from what money brings.

So when Joanna made her parting with the Falcon and moved into Crown Dips she sweepingly dismissed Mrs. Wicken's boy, and installed Mr. and Mrs. Root in the care of her farmyard. Indoors, she kept a girl, to cook and scrub and help her with the baby. Her parlormaid was still some years ahead.

VI

THE neighborhood was inclined to be curious about the new owner of Crown Dips.
As a rule when a farm changed hands the in-
comer was already known by repute, having
come from a spot within twenty miles at farthest. There was but little movement in the
settled population of the Manhood Peninsular
—it was as if the stream of visitors flowing to
and from Selsey Bill drew off all the energy
of the district, leaving the local life stagnant.
There was but little buying and selling of land,
except in building plots to Bungalow Town, and
the farms, great and small, dwelt in unchanging
stillness, rotting like red fallen apples in the
green freshness of the marsh.

Crown Dips had been built sixty years ago,
by the father of the late owner, therefore it
was still talked of as new, and its shifting for-

tunes considered no more than was to be expected in such a place. Nevertheless, it was a surprise to find that the new owner was a woman, who had appeared suddenly out of nowhere, and had no kith or kin on Manhood, nor, apparently, west of the Downs.

No one could discover anything of her past except that she was a widow and had lived for the last six months in Chichester. Her husband had been killed in a railway accident—on a threshing machine—out hunting—had been drowned at sea—had fallen down dead in his own kitchen—had died in his bed of pneumonia—cancer—consumption—kidney disease. Joanna herself gave no help to conjecture. She was rather gruff in the face of inquiry, as was only seemly after so recent a sorrow.

She did not think it right to invent any story about herself, though Martha had often urged her to do so. To call herself Mrs. Godden and wear a broad gold ring on her wedding finger belonged to a different order of deceit. It was not so much a lying statement of respectability as a refusal to issue an open challenge of disrepute. Besides, in Joanna's world, "Mrs." was often a purely honorary title, the reward of established spinsterhood. She told herself that anyhow she would have been "Mrs. Godden" in due course; she was merely anticipating her title—though anticipating it in circumstances that destroyed her right, as her heart was not slow to tell her when she let it speak.

Martha had wanted her to call herself "Mrs. Hill," as if she had been Bertie's wife in name as well as in fact—it was not so very difficult to imagine. To Martha it was more in accord with things-as-they-were, and also gave a better disguise. But Joanna would have none of it; her mind worked differently from Martha's, and she saw her chosen course as the less ignoble. As for safety, there was many a Godden in Sussex, Kent, and Hampshire; it was a good old country name, widespread now like all the best. It would give her a better shelter than any foreign Hill. Besides, suppose Bertie were ever to come into the district, and find her using the name she had so scornfully rejected—the mere thought of such a contingency made her scarlet with shame, and it did not seem unlikely to her fear.

Besides, she would be less prone to muddle things if she kept the name she was used to. With a new one, her tongue might trip and give her away. Apart from Martha's warnings, Joanna knew that she was likely to give herself away, and for the boy's sake she avoided occasions of self-betrayal. She adopted an almost cloistral life—the red and brown and golden roses blushed unseen, and the Nottingham lace lay like a veil between her and the rest of the world.

This again was all that it should be, and the neighborhood felt disposed to approval. It is true that Mrs. Godden had quarreled with the Falcon and stolen Mr. and Mrs. Root from Owledge. But the Falcon was not held in any great local repute, and Owledge had lately passed into the hands of a new owner—not a stranger it is true, since he came from Appledram, setting up for himself on marriage, but nevertheless subversive of the ways of Owledge and giving Mr. and Mrs. Root a lawful reason for complaint and removal, apart from the briberies of Crown Dips.

These briberies and the price she had paid for the farm, improved by gossip's multiplication table, added greatly to Joanna's credit, and gave her the reputation of being a rich woman. Her husband had owned a fine place over by Horsham—he had made a lot of money out of live stock, and left his widow rolling, as you might say. She was only running the farm as a hobby—she had done up the house so as it took your breath away, and was living in it like a lady.

Joanna heard the echoes of these rumors, and they made it sometimes difficult for her to maintain her seclusion. She would have liked to see local feet—the feet of Mrs. Boorman of Owledge and Mrs. Gill of Solegate and Mrs. Gain of King's Court—treading her roses. It was real pain to her that her silver teapot, saved from the wreck of Ansdore, should never be the central sun of an admiring female system. She felt like a lonely queen in the midst of her splendor.

But she would not relent towards herself. If she grew friendly with the neighbors she would either have to involve herself in more falsehood or else give herself away—possibly she might do both. Also there was a queer moral complication. It was right that folk should be impressed by her wealth and skill and enterprise, for she was wealthy and skillful and enterprising, but that they should take pleasure in her society involved a lie, because, according to her code, she had forfeited her social claim. If all these people, the Mrs. Gills and Mrs. Boormans and Mrs. Gains of the district, knew her story, they would no longer seek her out, but regard her with contempt and indignation and, since they must not know her story, they must not enjoy her company under false pretenses. Joanna was hard on herself, as she had been hard on others.

VII

THAT winter was the dreariest she had
known. The winter before had been
more catastrophic, more remote from experience, as she had sat and watched it go by from
her window in Chichester—going by in flurries
of rainy wind that passed down West Street, in
cold gleams of sunlight on the Cathedral tower,
in the smell of moist earth in the Canons' gardens, in the queer many-colored jostle of a town
at Christmastide, and the first drawing out of
the days in a gaslit dusk. But it had never
wearied her—it had been so like a procession
passing by, a procession of hours and days and
weeks going gallantly forward to the hope of
the spring. She herself had seemed to lead winter onward, going before it in expectation. . . .

But now, winter was no path to spring, no
procession, nothing that moved, but a weight

upon the land, a heavy cloud that shut her into her empty house. There could be no developments on the farm till warmer, lighter weather. All she and her servants had to do out of doors was to keep things going as they were, and that was an easy job for the three of them. There was far too much time left to spend indoors, by the fire, thinking and remembering, while the wind howled over the marsh and through the bending reeds of the dips, and the sea, unaccustomedly near, bellowed and pounded at the sandbanks, uttering hoarse threats to Crown Dips, shouting "What if I came nearer? . . ."

The roughness of the weather—climate made the chief difference between Manhood and Romney—combined with the difficulties of railway fares and the inconvenient hours of winter trains, kept Martha Relph away in the sheltered town. Joanna, who had hoped for her company, felt neglected. She did not find in her son either the occupation or the companionship that other women's remarks and her own thoughts had taught her to expect. It is true that a good deal of her time was spent in washing, dressing, and feeding him, and that every day she could watch some fresh marvel of growth; but curiously enough, he seemed to intensify her sense of loneliness.

On the whole, she felt, she had loved him more before he was born. Then he had been a cherished mystery, a part of herself so intimate and dear that it had never occurred to her to want another human being to share her love. Before his birth she and her child had been one, a single unity. Now they were separate, a pair. But this was wrong. The number of love is not two but three, a trinity—father, mother, son. Her love was incomplete because a part of it was lacking—the father's part. Oh, deary me, what am I to do without a father for little Martin?—To work for him and watch him grow—I was never meant to do it alone.

This was a new discovery for Joanna. Hitherto she had imagined that when her child came life would be complete. But now it seemed even further from completeness than when she had been single. More than ever during those days of quest and yearning, she wanted a man, a husband, a keeper of her household, a father to her child. And now she knew that she could never have him. According to her code no decent man would look at her. It would not be right—she herself would disapprove if he were lax enough to want her in spite of all. But no one would want her—if ever anyone did she would have to tell him everything, and then he would go away. Better not meet anyone—better live alone as she was living—she would grow used to it in time.

She found a certain companionship in Mrs. Root. The man himself was too inarticulate even for Joanna; he plodded on at his work without speech and, it would seem, almost without thought, toiling not of plan and care but of inherited instinct. Mrs. Root, however, had moments of conversation, in which she told Joanna about neighbors past and present—how they were going to start sheep next year at Slivericks and were engaging a shepherd from the Downs (as if he'd know anything about it); how Solegate Farm had been given Mrs. Gill as a wedding present by some earlier lover, whose name nobody knew, her having met him when she was in service at Brighton; how Mrs. Ades was expecting her eighth child in May; how they were getting a new couple in at the Falcon, as the brewers were shocked at the way Mr. and Mrs. White had run the place. And did Mrs. Godden know, but a murder had once been committed there? Not in the days of any-one living, but a young man hanged for it all the same.

Joanna found that Mrs. Root was nervous of going out after dark and would never walk home without her husband, for fear of "ghosteses."

"You don't mean to tell me this place is haunted!"

"Not the house, ma'am, nor yet the pläace. But you sometimes meet Them on the road. 'Tis ghosteses out of the sea."

"Drowned folk?"

"No, ma'am—folks that used to live under the sea, or sooner, I shud say, that lived a dunnamany years ago in a forest where the sea is now."

Joanna caught her breath in a pang of memory.

"In the place where I used to live," she said, "there was a whole town under the sea. Someone once told me about it, a town of fifty taverns, he said, and twelve churches—all drowned when the floods came, way back in old times. You can see the marks of the waters in New— in one of the churches—leastways of the mud the waters brought. Was it a flood that drowned the forest here?"

"Reckon it was—an unaccountable gurt flood, that came upon them when they was all eating and drinking and giving in marriage. You can read about it in the Bible."

"Oh, no, Mrs. Root,—surelye. The Bible ain't about people like us. That was Noah's flood."

"Maybe you're right, ma'am, but I always

understood as it wur ourn. There wur a king drowned in it—while he was out hunting—and sometimes still you hear his horn."

"And at—at home you hear the bells—the bells of the churches under the sea. . . ."

In that moment Manhood and Romney flowed together in the waters of a common doom. The whole of memory was as a land drowned under cool green water.

VIII

WHEN spring came the child ailed. He had always been a comfortable baby, calm even in his teething, but at the coming of the spring winds he grew peevish, tossed and whined, refused his food, and made Crown Dips stormy o' nights. Joanna was not used to children, and her inexperience fed her alarm. She thought Martin must be terribly ill, that he would die; she sent for Martha, she sent for the doctor who had attended her in Chichester, recklessly paying his town fee in preference to the more modest one of the local practitioner, whose skill she doubted. Both the doctor and Martha agreed that there was not much wrong with young Martin, who was merely cutting his double teeth, but there was a great deal wrong with Joanna, who was worn out by her frets and her bad nights, and had, moreover, been revisited by the rheumatism which had first mocked her age three years ago on the other marsh. The doctor told her she ought to take a holiday—go inland to some dry, bracing, cheerful place, and if possible leave the baby behind her.

"That's good sensible advice," said Martha, "and you should ought to take it."

"What! Leave a chicken farm in the spring? I don't call that sense."

"If you go at once, you can get back before the real work starts, and reckon Mr. and Mrs. Root can manage till then. As for Martin, if you go now I can come here and stay with him, seeing as my rooms aren't let till Easter. Georgie can manage by himself for a week, and a week ud be all you'd want to set you up again."

"It ull cost a lot of money, which I can't spare till I know how we're going to do this spring."

"You won't do nothing this spring unless you go and get a bit of change first. You've gone

and moped and worried yourself ill, down here
alone by yourself all the winter, and if you
ain't careful the rheumatiz ull get you fast, seeing as you're Marsh bred."

In the end a compromise was effected, a
rather expensive compromise, since it involved
taking both Martha and the baby with her to
lodgings in East Grinstead.

"There's no use talking. I'd fret myself silly
if I left him behind, even though I left him
with you—and I'd be lonelier than ever I was
at Crown Dips."

"But you should ought to go to a hotel—
you wouldn't be lonely there. You'd see life."

Joanna shook her head. Hotels were outside
her existence as she viewed it now, as a thing
austere and apart from her fellow men. Staying at a hotel had been the beginning of sorrows—she would never forget that it had been
because of her going to stay for a fortnight at
the Palace Hotel, Marlingate, that she had first
met Bertie Hill. Similar traps for those who
forgot the good ways of the Marsh—according

to which no woman stayed alone except in lodging-house seclusion—might lie at the Dorset Arms, East Grinstead, or the Beacon Hotel, Crowborough. So she renounced the temptations of their comfort and social altitude, much as she would have enjoyed boasting of these even to no other audience than Mr. and Mrs. Root. Martha knew of quiet lodgings in Brambletye Road and, as she would take charge of young Martin, Joanna could get her sleep at nights and some freedom during the day, and at the same time feel that her most precious treasure was under her eye.

She had never been successfully idle, and by the end of the week was eager for her return to Crown Dips, apart from her conviction that the Roots in her absence had destroyed it entirely. But she was substantially better for the dry bracing air of the Sussex highlands, and for a week's good sleep. Little Martin was better too—Martha's less emotional methods suited him admirably. His yells did not wake her the first night, so he did not trouble to utter them the second. He and Martha understood each other.

On the day of her departure, feeling cheerful and invigorated, chiefly by the thought of going home, Joanna walked up to the Dorset Arms to order a cab to take them to the station. An open touring car was just pulling away from the hotel and, looking into it, she found herself looking straight into the eyes of her sister Ellen.

For a moment both women stared powerlessly at each other—then the man who sat beside Ellen called to the chauffeur to stop.

"Why, Joanna!" he cried, "here's a surprise. Who'd have thought to meet you here!"

It was Tip Ernley, Ellen's husband, a bit shy and startled, but with all a man's desire to regularize an irregular situation.

Ellen had by this time recovered, and rose to the occasion in her turn.

"How are you, Jo? I thought you were at Chichester."

"I've been staying here for a week with

[58]

Baby, seeing as we'd both got run down with the winter on the marsh."

"Which Marsh? You haven't gone back to—?"

No madness of Joanna's seemed improbable to Ellen.

"Oh, no—not Walland Marsh. I'm on Manhood, over by Sidlesham. I've got a little farm there."

Joanna was the most flurried of the three. She stared at Ellen sitting there like a queen in her fur coat, and for the first time doubted the perfection of her own coat and black-plumed hat. Though Joanna infinitely preferred her own way of dressing to Ellen's, her sister's clothes never failed to make her feel either shabby or outlandish.

"We're on our way to Brighton for the week-end," said Ellen with unexpected graciousness.

"Is that your car?"

"Yes—do you like it?"

"It's fine. I'll be getting one of my own before long, I reckon."

"I hope you will," said Ellen, while her smile added "but I doubt it."

For another moment the sisters stared at each other without words. Joanna felt the color mounting on her cheeks. It was just like Ellen to sit there talking of nothing that mattered, instead of having things out. Joanna had always set great store on "having things out," such circumstances as spectators and occasion counting for little.

Ellen saw the color rise and deepen, and as she gazed found herself quivering with a sudden undesired response. That flushed face under a towering black hat . . . it seemed to link her up with a past she had thrust away, with her own childhood on the Marsh, with a little girl who had hidden her face in a big motherly breast, who had coaxed and kissed and quarrelled with a kind big sister. . . .

The situation once more required regularizing.

"You haven't told us where you're living,

[60]

Joanna," said Tip Ernley. "What's the name of your farm?"

"Crown Dips, near Sidlesham."

Ellen had recovered herself.

"How's the baby?" she asked. "He must be quite big."

"Reckon he's getting big." Then "things" had to come "out"—Joanna could not help it if the whole town was looking on.

"Ellen . . . Ellen . . . won't you come and see him?"

For a moment Ellen hesitated, then she said quite gently:

"I can't come now, but I will some day."

"You will . . . you promise?"

"Yes—some day. Good-by, Jo."

The car drove on. Tip had felt that it might properly do so now. Both he and Ellen turned and waved to Joanna, who stood motionless— like a monument to Good Will Frustrated by Good Manners.

IX

LITTLE more than three months later England went to war.

The matter came as a surprise to the people at Crown Dips, and indeed to most of their neighbors. Cause and effect were difficult to trace—somebody had murdered a foreigner in Servia. Why not? Murder was the common lot of foreigners, since rumor said that there were no policemen in foreign parts. Joanna had no love for foreign parts, though long years ago she had dreamed of a Parisian honeymoon. It was just what you might expect of foreign parts, to conspire so formidably to wreck the peaceful process of day-by-day.

"Surely we're not going to war about a lot of blacks," said Mrs. Root.

"Belgiums ain't blacks," corrected Joanna's enlightenment.

"Those I saw was," persisted Mrs. Root.

"Where did you ever see any?"

"In the sea—" with which remark she cryptically closed the conversation.

But on the whole Manhood approved of England's decision. War was a good thing for agriculture, sent up prices, and gave landowners a chance, which the Lord knew they needed. Besides, it would be all over in a month or two, and good fun while it lasted.

There was some private dismay when one or two local lads marched with the Territorials, and still more when some others who were not Territorials went to enlist at Chichester. Those in the district who remembered war remembered it only in South Africa, an affair of distant drums. They at first imagined that the new war would be like the old one, would come no nearer to them than the newspapers, and take no more of their youth than a few adventurers, or of their money than a tax easily payable out of agricultural fullness.

As the drear days of the autumn closed in

over a sea unlighted by the watchful eyes of the
land, as the disaster of Mons forced its way
through suppression by channels of rumor and
report, and the turning-point of the Marne
proved no decisive victory and conclusion of
the whole matter, the spirit of the country
changed, and the change penetrated even to
Manhood's End, where there had been no flags
or national anthems or Belgian wounded—even
there the change was as of a shout dying down
into a sigh.

Joanna felt it all remotely. She had never
been much of a reader of newspapers—a glance
at the headlines in the Sussex *Gazette* had suf-
ficed. Now for the Sussex paper was substi-
tuted the *Times*. It cost more, but she felt convinced that it knew everything. She could
scarcely believe that any Censor dared check its
utterances; any suppressions must be due to a
mighty submission of its will in the interests of
safety. No one else in the immediate neighborhood took in so august a journal, preferring a
penn'orth of pictures to two penn'orth of solemn

words, wonderful and incomprehensible as spells. Joanna felt appreciably nearer the heart of the Empire's struggle than any Gills or Boormans, and the feeling gave her a secret pride.

But something was to make her feel even nearer than reading the *Times*. Hitherto she had had no personal link with the War—except when in a moment of sudden dismay at its continuance over the scheduled two months, she had wondered whether it might not now go on for twenty years, eventually to involve Martin in its carnage. But during the autumn Ellen wrote to say that her husband had succeeded in getting a commission in the East Kents, and would be over in France very soon. When he was gone might she come down and see Joanna? She had heard that there was a very decent hotel at Selsey Bill.

Between the rather indifferent lines Joanna read, or at least imagined, the anguish of her sister's soul. Ellen loved Tip Ernley. It was because she loved him so much that she had

[65]

been cruel to Joanna. Love makes you cruel sometimes—Joanna knew that. Her love for Ellen was no longer cruel, no longer fierce with outrage. She wrote and begged her sister to come to Crown Dips, to make it her home while her husband was away—"To be just as we used to be, duckie, you and I."

But Ellen remembered what "just as we used to be" was like, and wisely avoided its renewal. No, she would rather go to the hotel—her comings and goings might be erratic—she would be better on her own. "But thank you very much, Jo, all the same."

So the estrangement of two years was to be over, and the most dreadful wound of Joanna's life was to be healed, in the midst of a wounded world.

X

ELLEN came down to Manhood's End in
the first days of the new spring. Tip's
going had been delayed until then. But now
he was gone, lost behind the dark curtain of the
smoke. It almost seemed as if Ellen's eyes
were following him there, so sad and far-off
was their gaze. Joanna was smitten when first
she saw her sister, and realized what she had
always known but had sometimes forgotten, that
Ellen's life had held nearly as much sorrow as
her own.

Of course Ellen had "done well for herself"
as they say. She had married unhappily, she
had disgraced herself with an elderly lover, but
she had somehow managed to thrust both events
back firmly into a quiescent past, and now she
was married to a kind and congenial husband,
well-to-do and a gentleman. She had a beauti-

ful London house and all the money she wanted for the clothes she loved. On the other hand, Joanna's past was not quiescent, it seemed to have traveled with her through life, gathering power and menace as it went. It was with her now in the concentrated shape of little Martin, whose ancestry was not merely the Bertie Hill of two years ago, but the Martin Trevor of fifteen years' remembrance.

Nevertheless, Ellen must have gone through her moments of overwhelming pain. She was going through such a moment now, and it was as well that her big sister was at hand to comfort and support her. Not that Ellen encouraged comfort or support. She seemed wonderfully able to support herself as she came into the lounge at the Selsey Bill Hotel where Joanna was waiting for her. Her dress and her demeanor started their usual challenge to Joanna's. It was disconcerting, that shout of utter quietness which Ellen's clothes seemed to give. Joanna did not possess an evening frock, vaguely connecting such raiment with hotels and moral downfall, but she had been pleased with her stiff black taffetas gown till Ellen's violet cloud proclaimed it a coarse and garish covering. There was the usual interval of incoherent and resentful embarrassment on Joanna's part and self-possession on Ellen's, then the two sisters linked arms and walked into the dining room.

They were reconciled. But not a word of reconciliation had been spoken. Ellen had seen to that. Their first meeting after the estrangement had been public by fortunate accident, their second was public of design. The almost empty dining room, in which every whispered word was common property, struck awe even into Joanna. They parted without any embarrassing confidences, regrets, or explanations. On the other hand, the first awkwardness of meeting soon was gone, and they fell into comfortable chat. They talked about Tip Ernley, about little Martin, about Martha Relph, about

[69]

old times at Ansdore without any chill sense of
estrangement over these things. Once or twice
Joanna had opened her mouth to utter forbidden words, but Ellen, more skillful now than
of old, was always able to silence them.

Her victory was so complete that when, the
next afternoon, she came over to tea at Crown
Dips, the position remained unchanged. Perhaps Joanna had been chastised into a new dis-
cretion—anyhow, her first attempts having
failed, she no longer sought to overthrow the
hard-won amenities. She made no further
effort to "have things out." She showed Ellen
the farm, the house, and the baby, feeling very
pleasantly proud of all three. Then they settled down to their good tea.

Joanna had sold all her household gods, feeling that she had desecrated their shrine, so there
was nothing in the room to remind them of
Ansdore. The roses were, of course, all part of
the Ansdore tradition, but Joanna's litter of
treasures—her mother's "ornaments," her

father's "Buffalo Certificate," all the framed colored supplements from Pears and the *Illustrated London News*, were gone, and as yet there was little to take their place. More sentimental memories than Ellen's might have regretted their absence, but Ellen could only feel glad that the riot she had always deplored was over, and yet that there was enough of the old Jo left in the carpet and wallpaper for her to feel herself at home.

They talked mostly of Tip and his adventures in France. He wrote home cheerfully to Ellen, but of course he could not tell her much. It was plain that she loved him dearly, and in her love was the self-sacrificing courage which is always a part of truth, whether in knowledge or love. Joanna could not analyze it, but she was conscious of this growth in Ellen—an inward growth, which might be hedged by hardness from the outer world, even from her sister, but which nevertheless was strong and ever more and more sweet towards her husband.

"Jo," said Ellen suddenly, "I hope you'll get married."

Joanna flushed. To answer directly would be to step on forbidden ground, and she was as anxious as Ellen now that this should not be trodden on.

"I don't know as I want to. Besides——"

"Besides what?"

"Well, there isn't anybody."

"Oh, I'm not meaning at once, but in time. You're the sort of woman who can always marry if she makes up her mind to it."

"I'll never do that. I'd sooner stay as I am."

"I'm not saying you're not very comfortable, but you must often feel it lonely here."

"I've got my child."

"A child's not much without a man."

Joanna grew angry because Ellen had echoed her thoughts.

"You've no right to say that, Ellen Godden . . . Ellen Alce . . . Ellen Ernley"—the whole past flew like a film before her as she fumbled over Ellen's names. "I've missed my man, but I'm no worse off than you who've missed your child."

To her surprise Ellen did not take up her challenge.

"You're quite right—I'm no better off than you, at least not much. I don't really know which is worse, to have a husband and no child or a child and no husband."

"Then you'd like to have a child, Ellen? I remember as how with Arthur Alce . . ."

But Ellen cut short her remembrances.

"It's different now. It's different with a man you love. I didn't love Arthur and ought never to have married him. But I love Tip, so I wish there was a child. But there won't be. That's certain now. So you're right, Joanna— I'm no better off than you."

Her mildness, accompanied by the revocation of what Joanna had considered the wickedness of earlier days, melted her sister's wrath. Joanna too revoked.

"I don't know about that, Ellen. I don't

[73]

know as I wouldn't sooner have a husband without a child than a child without a husband."

They debated the matter amiably for some time, coming to the conclusion that the first was best, since a husband was always more or less himself one's child.

XI

O N THE whole Joanna, like most women, enjoyed the War. As it went on through the months she enjoyed it better. The new experience of having an interest outside the round of one's daily life was too pleasing and vital not to be clung to. She had now grown used to the *Times,* and could understand much that had once mystified her in its language and point of view. She was able to talk about the War not only to Mrs. Root, but to the Vicar when he called, and to Tip Ernley on the one occasion that Ellen brought him down to Manhood's End.

Ellen brought him only once. Joanna could see that she did not mean the reconciliation to be more than formal where he was concerned. She had never quarrelled with Tip as she had quarrelled with Ellen, he had merely been kept away from the doubts and embarrassments of her acquaintance. Now he was still to be kept away. His life was not to be complicated by the misfortunes of Joanna's. But Ellen and Joanna were sisters again—nothing could alter that; they belonged to each other once more, and nothing else mattered. Not that Joanna saw much of Ellen during these times, for Ellen was busy in London, doing War Work. She went through a course of training and became a voluntary nurse in a big hospital. She sent Joanna a photograph of herself, looking almost nunlike in a white veil, with a red cross on her breast.

Joanna did not do War Work. She was too busy with her household and her farm. But she gave to her country ten of the twenty acres she had meant to reclaim from the Marsh for her own delight and ornament. She had meant to convert the land nearest the house into an orchard and flower garden, as part of the scheme of developing Crown Dips as a country house rather than as a farm. But now she foresaw a new need, greater than her own. Before the Ministry of Agriculture had begun its arguments with rural prejudice, Joanna had refilled herself with the glamour of an earlier exploit and put ten acres of grassland under the plow.

It was true that this plow was a hireling, and the ground when sown did not yield with the rich fruitfulness of the eastern marsh. But the excitement roused by her deed was much the same as that roused by the same deed at Ansdore. "Them as breaks grass shall themselves be broke"—thus at her inspiration Furnese of Misleham had created a new proverb in the bar of the old Woolpack, and much the same was soon being said in the bar of the Falcon on the Wittering Road, in the bar of the Lion, Sidlesham, and the Crown, Bosham, and the Queen's Head, Appledram.

She did not give the neighborhood the lie quite so triumphantly as before, nevertheless, she gave it and some sixty quarters of grain to her country's need. She came to be looked upon with wonder as well as curiosity—the marsh talked of her prowess, and of other things connected with her which she would not have been so pleased to hear discussed. Hitherto it had accepted her as a well-to-do, stand-offish neighbor, who wanted to amuse herself with farming in a small way. The last thing it had expected was to find her competent and, now that she had proved herself so, it was perhaps inclined to view her less favorably than when it had considered her the usual ineffectual sort of lone woman. But whether or not it approved, it was impressed—and Joanna knew that it was impressed, and tasted triumphantly of sweets she had long forgotten. When those in high ministerial places passed from the cajolery of the English farmer to his discipline, then was Joanna's head exalted above her neighbors. It was pointed out that where she had succeeded, others at least ought to attempt. She had, in fact, discredited the local Providence hitherto supposed to be set in judgment on those who force the earth.

She had forced the earth, and the earth had

yielded. She knew that in spite of herself she had become a farmer once again. Her ambition lost its merely household quality, and became agricultural. She would forego all thought of "grounds" outside the house and a parlormaid within; instead she would buy more land since things were going well and the war was good for farmers. She would break up another ten acres and at the same time increase her pasture for more cows . . . she'd give the Falcon and the others something to talk about. . . . The War had brought a dead Joanna to life again.

XII

BY THE summer of 1917 Crown Dips was a farm of fifty acres, half dairy, half grain, Mr. and Mrs. Root were reinforced by a plowman—Tom Addis, a bad-tempered and obstinate old fellow, but all that could be obtained in such times of dearth. The dearth of butter, milk, and eggs was more satisfactory to the farmer than the dearth of able-bodied men. Joanna's milk-round could have been twice its size, and people came all the way from Chichester to beg personally for her butter, until she found that it was not worth her while to make it. She herself and Mrs. Root had charge of the fowls and dairy, Root—finally relinquished to her after sundry tussles with sundry tribunals—being required to help Addis with the beasts.

Joanna worked from six o'clock in the morn-

ing till eleven o'clock at night, toiling as she had
never toiled in personal sweat and backache.
She never left the farm, except when its interests took her to Chichester. She had no time to
be lonely or weary, no time to have rheumatism,
no time even to hear the wind as it wailed down
the Marsh. All her life was work, driven by an
urge which was partly agricultural ambition,
partly the first growth of her class's love of
money, and partly mere energy, inspired by the
great unrest around her and the great need.

In the house her joyous roses faded. The
one girl—who was never added to, but occasionally replaced by an inferior specimen, as the
call of the munition factories was heard on
Manhood's marsh—had no time to keep the
dust off the carpets nor the blinds drawn against
the grin of the sun. The house, which Joanna
had planned to be so marvellous, began to look
neglected and shabby. It was being sacrificed
to the more importunate farm.

There was another part of her life which was
being sacrificed in those days, and that was little

Martin. Sometimes she lamented it, sometimes she resented it, but she could not deny it. He was not neglected—his washing, feeding, and other cares were all a normal part of her day —but she had no time to play with him, no time to discipline him, and the little boy needed both play and punishment. He was four years old now, and trotted with her round the farm, putting his hand with hers into the nests, standing beside her while she milked—a new experience even for Joanna—holding a little besom and pretending to help her clear out the sties, for she now kept over a dozen pigs.

There was no harm in all that, indeed it was good that he should get to know the farm so early, and have as toys the animals which in twenty years would be to him mere pounds, shillings, and pence. Joanna encouraged him to hold the little April chickens and scratch the backs of the young pigs. "Mumma will give you a puppy dog," she said a few days before Jennie the spaniel-retriever was due to have her litter. In that way all was good, but there were

other aspects that were more disquieting.
Sometimes Joanna said to herself, "He's growing like his father." He was not a bad little
boy, but he had a strong will and a fierce temper, and she owned that she could not manage
him. She told herself that she could have managed him if she had had time; but she had not
time, and there was nothing to be done about
it.

She had not much time to think about it
either, but when she did think she was disturbed.
There was so much against poor little Martin.
First of all there was his father—Joanna believed implicitly in heredity, and expected to
find Bertie Hill's rather pathetic selfishness in
his child as a matter of course. She also believed in prenatal impressions, and sometimes
grieved to think that the whole time he had
been "coming" she had been at issue with the
world, all conflicts and alarms. Besides, Martin was very nearly a war-baby—only a few
months of his life had been lived out of the
sound of the great guns at Portsmouth, thun-

[83]

dering in the west, shaking the doors and windows of Crown Dips, shaking the very air. . . .
It was only natural that the child should be
restless and excitable. But it was bad. If she
thought about it much she would get like what
she had been in her first winter on the Marsh,
frantic and miserable. Just as well she had no
time to think. . . .

XIII

EARLY in July the Sidlesham Flower Show
took place. It had been in abeyance for
two years, but now it was considered expedient
to revive it for the encouragement of local
effort. Just as the farmers were being driven
to break up their grass for grain, the cottagers
were being urged into growing vegetables in
their flower gardens. The Roots' front door
was buried in a jungle of giant rhubarb, cauli-
flower run to seed, peas bearing one pod to
every coiling yard of stalk, and other fruits of
good will. They had sown their seed, but had
been unable to do more in the pressure of their
day, and now Mrs. Root privately considered
the results inferior to the rows of many-colored
asters, clumps of phlox, and bee-humming sun-
flowers that had preceded what she called her
War Vegetables.

Certain efforts had been made to turn the Show into a carnival. There would be fancy dress, and prizes, a band, and dancing after tea. Joanna was inclined to regard all this as degradation—on Romney Marsh people didn't have to be invited to make exhibitions of themselves before they would do the same for their fruit and vegetables. But of course she would go to the function—she had one or two exhibits in the poultry class, and besides must give her countenance to all agricultural effort. She decided to bring the boy. It would be a change for him and the first real treat he had ever had.

This was Joanna's first public appearance since leaving Ansdore. For five years she had stood resolutely by her rule to go softly, and not to enlarge the scope of her lying by seeking many acquaintances or social occasions. But this revival of Sidlesham Flower and Vegetable Show in the interests of her country definitely seemed to require her presence. She must come forward, since without her all would be flattish. Crown Dips was far from being the largest

farm in the district, but it was in many ways the
most important, and had a pioneer glamour
about its new-sown wheat. Joanna Godden in
her black was a towering figure among the
tents, an intended rebuke of fancy dress, and
a lure to the eye of the gallant colonel who
rather incoherently opened the Show.

When he had finished talking about "doing
our bit" and "backing up the boys," Joanna es-
corted him round the stalls. In reality they
were accompanied by the Committee, but somehow that collection of war-rejected males was
lost in the glow of the one woman. The colonel
noticed that Joanna's clothes were odd—rather
startling even if they were black, and a bit old-
fashioned too—but he also noticed that her eye
was bright and her cheek was warm and her
step was full of life. He began to wonder who
she was and how old she was, and why was she
in mourning? A widow, he supposed—maybe
a war widow. He'd like to know something
about her—what was she doing on a farm in

this one-horse place? Did she ever come to Brighton?

When they had been the round of the tents and stalls they came back to where little Martin waited in the charge of Martha Relph and Mrs. Root.

"Mumma!" shouted Martin.

"Hullo, my duckie."

"I wan'er dress up, I wan'er dress up as an ash-heap."

"He's just seen little George Sell, ma'am," said Mrs. Root, "all done up as an ash-heap, wud a pail over his head and bits of muck hung around him. You never saw the like. He'll be first prize, I reckon."

"He should ought to be spanked. I never heard of such things."

"I wan'er dress up as an ash-heap."

"Ha! Ha!" laughed the colonel—"that's a fine idea he's got."

"It's a shocking idea. I can't think how people can do such things. No, you've got your new suit on, dearie, the nice new suit that Mar-

tha made you. You look unaccountable smart.
You be satisfied with that."

"I wan'er dress up as an ash-heap"—and
Martin took a flying kick at the black folds of
Joanna's skirt.

"Now, now, young man!" said the colonel
severely.

Martin quailed at once, and the incident ab-
ruptly ended. Joanna, who had prepared for
a long battle, looked surprised.

"He's a bit of a handful, that little chap of
yours," said the soldier.

"Yes, a bit . . . sometimes. Not always."

"A boy's sometimes too much for his mother.
I expect my two are running pretty wild now
I'm away. Ever come over to Brighton?"

The question startled her, and she looked
into the man's eyes. In them she saw his honest, rather inquisitive admiration. Her color
mounted. She suddenly felt angry and, seiz-
ing Martin by the hand, pulled him away.

"No, never—and if you'll excuse me, I must
go and look at my fowls."

The Committee came to life around him, told him that nobody knew Mrs. Godden very well—she was stand-offish and went her own way. No, her husband had not been killed in the War—no one knew anything about him— he had died before Mrs. Godden came to the Marsh . . . and some queer things were being said.

Meanwhile Joanna went into the enclosure where the poultry and dairy produce were on view. She herself had several exhibits in this class, and had only expected that her brood of chickens and her brood of ducklings, as well as her milk and her butter, should take prizes. To keep him quiet, Martin was allowed to play with the little ducks. There were ten of them in a basket, yellow, fluffy, funny things, their faces full of intelligence and good-humor. Martin loved them and fed them delicately with little bits of corn.

Relieved to have him quietly occupied, Joanna went about her business, then when the shadows of the tents were lengthening upon the grass, and the thought of dancing was invading less well-ordered minds, she turned peacefully to the idea of going home.

"Time to go home, darling. Baby must have his tea."

"I don' wan'er go home. I want my tea here."

"Better have it at home, duckie. It's such a squash in that tent, and no nice milk for you. Come on, and we'll all have tea with Martha."

Martin was fond of Martha and his countenance lifted. Then Joanna spoke the words that opened hell.

"Say good-by to the little ducks."

"They're coming home with us."

"Not to-day, darling, they're sold."

Martin clutched the handle of the basket which stood at the edge of the stall.

"I won't go home without my ducks."

"They never were your ducks—they were mother's, and now she's sold them. They belong to Mr. Gain."

[91]

"They don't. They belong to me. I want my ducks."

Joanna grew heated. Their voices had by now attracted a small ring of spectators.

"Be a good boy, Martin," said Martha, "and go home. You'll have plenty more ducks to play with there."

"I won't. I won't. I won't. I stay here for ever and ever. I want my ducks."

"How dare you be so naughty!" cried Joanna. "Come along at once."

She seized him by the arm, and his anger blazed at her. One vigorous tug and the basket of life was on the ground, one vigorous stamp and at least one life was death.

"No one shall have my ducks, I'll—"

Joanna was nearly sick. She snatched Martin up bodily in her arms and held him there, kicking and screaming, while Martha and Mrs. Root picked up the basket, to discover that one other duckling was dead besides the one Martin had stamped on.

"For shame—shame," murmured the crowd.

[92]

"What a naughty little boy—so cruel—and prize ducklings too."

"I don' care! I don' care!" screamed Martin.

He kicked and struggled so that Joanna was forced to put him down. She noticed that his face was no longer red, but white. Nevertheless, he went on shrieking:

"I don' care."

"Then you should ought to care. Look at the poor little things."

A hand was extended on which the two little bodies lay limply. Martin still shrieked:

"I don' care. I don' care. They don' mind. They've gone to heaven."

"Oh, hush!" cried Joanna, horrified that her offspring should add blasphemy to his misdeeds.

She was nearly weeping herself. She was overwhelmed with shame, and a shame which was not only for Martin, but for herself and her powerlessness to cope with him. The spectators were predominately female—they whispered and nudged and clucked—four male years were able to hold them at bay.

Then suddenly old Tom Addis the plowman came pushing his way through the little crowd. He did not speak, merely picked up the yelling Martin and carried him off under his arm.

"I don' care. They've gone to heaven. They've gone to heaven," shrieked Martin.

But old Addis took no notice of him at all. He merely walked off with him homewards at his usual stolid gait, while the three women followed, trotting helplessly.

XIV

WHEN they came to Crown Dips Addis
delivered young Martin to his mother.

"You're a bad, naughty boy, Martin. You
shan't have any tea to-night."

"He should ought to have a good spanking,"
said Martha, "and what queers me is why you
don't give it to him, mum."

Joanna shook her head.

"Why, when I remember you and Miss
Ellen," continued Martha—"and Fuller, your
looker, that you sacked before all the world in
Romney Market—"

"Hold your tongue, you fool," cried Joanna.

She felt humiliated by her own want of spirit.
How was it that she who had dealt so drasti-
cally with her sister and her shepherd had no
power to deal with her son?

"I don' care! I don' care!" shrieked Martin. "They're in heaven. They're with the Lord."

"You'll end up somewhere else, you young devil," said Martha grimly. "You're getting ruined, you are. It's all true, what I told you, mum. You can't bring up a boy without a man."

Between them they managed to undress him and put him to bed. His own struggles exhausted him in time and his screams died into whimpering.

"There, you naughty boy," finished Martha, "there you are and there you stay. It's less than you deserve after what you've done."

"They've gone to heaven," wept Martin—"they're around-the-throne."

His wailings had all latterly been concerned with the ducklings' eternal state. Joanna's first feelings of horror at a heaven which included animals had been purged by the sudden realization that Martin was saying all this not to vindicate but to comfort himself. She had begun to see his rage not only as a thing which hurt her but as a thing which hurt him. He was trying to comfort himself as grown-up people try to comfort themselves—by imagining the poor corpses revived in glory. She became convinced of this when, as she and Martha went downstairs they heard him singing in a voice choked by tears:

"Around the throne of God a band
   Of glor'ius angels ever stand—
   Bright things they see, sweet harps they hold,
   And on their heads are crowns of gold."

"He's sorry," she said to Martha.

"Imphs," said Martha.

Joanna went wearily through her evening's work; in spite of her prize winning she felt overpowered by a sense of failure and pity. It was all being brought home to her again—the necessity of Man. Man was made for woman's suffering—that was of experience—but he was also made for woman's need, and for her need in those circumstances in which one would think she stood most triumphantly alone. Mother and child—surely that was enough. No, it was not—without a man. Ellen had spoken truly when she said that you did better with a man and no child than you did with a child and no man. Perhaps if she'd had a girl . . . but she hadn't, and poor little Martin was suffering for want of a father. Perhaps after all it would have been better if she'd married Bertie. . . . Oh, no! no!

She went up to bed with her heart full of pity for the child who had made her so angry. Poor little fellow—he was his own victim—and her victim too. She had been unable to mother him as she ought because she had been busy with the man's business of working for him. She had been weak with him, too, because to be strong for her meant effort—temper—tears . . . so different from the strength of that old soldier at the Show, who with a sharp word or two had brought him to obedience, or from the strength of Tom Addis, who had just used muscle and silence. . . . Yes, it was

through his mother that he was suffering now—
and would suffer again.

She leaned over the little bed beside her big
one, her heart swollen with pity and anger—
the pity for him, the anger for herself. Poor
little fellow! What a life lay before him if
she could not save him from his own passions.
He lay on his side, his face flushed and the
tears still wet. She suddenly knew that he
was not asleep, and fiercely gathered him to her.

"Oh, mumma," he mourned against her
breast—"oh, mumma—the poor little ducks."

XV

TOWARDS the end of the night, just as day was beginning to break, a horn sounded in Joanna's dreams, and she woke suddenly, in the midst of a stillness. The stillness seemed to wait, as if for a sound to break it. She leaned upon her elbow and waited too, her body tense with dread, expecting once more the note of that horn under the Sea. Then suddenly the breaking came—as the breaking of the whole world. The room seemed to crash about her, the earth to rise at her through the floor, the sky to rush in through the window. Automatically, her arm shot out over the child's bed, and in the shock she fell forward gasping. Then another stillness came, more dreadful than the first.

It ended less impressively, seeming to fray

out into screams—whimpering screams from
the baby's bed, loud shrieks from the servant
girl's room, and far-off screams on the Marsh.
Joanna straightened herself, gathered the terrified child into her arms, and gazed wildly
round the room, feeling that if she did not look
now to see what had happened, she would not
ever dare to look at all. It was not so bad as
she had feared. The remains of the window-
pane hung in a row of ragged teeth from the
frame, the ornaments and pictures were on the
floor, and broken glass seemed to be everywhere,
but the walls stood firm, contrary to first impressions. The next moment there was a bat-
tering at her locked door.

"Oh, ma'am, let me in! Let me in!"

Joanna had the sense to put on her slippers
before she set her feet on the carpet. Then she
stepped gingerly over the broken glass and
opened the door. Outside stood her servant,
Rosie Pont, in a pink cotton nightdress, clutch-
ing a bundle of mixed possessions, her hair in

[101]

the discipline of curlers, the rest of her abandoned to fear.

"The Germans have come. Oh, ma'am, where shall we go?—whatsoever shall we do?—Oh save me!"

"Keep off the broken glass, you foolish girl. It ain't the Germans—they's never make a noise like that."

She went across to the window and looked out. The dawn was leaden, gray and black, and dullish white, with a steely gleam on the sea and on the water of the dips. Nothing was to be seen, and nobody. It was dreadful, this loneliness of Crown Dips. Here she was, alone with a baby and a girl who was little better than an idiot. Her house felt devastated, and she found herself almost weeping.

Then she caught sight of a man below the window, and her heart beat less wildly. Once again Tom Addis had met her need.

"That you, ma'am?" came the comfort of his steady drawl—"that was a mine went up—off the Bill."

"Anyone hurt?"

"I dunno. There must have bin something hit to make it go off, I reckon. But you can't see nothing now."

A few dark shapes were beginning to assemble on the beach.

Joanna shuddered.

"I'm coming down," she said. "Rosie, you stay here with Martin. He'll be quite good if you don't take on. There ain't no Germans here, and if there was they wouldn't waste any time on *you*."

She soothed and kissed the child, hastily put on a few clothes, and ran down into the growing light.

Nearly a dozen people had assembled on the ridge of sandhills between the dips and the sea. Owledge, the Falcon, and the Roots' cottage had given forth their population to greet the night's adventure.

"I can see spars floating," said Mr. Boorman of Owledge. "Some poor blighters of fishermen must have struck a mine and gone down.   Didn't nobody see it happen?"

Nobody had.

"I wur dreaming as I wur out rabbiting, and just as I wur going to put up my gun I saw old Mus' Pokehill of Weddersham a-putting up hisn—at me.   I throwed myself down on the ground just as it wur a-going off—bang!   And there I was laying in bed wud the house shaking and bits o' glass all over me."

Thus Hickman, their stockman at Owledge, gave his version of the disaster.

"There's my poor boy home on leave before he goes out again," said Mrs. Light of the Falcon—"him that was wounded at Popperingy. And would you believe it, he's under the bed now, screaming and crying like a baby, and saying he'll never come out, or go out—I can't make sure which."

"Look!" shouted Joanna.

The gray light was whitening on the sea, and flat far-away coasts were coming out of western fogs. On the near waters tossed a black object, shaped like a log, or spar, or perhaps an overturned boat, and from it shot up suddenly—again—a human arm.

"Lord! Lord! There's a poor chap in the water."

"Quick! Somebody get a boat."

"There's one at Sharps', before you come to Wittering."

"It ud take an hour to get it."

"Can't anybody swim?"

"Oh, somebody help the poor creature!"

And like an echo a voice came over the water—"Help!"

All, men and women, ran down to the beach. Nobody, apparently, could swim. Mrs. Light said her son could and offered to fetch him from under the bed, but her husband told her not to be a fool. Then Hickman of Owledge rushed in and stood up to his chest in water. He shouted to them words that they could not hear. Then they saw him struggling. He was holding something in his arms, and the next minute

Light ran into the sea, followed by Addis. Everything happened so quickly that Joanna had not time to think before she found herself looking down at a man who lay limp and unconscious at her feet.

XVI

"TAKE him to Crown Dips."

The words came out of her mouth almost before the thought came into her heart. In a sudden vision she saw him warm and tended, dry and comfortable between clean sheets.

"He's dead," said somebody.

"Nonsense! Not he!"

"He's been wounded though! Look! There's blood!"

Once more the ineffective little party was quickened into use by the call of human need. Mrs. Light produced a handkerchief, and Mrs. Boorman remembered some first-aid lectures she had attended at the Women's Institute. A broken arm was bound up not too clumsily, and during the operation the men fetched a hurdle from Joanna's paddock, so that when it was over the sufferer could be gently carried across her land to the refuge of her house.

Mrs. Light and Mrs. Boorman helped her make up the bed in the spare-room, light a fire, and put on the kettle. At the same time Boorman went off to the doctor's at Sidlesham. All the while the patient lay unconscious—only his deep breathing told them of life. He was a middle-aged man, lightly grizzled about the temples, and lavishly tattooed all over his body and arms. His undressing—performed by the matrons, for Joanna still considered herself a spinster and more suitably occupied in making tea—was a revelation of ships and anchors and flowers and love-knots and girls' names.

"You can tell he's a sailor," said Mrs. Light, clucking her tongue.

Joanna was glad to see him comfortable, lying there bronzed and still between her sheets. She hoped that he was not seriously hurt, that he would not pass from one stillness into another. She was also curious for him to wake and tell them about himself and what had happened to him in that terrible dawn at sea.

When the doctor came he was reassuring. The fracture of the arm was quite a simple one, the concussion not serious. He had been struck on the temple by the spar to which he was clinging when Hickman reached him—that and exhaustion only were responsible for his present state. The doctor thought he would soon regain consciousness. Meanwhile Mrs. Godden had done exactly what was best.

Mrs. Light and Mrs. Boorman went home to their breakfasts, and Joanna, feeling suddenly hungry, set about preparing her own. Rosie was now once more a sober handmaid and Martin, though full of questions, had recovered from the night's shock. Of course there would be the house to clear up, the insurance people to visit, new window-panes to put in, and endless trouble, but at the present moment Joanna felt her spirits rising. Adventure and man had come again together into her life, and though she would not have acknowledged that this was the seat of her content, nevertheless, she felt a new buoyancy in her outlook, a new expectation.

While they were having breakfast two coast-guards arrived to inquire into the disaster. A trawler had struck a mine off the Bill, they said, and apparently there were no survivors except the man who had been brought to Mrs. Godden's house. He was not able to speak to them, but she promised to send to the coastguard station as soon as he came to himself. Meanwhile her sense of her importance grew. Neighbors called—on flimsy pretexts or boldly to inquire. She received a telegram from the Shipwrecked Mariners' Association at Portsmouth. For the first time for years her morning was not entirely occupied with cows and poultry. Indeed, she left the latter almost entirely to the Roots, and fussed about the house and her patient, looking in upon him every other minute in hopes that his change had come.

It did not come till the evening when, as she was putting a newly filled hot-water bottle into the bed, he suddenly opened his eyes.

"Hullo," he said weakly.

"Hullo," said Joanna, taken by surprise in spite of her hopes.

"Hullo, ma'am," he repeated.

She felt that the conversation might go on indefinitely like this.

"How are you?" she inquired, coming round to his pillow.

"Oh, I'm fine. Leastways, I've got a bit of a headache . . . and my arm . . . Lord, what's happened? Where was I last night?"

"You were blown up," said Joanna soothingly.

"Blown up. . . ."

He stared at her. Then suddenly the gap in his memory was filled. He tried to sit up in bed, but fell back with a groan which turned unexpectedly into a laugh.

"Good Lord! So I was. Blown sky high— that's it, ma'am. But came down on my feet, seemingly. Where are the other chaps?"

"I dunno. There was nobody picked up but you."

"My God, you don't say they're gone! Old Gunning and the boy, and Phil . . . not anybody saved?"

Joanna feared his distress.

"Don't fret yourself or you'll be ill again. Maybe they've got ashore somewhere else."

"Maybe—I hope to God they did. I remember now . . . no time to launch a boat. She just broke in two. We were all in the sea. Gunning could swim. . . ."

Joanna went out to send Root for the doctor. She feared that the patient was growing excited and would make himself worse. She tried to persuade him not to talk. But his mind was seething with curiosity, anxiety, thankfulness, and disgust. She realized in time that it did him good to talk—that he was better talking than thinking.

"What a bust up! . . . Well, I never! And scarce a mile out, all as quiet as sleep . . . a mine . . . well, I'm damned. We thought we was as safe as houses. I've been on bad jobs— I've been on a mine-sweeper, and got sent up in that. That's why they'd given me a spell ashore. And then I go up again, in my own boat this time. Did you ever!"

He was a Portsmouth man, he told her, and owned a couple of trawlers. His name was Carpenter, he was in the Royal Naval Reserve and had done a lot of secret and dangerous war service in home waters. No, he was not married, but he'd be obliged if she'd send a telegram to his sister, Mrs. Beaton at Seaford, in case the tale got round. Oh, the *Princess* was insured all right . . . but he was miserable about the lads—a mate, he had, and a man and a boy besides. Something would have been heard by now if they'd got ashore anywhere else. . . . And might he take the liberty of asking the name of his kind friend here? . . . Indeed—he was obliged to Mrs. Godden. She'd done him more than a kindness. He could never repay her for what she'd done . . . and the chaps who'd pulled him out—he'd like to see them sometime.

Thus he rambled on until the arrival of the

[113]

doctor, whose only treatment was to send him back into the sleep he had come out of. His mind was working too hard over the broken pieces of the past—the puzzle must not be put together yet.

XVII

HIS recovery, though never in doubt, was a slow one. Owing to his war experiences he was not a robust man, and for a few days pneumonia threatened. Joanna waited on him untiringly. A week ago she would have denied that one single minute more could have been squeezed out of her day, for any purpose whatsoever. But now she found time for continual runnings to and fro, bed-makings and meals— even for times when the patient wanted her to sit and talk to him, or listen while he talked to her.

When she learned that his stay was likely to be a long one she had ordered Mr. and Mrs. Root to come up from their cottage to the house. She considered it unseemly that she should be left alone in attendance on a sick man. But the Roots were merely there to regularize the situa-

tion—nothing more clinical was, perhaps fortunately, required of them. Joanna herself
may not have been a very good nurse; but she
was at least a pleased and pleasant one. At
first he had made some offer to go into a hospital, but she had indignantly rejected it. She
would feel ashamed if he left her, she said.

So he stayed, and in time she grew to know
that she liked his staying. It was not only pity
for his misfortune or the sense of her own importance in the disaster. She liked having him
there to nurse and talk to. He gave her an interest and a society which she could enjoy with
a clear conscience. . . . She would be sorry
when he went.

She had never met anyone quite like him before. The men of her world were the farmer,
the parson, and the squire. Here was somebody altogether different—a seafaring man,
who yet was not quite what she expected a seafaring man to be. He was not a "gentleman,"
but he had ways which she had associated ex-

clusively with gentility until now. For one
thing, he read books.

"Have you got anything that I could read?"
he had asked her one day, just as he was beginning to mend. "I feel like a bit of reading if
you could oblige me."

Joanna brought him the *Times,* a volume of
the *Farmer's Encyclopædia,* and *Little Lucy's
Prayer* as light relief.

He received them politely, but before long
she discovered that they were not the sort of
thing he wanted. He asked her if she had any
of Dickens's novels.

She shook her head.

"Anything by Sir Walter Scott?"

"No. I'm unaccountable sorry, but that's all
the books we have in the house, except Robert-
son's *Sermons* and the *Pilgrim's Progress.*"

"I'd be glad if you'd let me have that one.
I've read it before but I could read it again.
It's a fine book."

"There's some terrible fine pictures in it.
When I was a child I would scarce open it for

fear I should see Satan. I had a lot of books in my old home, but I sold them when I left, all except these few."

Once or twice he had asked her questions about her "old home," but Joanna had frozen into silence, and he had not persevered. On the other hand he told her a great deal about his own past life, where he used to live and the places he had seen.

As he recovered his health his conversation opened a new world to Joanna. He had been a seafaring man all his life, chiefly in the Merchant Service, and had sailed over every ocean before the war called him to service at home. He told her strange tales of the Indies, of Australasia and the cold seas by the Pole, of the grim coast of Tierra del Fuego, where the fires go up from a hundred craters, of little coral islands like rings of ivory in a sapphire sea, of huge pink temples towering over palms, of Buddhas ninety feet high, sitting in eternal contemplation, of lanterns and dragons and gongs in a Chinese city, of devouring jungles in Yucatan where the forest eats the towns. Joanna listened delighted. She always expected the male to be informative, and Jim Carpenter was in the true tradition here. She might be listening to Martin Trevor telling her stories of the drowned marsh. . . . Hitherto foreign parts had meant no more to her than Paris where she was to have gone for her honeymoon, the Riviera to which Ellen had wickedly escapaded, and Africa where Martin's brother was a missionary. Even the recent upheaval of the map of Europe had not brought it much into her notice. To her the combatants were men —brave Englishmen, gallant Frenchmen, dashing Italians, noble Russians, brutal Germans, cowardly Austrians—there were no actual territories involved, nor national characteristics beyond good and evil.

But now she began to catch glimpses of a life beyond her own, whether as lived in her house, her poultry yard, her past, or the pages of the *Times*. She too began to read. He sent for some books on foreign countries that he had in his lodgings at Portsmouth, and she read them with difficulty and delight. Her mind and imagination were beginning to disturb her with the pains of growth—now that she was forty and had put the first part of her life behind her like a tale that was told.

There was no denying that she would miss him when he went. She was determined to keep him till he was completely recovered and able to go to sea again. He had no home of his own, only lodgings, and his sister, who came over to see him once or twice, was, she discovered, the mother of many children in a cramped house. Manhood was near enough to Portsmouth for him to be able to transact without much difficulty the business attending the loss of his ship. He was very well off with her, she told herself, when she sometimes had qualms at her clinging, and was of infinite use to her, with entertainment and advice, and often with the care of little Martin, who would sit for long hours playing on his bed, and, even so, picking up a certain discipline. . . . Ah, the Man in the House.

On one occasion it suddenly struck her that, though he talked to her so much about the foreign places he had been to and the queer people he had seen, he had never told her anything really personal. How was it that he, a man of past fifty, was a bachelor—owned two trawlers and yet had no home? . . . and all those girls' names tattooed upon him. . . .

The sleeve of his sleeping-suit fell back as he took the cup from her hands, and she read "Milly" over a heart. They were on easy terms now, and he sometimes teased her. She tried to do the same to him, but Joanna's tongue had never been light enough to tease.

"Aren't you ever going to tell me about Milly?"

He looked at her with a smile.

"Yes," he said, "the day you tell me about Billy."

"Billy? Billy? What d'you mean?"

"Well, whoever in your life matches my Milly. There must have been someone."

"I—I—I don't want to tell you about myself."

"Very well, then I won't ask you. But you mustn't ask me either. I don't know anything about you, so why should you know anything about me? No questions asked, no questions answered. That's fair."

"I shan't ask you nothing."

Her face was crimson, and she quickly set down the tray because her hands were trembling. He had shown her. He had shattered her content. He had shown her that after all it would be a good thing when he went away.

XVIII

HE WAS well enough to come down to meals, and they were sitting at their supper together when the post arrived. It was the one post of the day; for a harassed government could not be supposed to worry about the needs of Manhood's End. After all, it brought only one letter—addressed to Joanna in a hand she seemed to know.

She turned it over slowly—yes, she knew that hand, but wasn't sure whose it could be. Not Sir Harry Trevor? No—it looked feeble somehow. She felt afraid—it awoke memories within her heart that made it beat uncomfortably. The letter had come a journey in search of her—first to her old lawyers, Huxtable and Son, of Rye, then to Ellen, since Huxtable was not allowed to know where she lived, then to herself. Someone was writing to her out of the past. Who could it be? Now suddenly, without reading it, she knew.

Carpenter saw her grow pale. Her face whitened under its tan and freckles, the corners of her fresh, hard mouth seemed to sag. She opened the letter, and as she read it she frowned and her hands quivered. She gave a little gasp, and for a moment—not knowing her—he thought she was going to faint.

He poured out a glass of water, and pushed it over to her.

"I'm afraid you've had bad news."

"No—no. Only a surprise. It's from a young chap I used to know, and he's been wounded."

"Dear me. I'm sorry. Not anything serious, I hope."

"I dunno . . . the writing seems queer. But he wants me to go and see him. He's at Bognor—only to think . . . and the letter's been to Rye and then to London, and here am I not ten miles off."

She did not seem to notice that for the first time she had slipped out a forbidden name.

"He seems bad," she continued. "I must go over and see him to-morrow. Reckon I was a fool not to give my address to Edward Huxtable, but I didn't want . . ."

She realized now that she had given away a secret. But her agitation was too great to be increased on any fresh count.

"I can easily manage it—I can go on the train as far as Chichester, and then get the bus."

She was talking to herself and had forgotten all about her guest. Supper was forgotten too —she rose and went over to the window. A flood of angry light was pouring across the sea from where in the west the sun's globe hung above purple fogs.

"If you'll excuse me, I'll go and see about the milking."

XIX

BUT of course she did not go to the milking. Her heart had been rapt out of everyday business. Milking was now a mere piece of routine that could quite successfully go on without her. Her whole being seemed to be focussed on the scrap of paper she held in her hand—Bertie's poor scrawl of a letter that had gone such a roundabout way in search of her.

She ran up to her bedroom for security, and there she dared read it again.

DENE CREST HOSPITAL,
BOGNOR.

MY DEAR JO,

I know that I have no right to write to you. But I hope you will forgive me when I tell you that I am wounded and in hospital at Bognor. I was hit on the Marne and they tell me I will have to have a tin inside for the rest of my days. Cheerful, isn't it? I have been lying in bed a long time and have

had six operations. I have been thinking of you a
lot and I see now that I have behaved like a swine.
I wonder if you got a letter I wrote you years ago.
You did not answer it and I heard afterwards that
you had left Ansdore. It struck me that I could
send this to your lawyers in Rye. I do want you
to come and see me, Jo, and tell me that you forgive
me for all that is past. I am very lonely. Mother
is dead and Maudie is married to a sergeant in the
Durhams. But perhaps you are too far away to
come and see me, and of course I shall quite understand.

Yours,

BERTIE HILL,
Lieut. 28th Middlesex.

For some reason Joanna had never thought
of the war engulfing Bertie as it had engulfed
Tip Ernley and a few million more. She had
somehow pictured him remaining eternally what
she had left him—a little singing clerk, busy
at his office, happy on his evenings out, eventually marrying his employer's daughter. . . .
That last ambition had not materialized, anyway. And here he was, wounded and done for,
one of a long list of names in the *Times* that

she never read, lying in hospital only ten miles away, pathetically longing for her to come and see him.

She would go of course—at once—and take Martin with her. That much she owed him, though she realized with a strange pang of fear that he did not even know the child had been born. It was all strange, and rather terrible—this—that the dead should rise. For years now she had grown used to the thought of Bertie in her past, but she could not adapt herself to the thought of him having power over her present. . . . Suppose he should want a share of the child. . . . Oh, but he couldn't have it. That was where the law befriended her, and rewarded her for having put herself outside the law. Martin was hers and hers only. Bertie could not claim him, except morally . . . and she was afraid, because she knew that claim was just. A father without his child, a child without his father—it was all wrong. Yet what was she to do?

XX

SHE started early the next morning, after writing out a telegram to prepare Bertie for her arrival. The farm must be abandoned to Tom Addis and the Roots. Jim Carpenter must be abandoned too and, as she went to fetch away his breakfast tray—for he still had breakfast in bed—she felt as if she were being deprived of some strength.

"I hope you'll find your friend much better," he said, wishing her well on her journey.

"I dunno . . . maybe . . . he says he's had a terrible time."

"Well, I hope it's over now. He's home in Blighty, anyway. Don't you fret, ma'am. I'll keep an eye on the youngster while you're gone."

"I'm taking Martin with me."

"Won't he be a bit of a nuisance to you? It's a difficult journey."

"I can't help that. He ought to come. Leastways—Mr. Hill used to know him when he was a baby. I reckon he'd want to see him now."

Her cheeks went crimson at the lie, which she felt, moreover, had not been a particularly good one. She swooped up the tray and went out of the room.

Martin was waiting for her, dressed in his new knickers and little blue jersey.

"I'm going in the train!" he shouted triumphantly to Rosie Pont. "I'm going in the train. Puff-puff-puff—to see a genplum."

"Well, you be good, that's all," said Rosie unsympathetically.

Joanna took his hand and led him skipping beside her down the drive and along the shingly road to the Falcon, where they were to catch their first bus. They would go by bus to Sidlesham Station, then by train to Chichester, and

[130]

then another bus would take them to Bognor more conveniently than the railway.

Martin was fortunately disposed towards good behavior. He was delighted at this unexpected treat, proud and satisfied to find himself in his new clothes, and off for a day's adventure amidst the wonders of locomotion.

"First we'll go in a bus," he shouted, "and then we'll go in a train, and then we'll go in another bus, and then we'll go in a bus again, and then we'll go in a train again, and then we'll go in a bus again."

"You'll be a good boy in the hospital, won't you, duckie? There's a poor gentleman there who's very ill . . ." she hesitated whether she should add "and he's your daddie," but the next minute even Joanna saw the madness of such words. Martin had not reached an age when he could be expected to keep secrets. . . . By the way, she'd better see Bertie alone first.

None of their different conveyances betrayed them, and they were in Bognor soon after one o'clock. It was a hot blue day, such as it always seems to be in Bognor—the sea was a great blue glare under the great blue glare of the sky, and the white parade and houses glared at Joanna, making her blink. There was no use going to the hospital till after dinner. Besides, she and the child were hungry, so they went into a pastrycook's and had buns and milk. Martin was luckily still cheerful and untired. He talked unceasingly and gazed about him—he had never been in a town or a big shop before —it was another delightful addition to the new experiences of the day.

Joanna scarcely heard his chatter. A strange abstraction had come over her, a strange weakness. Incredible as it seemed, she was trembling at the thought of meeting Bert. A kind of sickness was in her heart, such as used to be there when she waited for him to come to her at Ansdore. But then the sickness had been nearly all joy, with only one part of fear—and now it was nearly all fear, a nameless fear of she knew not what. A fear of her own memories . . . of the resurrection that was taking place within her? In Joanna's heart the graves were opening, and long-buried emotions were rising again. Perhaps they were only ghosts, but they troubled her none the less as she sat drooping there over the marble-topped table at the pastrycook's, amidst all the tinkle and clatter of china and glass and human tongues, gazing out through the open door at the blue and white glare of the seaside: passion, the unforgettable . . . troubling her once more with memories and desires . . . so brief and so long dead . . . it seemed to enfold her and Bertie once more in a dark veil, and within that veil with them now was the child Martin . . . he was part of that passion, that darkness—part with her and Bertie . . . they were three together. . . .

She paid for their food and went out. There were many soldiers in the street, and more than one turned round to look at the tall, handsome, weather-beaten woman in black who walked up Aldwick Road, leading a small child by the hand. But none of them called after her.

They were perhaps afraid of her mourning, and they may have guessed that her way was towards the hospital.

When she came there she could hardly speak, and it was in a voice unrecognizable as Joanna Godden's that she asked for Lieutenant Hill.

They told her that she could see him at once, and she followed the young Red Cross nurse down a number of clean bare corridors, smelling of beeswax and disinfectant. A door opened, and she was scared by the sight of many beds. Somehow she had never realized that their meeting might be in public, and she had forgotten to leave Martin outside the room. She followed the young nurse past the beds till she came to one close to the window. Then she found herself looking down into a man's face.

It was just that—a man's face, drawn in its outlines, with a queer yellow taint in the skin and a queer glow in the eyes, the face of a man who has suffered—who is suffering still. But it was only a man's face. It was not Bertie Hill's face which had so rapt and troubled her years ago, with its secret saucy eyes and the hair that sprang thickly from the broad low forehead. There was nothing in this face to make her heart beat quicker or the darkness rise. On the contrary, as she gazed down speechlessly she knew that her re-born passion was dead, or rather that it had never been re-born, that it had merely "walked" as a ghost. . . . She had dreamed—that was all—and was now awake.

"Jo," said Bert.

His voice struck certain chords, and she shivered. But the past was dead.

He looked at her, and then slowly smiled—a comforted smile, as if her presence brought relief and strength. Then his eyes fell on the little boy.

"Who's this?"

"Martin," said Joanna, her mouth dry.

He seemed to understand her at once.

"Jo—he's—is he yours?"

"Ours."

For a moment neither of them spoke. Their

[135]

low speech could not be heard by the man in the next bed, which was lucky, as they both had forgotten him. Then suddenly Joanna felt violently, overwhelmingly silly. She must behave naturally—ordinarily—or she wouldn't be able to bear it any longer. She picked up Martin and sat him on the bed.

"Speak to the gentleman, Martin. Show him your new suit."

"Are you a soldier?" asked Martin.

"Yes, I am, or rather, I was once." Then he seized Joanna's waist and dragged her down to him.

"Jo, this is dreadful. Why didn't you tell me?"

"Shut up! Don't be a fool."

"You ought to have told me."

"I couldn't. Do hold your tongue."

"Why are you lying in a tunnel?" asked Martin, shaking the arched bedclothes.

"Because my tummy's hurt and the bed-clothes mustn't touch it. Take him off, please, Jo. I can't stand anyone on the bed. Send

him down the room to talk to the other chaps—
they'd love it—and I want to talk to you."

She had to do as he asked, though she
dreaded to be alone with him. Martin was sent
off to talk to a cheerful boy at the other end of
the room, and she drew up a chair and sat close
beside Bert.

"You haven't changed a bit," he murmured.

"What nonsense!"

"You haven't—you're the same strong, beautiful Jo. When you came into the room I felt
as if someone lovely and strong had come to
comfort me."

That was not how he used to think of her,
long ago in the health of his young, ardent,
selfish manhood. The war had broken him—
he was cowed by all he had been through, and
wanted desperately someone to cling to. He
told her that he had joined up in the Autumn of
1914, had been given a commission in 1916,
and promoted six months later. Then a shell
had done for him—he was terribly smashed up,
and had been moved from hospital to hospital,

[137]

operation to operation. He had wanted Jo from the first, he said, but hadn't dared write to her till a week ago. He had not really expected his letter to find her—he had been half-dead with delight when her wire came that morning.

"It was just like you, old girl—generous as ever. Oh, Jo, it was good of you to come."

She felt nothing but his infinite pathos. He seemed to her broken and refined out of knowledge—he had lost all the swaggering qualities that had endeared him to her. His beauty too was gone—how could she ever have thought him like Martin Trevor?

They sat talking together till the patient's tea was brought in, and it was time for the visitors to go away. She told him about herself and her life at Crown Dips; after a while she lost her sense of constraint and felt friendly and free once more, though quite unstirred—rather like a woman talking to some close but not particularly well-loved relation.

Though desperately ill, he was full of talk

of his recovery. He thought he would soon be
discharged from hospital—"they want the bed,
and there's nothing more they can do." He
would have a gratuity, of course, and a pension.
He wouldn't be so badly off. "But I shall be
lonely, Jo—I shall be lonely. The old home's
broken up—poor mother died three years ago,
as I told you."

Joanna remembered that he had not seemed
particularly to love or value poor mother when
she was alive, but she was beginning to see that
here was a Bert wholly sentimentalized. Suffering and fear had had that not unusual effect
upon him. He was dwelling in the past—in a
past he had made beautiful to receive him—a
past in which the drab and quarrelsome household Joanna remembered had become a happy
home for mother and son, a past in which their
disastrous, disillusioning love had become an
idyll of fragrant memory.

It was all very strange and very pathetic,
and she herself was so touched with pity that
she could not refuse to enter that past with him

and treat it as if it were real. She was both glad and sorry when she had to go. Bertie kissed Martin and looked long at him for a likeness.

"You'll come again soon," he begged Joanna.

She promised that she would.

"And bring the child."

"Oh, yes, I'll bring him as often as you want."

Bert wanted Martin. The boy had become a part of his dream. The first surprise and concern had given way to what seemed to Joanna a strangely easy acceptance of the situation. His thoughts did not linger over what must have been her certain anguish, but dwelt instead in the new pride of his own fatherhood. Coming as it did to a man prostrated, shattered, and weak, this realization, this vindication of his broken manhood was like a drug, an exalting wine. A flush had crept into Bert's haggard face and a look that was almost triumphant.

"You've done him good," said the nurse to Joanna as she showed her out.

"Is he very ill?"

"Very ill, I'm afraid."

"He'll never be quite well, I suppose."

"Never. Still, we may be able to do wonders for him with this new appliance."

Joanna did not bother to inquire what the new appliance was. She was full of a more vital question which she did not dare ask.

XXI

"WELL, I hope you had a good day," said Jim Carpenter on her return.

"Oh, yes, thank you."

"And the man you went to see—doing nicely? I hope."

"Oh, yes." . . .

She could feel his eyes upon her. Though she looked down at her plate, she seemed to be watching their gaze as he and she sat at supper together. She saw them blue and living, set rather deep within a radiation of fine, kindly lines. She knew that he was not smiling with his mouth, but that he was smiling with his eyes. He was saying to himself, "That's another thing I mustn't ask her about." . . .

And she could not help it. She longed to protect herself from him, but she was powerless

[142]

to improve her defenses. Oh, for half an hour of Ellen's cool easy dealing!

"I've been out quite a bit to-day," he remarked. "I'm quite steady on my legs; and not too stiff with my arm and I've been thinking, ma'am, that it's time I gave up trespassing on your hospitality."

Oh!—Did he know what he was saying?

"You're more than welcome," she said, "and I'm sure you've been no trouble, but a lot of help—with the child."

"It's uncommon good of you to put it that way."

"But I mean it. I—I'd be sorry for you to go."

"I'll be sorry too, but reckon all good things ome to an end. I've my boats and my men to see to, and I'll do it better in Portsmouth. I can't call myself a sick man any longer now."

She answered him almost at random, desperately striving to pull the conversation to another subject, for fear that he might see how she was shaken. To have him go now—now, of all times—now that a man's weakness was dragging at her strength and she must herself take strength from someone, or fail . . . What a wicked fool she was! What a mercy he was going! She saw herself as a wanderer on a wrong and pleasant road—in mercy brought back. . . .

The next morning she felt quite settled and calm about it. She was glad that he was going, glad that a complication was to be removed from her life, and that she would be able to return to the old ways—the old ways of austerity and reparation—to "go softly" once more. For two whole days the peace lasted. She spent her time in quiet busyness, her heart numb and calm within her. When on the second evening the post came and brought her a letter in Bert's handwriting she felt no alarm or distress, merely relief that it had found her alone.

She had met the postman in the drive, and walked up to the house reading her letter.

It was so lovely seeing you again, my dearest Jo. You were just your old self, not a day older. And

the child. Oh, Jo! You don't know what I felt
when I saw him. Since then I've been thinking a
lot about you, and I've come to see that the past
can be undone. Dearest, it's not too late, if you will
be noble and generous, as I know you are by nature.
We've hurt each other, but we can heal each other
now. Let's get married and forget all these miserable years. I know I can't be much of a husband to
you, but I feel sure I could make you happy, and
I shall have my pension as well as a gratuity, so I
shan't be a drag on you anyhow. Besides, there's
the child. We ought to get married for his sake.
If I'd known he was coming I'd have made you
marry me long ago. Oh, darling, I want you so.
Do be kind and forgive me for not understanding
you when we first knew each other. I feel you are
quite unchanged, and are the same old kind, forgiv-
ing, tender-hearted Jo.

Your repentant and loving

BERT.

P.S. Please don't write and say you won't have
me. Come and see me anyhow.

The corners of Joanna's mouth drooped.
She thrust the letter deep into her apron pocket.
She hated it, somehow, and despised the man
who had written it; but, oh, she was sorry—

she was sorry—for Bert. He was the utterly
selfish man thrown out of his security into the
utterly selfish world, and crying for his mother.
He wanted her to mother him and take care of
him for the rest of his life, that was bound to
be full of helplessness and pain. When he had
seen her bending over him as he lay in bed at
the hospital he had seen his mother bending
over his cradle. Poor little baby! And, of
course, it was all nonsense about her not being
changed or a year older. It was just because
she had changed so much and was so many years
older that he wanted her, since he wanted her
for mother and not for wife. Poor Bertie!

There was that bitter, twisting compassion for
him in her heart all the evening, and at night
she took it with her up to bed. But as she lay
awake with it in the darkness, its quality
changed. It became a queer distress of her
whole being. It became her response to Bertie's
call. She remembered him then as he used to
be, her little singing clerk—handsome, saucy,
confident, full of his own business and impor-

tance. She had made a prey of him—she had pounced. . . . Oh, there was no good denying it—it had all been her doing. Not that she ever denied it—indeed, she had acquired a habit of self-reproach, but she might just as well remind herself again of her wickedness. She had wanted him so. . . . She had caught him, and he had struggled, and he had escaped . . . and, oh, she had been angry! But it was her own wicked fault—expecting to find her lost lover in the arms of any other man. What a blind fool she had been—spoiling three lives with her folly. . . . And now Bertie really wanted her. He had not wanted her while she held him— he had been half afraid of her, as she knew now—half afraid of her vehemence and violence, the pull and strangle of her love. Now he was no longer afraid, for she had come to him in a capacity that drives out fear. He really wanted her now.

She sat up and lighted her candle. Her apron hung from a nail on the door, and Bert's letter was still in the pocket. She took it out and read it again in the wavering light of the candle. The candlelight threw her head and shoulders monstrously upon the wall, making of her as she crouched there a huge shadow of motherhood—protection and tender strength.

The appeal of the letter came more terribly this time. Not only Bertie, but her whole past seemed to cry to her from it, and she knew now that she could not refuse that cry. For Bertie's sake, for the child's sake, for her own sake, she must pick up the ashes. This was what God wanted her to do—this was her chance of reparation. She was no more to "go softly" in her quiet lonely ways, but turn once more to her woman's striving. Passion was dead, but pity lived as it had never lived before. She could give Bertie no longer the frenzy and flame of her love; but he did not want that now, if indeed he had ever wanted it. He wanted her kindness, her support, and he should have them, and in giving them she would find peace and humble hope. . . .

When she had parted from Bertie the lover

that dreadful morning five years ago, she had
said, "You're not man enough for me." That
had been true, and it was true still, but it did
not matter now. You want a man for a husband, but you don't want your child to be a
man. Bertie was to be her child—she would
have two children instead of one. It would
all be for little Martin's good—he would grow
up with a father's name. And she—it would
all be for her good. It would put her out of
reach of such moments as that which had come
upon her the evening before, when she had
tried to make Jim Carpenter stay. He would
have to go now. He would have to go at once
—to-morrow. She could not carry this thing
through unless he went.

XXII

SHE told him so the next morning, just
before she set out.

"I hope you won't think me rude, but I find
I—I can't let you have . . . I mean, I want
the room . . . since you are going soon anyhow, do you think you could go at once?"

He eyed her calmly in the way she dreaded.

"Yes, I could go at once."

"Will your lodgings at Portsmouth take
you?"

"Yes, I can go to them anytime I want."

"Could you go there to-day?"

"Yes, certainly—whenever you like. You've
been too good to me, keeping me all this time."

"Rosie ull pack up your things for you and
get you a trap. The trains are quite easy once
you're at Sidlesham. I've got to go to Bognor."

"That's quite all right ma'am. When you

return you'll find I've gone. But I don't promise not to come back."

He had been so smooth and obliging in his talk that his last words, uttered in exactly the same agreeable tone, surprised her.

"Eh?" she gasped.

He surprised her still more. He seized her two arms and held them against her sides, while his eyes laughed into her horrified ones.

"You don't think you've done with me yet?"

Joanna broke from him, dashed out of the room, a whirlwind of outrage, and banged the door after her. She was shocked and frightened. She had never thought this could happen —and, oh, why had it happened now? Just when the empty way of expiation stood waiting for her devoted feet. . . . She did not dare even be angry, because to be angry with him obliged her to think of him, and she did not dare think of him to-day.

But the incident made her stronger in her resolution to marry Bertie. The touch of another man's hands, the hint of his pursuit, had only shown her more clearly that it was to Bertie she belonged. She belonged to him by law of nature—he and she were father and mother together. They were part of a trinity which she knew now could not be divided. Already she belonged to Bert; nothing—not all the renunciations nor all the years could alter that. The other man was merely the lover, the outsider, the thief. She was Bert Hill's, and it was only natural that she should go to him.

Nevertheless, there was no joy in her heart. As she journeyed across Manhood to Chichester, and then once more back to the coast, she could picture no happiness in the years ahead. A future of nursing and caring and giving her strength. . . . Well, it was only right. It was her reparation to Bertie, to Martin, and to God. She still thought she had done well to refuse to marry Bertie before Martin was born, but things were different now. That selfish, overbearing temper would now be a mere querulousness that she could soothe, that failure of love for Joanna the bride would give place to his loving dependence on Joanna the mother. She would bring him to Crown Dips, and her marriage would give her a right to go among her neighbors; little Martin would no longer be cut off from other children, or his home from other homes. Local custom would give him his supposed stepfather's name . . . no more struggles with "Mrs. Godden" or fears of discovery. She did well by Martin as well as by Bert.

It was only by herself that she did ill. As she walked up the shady road to the hospital she was reminded of an old Bible story in which Abraham walked to the sacrifice of all he loved best on earth. The Lord had said unto him, "Abraham," and he had said, "Here am I." But the Lord had spared him in the end—the story had a happy ending. There had been a ram with its head caught in a thicket which he had offered instead, and the Lord had said to him, "Because thou hast done this thing, I will bless thee." . . . Joanna came to the hospital.

"Can I see Mr. Hill? . . . I won't be staying long."

She had remembered that it was dinner time, and there might be objections to her seeing him now.

The nurse hesitated.

"Haven't you heard?"

She was very young and pink.

"Heard what?"

"That he—he died last night."

Joanna burst into a storm of tears. She sobbed rackingly and wildly. The little nurse was frightened.

"Oh—I'm so sorry. I—I didn't know. I'll fetch Matron. Do come in."

She almost pushed her into a small green-distempered room, where Joanna sank down on a chair, hiding her face in her arms. She could not stop crying—it was no good—she could not help it; nothing would stop those tears of gasping, blind relief. When the Matron came in she was half lying across the little table, her face still hidden, her shoulders heaving and arching with her sobs.

[154]

"My dear, my dear," said the Matron kindly. Then, "Drink this."

Joanna drank it, whatever it was.

"I'm dreadfully sorry," continued Matron, "the news shouldn't have been broken to you like that. But of course you know that it was a release for him—a happy release."

Joanna sobbed on.

"The nurse had no idea that you were a close friend of poor Mr. Hill's. Perhaps she might have stopped to think . . . but he was dreadfully ill, you know—he could never have got better."

"I was going to marry him."

"Oh, my dear!" The Matron was shocked. She laid her hand for a moment on Joanna's heaving shoulder. "How dreadful for you to be told like that; but we didn't know. He gave us only one address—his sister's. You know when men come here we have to have an address to write to if anything happens."

"He'd only just asked me. I'd come to tell

[155]

him I would. And now—and now—he'll never know."

The Matron made an inarticulate sound.

"The posts are so bad," continued Joanna, who had re-found her tongue, "I only got the letter last night."

"My dear," said the Matron very gently, "he never could have married you. He was far too ill—it's surprising he lived so long."

Joanna was astonished.

"But he didn't think he was going to die."

"I know he didn't. They're sometimes very hopeful, these poor boys, and it's pathetic to hear the way they plan ahead for years we know they'll never live to see. But often it's happier for them when they die. It's the poor things who live . . ."

She went on with her talking and soothing. She patted Joanna's hand; in the end she ordered her a cup of tea. Joanna felt uneasy with her kindness, a hypocrite unworthy of it. But she could not possibly tell her that her tears had been tears of relief—that she had sobbed and cried like that because after all she had not to marry Bert, because after all her sacrifice would not have to be offered. "And the Lord said unto Abraham . . ."

XXIII

WHEN she came home the house felt empty.

"Has Mr. Carpenter gone?" she asked Rosie Pont.

"Yes, mum, he went this afternoon."

Joanna sighed, then sharply chid herself. All this that had happened made no difference to herself and Carpenter. Indeed, it was a good thing that in her panic she had sent him away. That question had been settled as well as the other.

But had it? She remembered his words, which she had forgotten in the stress of her sacrificial journey towards Bert, "But I mean to come back" and "You don't think you've done with me." She seemed to feel his hands, warm and strong, pinning her arms against her sides. She had been frightened then. Her passion for

Bert had proved itself a ghost, a memory, but *that* had been no ghost . . . her heart had been living then as it had not lived for years. She told herself that he would not come back—she had been too rude. But she did not believe what she told herself.

Perhaps, after all, he had better come, and end this absurd frenzy of her spirits. She would never be able to go back to the old hard ways of reparation—she was too unsettled, too disheartened by all that had happened. She ought to marry for steadiness. . . . All that evening little Martin was crying and fretting for his lost friend—she ought to marry for the child's sake. But what nonsense she was thinking! Her thoughts flowed as if there had never been any Bertie Hill, as if he was not only dead, but had never been born. Jim Carpenter wanted her because he knew nothing about her. If he knew, he would not want her any more. Bertie was the only man she could have married, and Bertie was dead.

Her tears flowed again, this time in sorrow.

She sobbed on and on, forcing her grief, feeling that she owed it to him because she had wept for joy when she heard that he was dead. Oh, Bertie, Bertie . . . dear lover of a dead June. . . . She knew it was wrong, but sometimes she could not help thinking of him as if he had been her husband, since love and nature had made them one.

XXIV

A WEEK later she received a telegram from Ellen, announcing her descent upon the Selsey Bill Hotel—and all that time Carpenter had not come. She had told Rosie Pont that if he came she was not at home. "Say 'Not at home,' Rosie—just like that, then it won't be a lie." But Rosie's powers of social evasion were never put to the test, and Joanna tried hard to convince herself that she was not disappointed.

Ellen arrived, looking rather peaked and pale after her hard-working summer in London. She was also anxious about Tip. Not that she had heard anything but good news of him, but he had now been three years at the war, and she could not believe that his good luck would continue. The calmness with which she had at first endured his absence was failing her now—and she was beginning to feel the strain of her work and of the racket of war-time London, where terror came with the moon.

Joanna tried to persuade her to come to stay at Crown Dips, partly out of a reviving maternal pity for her little Ellen, looking so wan, partly out of an unformulated desire to have her spare-bedroom occupied, and a ghost driven out by flesh and blood. But Ellen still clung to her freedom.

"It wouldn't do, Jo. I'm tired to death and want to stop in bed all hours."

"Well, you could do that here, duckie, and welcome."

"No, I couldn't—you'd disapprove of me inside, you couldn't help it, and I'd end by getting on your nerves just as I used to do. For there's nothing the matter with me, only tiredness, and tiredness of mind at that."

"I had a man lying in bed here a fortnight and I didn't disapprove of him, inside or out."

"But he was really ill"—Ellen had of course heard of the adventure—"and you felt you were

[162]

doing your bit in looking after him. Besides—
he was a man. Oh, no, Jo, don't start denying
it. I know so well why you could bear with him
and could never bear with me."

However, she came a great deal to Crown
Dips, and they were sitting comfortably at their
tea together one evening when Jim Carpenter
walked in.

Joanna's first emotion was rage, and her first
impulse to devastate Rosie Pont even before she
greeted her visitor. But she suddenly remembered that Rosie had gone off to her mother's
after laying the tea, and he would have been
admitted by Mrs. Root, who had received no
training in such matters. So there was nothing
to do but shake hands and introduce him to her
sister.

Carpenter seemed quite at his ease and completely unaware of the disruption caused by his
visit. Had the man no memory—or no shame?
Did he really think that you can seize a woman
by her two arms and tell her she hasn't done
with you yet and then drop in to tea as if noth-

[163]

ing had happened? He had been to see a man
at the Coastguard Station, he said. He had to
prepare a report on the loss of his boat. Yes,
he'd get his money all right, but he'd have to
wait for it—you always had to wait when you
wanted anything out of the government.

He spoke mostly to Ellen, not because he
was shy of Joanna, but because she sternly refused to join in the conversation. She sat bolt
upright, her arms folded, her eyes scowling
from under the high-piled riches of her hair.
He and Ellen seemed to get on together rather
well. They spoke of books and of things in the
newspapers. She could see that Ellen was
pleased with him. And he, no doubt, was
pleased with Ellen. . . . Joanna's scowl grew
deeper. She remembered some words of her
sister's, spoken long ago: "Poor, dear Joanna.
I'm sorry if I've taken another of your men."
She had spoken like a lying minx, for she had
taken no man of Joanna's except such as her
sister had given her. Neither, of course, did
Joanna want Jim Carpenter. . . . Nor could

[164]

Ellen take him, seeing that she was married. All the same . . . suppose Ellen's low spirits were a part of true premonition, and Tip was killed. . . . Ellen was the sort of woman who was sure to marry again.

Her sister, however, was cherishing no such thoughts for herself, for when he had gone she said to Joanna:

"That man admires you, Jo."

Joanna grunted.

"I hope you're not being a fool about it," continued Ellen.

"What d'you mean?"

"I mean you were extremely gruff and un-friendly this evening. I hope you're not trying to drive him away."

"Yes, I am."

"Then you're an idiot. He's absolutely the right man for you."

"How do you know?"

"Well, he's the right age for one thing, and in the right position. You probably won't agree with me, but I feel sure you wouldn't be really happy married to a pukka gentleman, nor would you be happy with a man who was inferior, like—"

"I know. Don't say it."

"I won't. You needn't be so cross. I'm only speaking to you for your own good. I like your Mr. Carpenter and I think he'd make you happy."

"He's too clever for me, and I don't hold with his ways."

"Nonsense, you love clever men. The reason you loved young Trevor was because he was clever and gave you ideas. You couldn't live with a stupid man two weeks, and as for not holding with his wavs—I don't know what you mean."

"I mean he's a fisherman—I've never had any dealings with the sea."

"No, you've loved the land—perhaps too much—but don't you see it would be best for you to have a man whose job's different from your own? Otherwise you'd always be arguing and wanting to be master."

[166]

Joanna rose and walked over to the window, which was full of the rusty twilight of September. Before her, like a sheet of beaten copper, lay spread the sea under which King Harry's forests were drowned. Oh, drowned land . . . was there no sea that would drown the life behind her?

She turned suddenly round.

"There's no good you talking, Ellen—there's no good us arguing. All that isn't the point. The point is that no decent man would marry me."

"My dear Joanna, what nonsense! Men aren't like that—not now."

"He thinks I'm a widow."

"Naturally; you want him to."

"But he can't go on thinking it if I say 'yes'."

"No, I'm sure you would never be able to keep it from him; besides, there might be legal difficulties in the way. But, Jo"—Ellen rose too, and came forward, laying her hand on her sister's shoulder—"You know—I was the same with Tip. He had to—had to understand, and

[167]

forgive. And never, never, by look or word has he ever cast anything up at me—Oh, Tip!" She suddenly thought of her husband in the Flanders hell, and her forehead sank down on her hand. Joanna's shoulders quivered.

"I—I can't help it, dear," she said more softly, "I'm different."

"Of course, there's the child . . . but I should think he could get over that. He knows you've got him, anyhow. And if he does mind —if it's too much of the other man about the house—Jo, I'd take Martin. I'd love to have him, especially now. Tip would like him too; we've always wanted a child, and we've spoken of adopting one, now we know we'll never have one of our own."

Joanna shook her head.

"I'd never give him up. And it isn't that."

"Bert isn't likely to bother you again, is he?"

"No—he's dead."

"Dead, Joanna! When did you know? You never told me."

[168]

"He was killed—in the War."

Ellen shuddered.

"Then, Jo, can't you let the dead bury their dead? Surely the past is over now. I'm sure Carpenter wouldn't be any less decent and kind than my Tip if you told him."

"It's just that—I can't tell him. If I married him I'd have to tell him, and I won't—I won't."

"But if it made no difference?"

"It would make a difference. I'd never marry the sort of man it would make no difference to. I don't hold with such ideas. Maybe he'd marry me just the same—he might and he mightn't—but he couldn't help thinking small of me. He'd know he'd been mistaken in the sort of woman I was, even if he still wanted me. And, oh, Ellen, I couldn't bear it. I'd rather he never asked me, or I said 'no'. I couldn't bear him to think small of me. There's no good us talking any more—I see these things different from you."

[169]

"Yes, you do, Joanna, but I hope you'll have some happiness all the same."

She took her hand from her sister's shoulder and walked back into the room, which was now nearly dark.

XXV

THAT evening, when Ellen had gone, Joanna sat down and wrote painfully:

DEAR MR. CARPENTER,

I am writing to ask you kindly not to come and see me again. Maybe you saw to-day that I didn't feel happy about it. I am very sorry to appear unfriendly, but I am sure you understand.

With kind regards,

Yours truly,

JOANNA GODDEN.

The next day was a day of thunder. The big guns were practicing at Portsmouth, and Crown Dips seemed to rock on its foundations as the sound sped over the sea. Joanna scarcely noticed the guns now—neither the big guns, nor that far more terrible pulse and murmur which could be heard in the silences, and which was the distant voice of the guns in France.

She spent the morning in her poultry yard, working desperately, as if in atonement for the hours she had lost in tender excursions. She wore an old straw hat tied under her chin and a big print apron over her oldest gown. So there may have been a twofold reason for the indignant start she gave when she saw Jim Carpenter come in at the yard gate.

"Good morning," he said cheerfully. "Rosie told me you were out here."

"But did—didn't you get my letter?"

"Of course, I did. That's why I've come."

The flame of her anger fed itself.

"How dare you?" she cried under her breath.

"It's a bit noisy out here, isn't it? I wonder if we'd hear the guns less in the house."

"I can't go into the house. I'm busy."

"We'd much better go in. I don't want to have to raise my voice"—and he glanced at the open door where showed the colored petticoats of Mrs. Root.

"I'm not coming in."

He went up to her.

"Do be reasonable—do be fair."

"I don't know how you dare talk like this."

"I shouldn't if it hadn't been for that letter of yours—at least not to-day. But when I got it I saw things would have to happen quickly."

"They won't happen at all."

"Perhaps not, but they must be talked about. You know, you've never given me my chance."

She saw the impossibility of getting rid of him, so she decided that after all she had better go into the house and have it over. Maybe she would have to go through the worst, but all the more reason to get done with it.

"Very well," she said slowly, "but you're unaccountable tormenting."

He opened the yard gate and she went through. The heavens roared.

"Ah," said he, "it was a bad day when Master Huggett was born."

"What d'you mean?"

"Master Huggett and his man John
They did cast the first cannón—

Don't you know the old rhyme? Reckon many a poor Sussex boy out there has reason to curse old Huggett and his forge."

Joanna made a vague sound. He had that disarming way of side-tracking her when she was angry—just as Martin used to, with his talk about the old floods.

"It was up over by Maresfield," continued Carpenter, "on the edge of Ashdown Forest. Sussex was the Black Country in those days—all hammers and cinders and forges and furnaces. Now we've got only the names."

XXVI

THEY had come into the parlor and sat among the roses. Joanna suddenly remembered the deficiencies of her costume.

"You wait till I've made myself decent. I can't sit in here like this."

"Yes, you can, and I shan't let you go. I don't trust you to come back. Besides, I like you ever so much better in those things than in the black you wear most times."

Joanna sighed.

"Don't sigh, my dear," he said tenderly, "I've not come to plague you. You know that. You know I love you and that you love me."

"I don't love you. How can you speak so?"

"You do, or why are you so anxious to get shut of me? There's no harm in a man showing you a little politeness, and I've done no more."

"Oh, how can you say such a thing? You know you've shown me you were courting."

"Maybe I have, then—but not till you'd shown me yourself how the land lay. Oh Joanna, why do you treat me like this?"

"I don't want you."

"You do."

She nearly wept in her helplessness.

"Haven't I tried to get shut of you time and again?"

"Yes, and it's just the way you tried to get shut of me that showed me you wanted me. But don't let's go arguing about it. Won't you tell me straight why you won't have me?"

She tried to say "I don't love you," but the words would not come. His brown face and blue eyes, his kind, puzzled smile, the very shape and set of him there, and the sound of his voice made such a lie impossible and silly. She could only plead:

"Don't ask me—please, don't ask me. I can't tell you. I couldn't bear to tell you."

"Shall I tell you, then?"

"Tell me what?"

"That what is past is past and can never come between us."

Joanna trembled.

"I don't understand," she said faintly.

He took her hand—she tried to pull it away, but he held it fast.

"There's something you think you ought to tell me, isn't there? Well, I don't want to hear it."

She burst out at him.

"I'm not going to tell you nothing. Why do you talk like that? How can you know? You don't know. You've only got some silly notion."

"It's you that have got the silly notion. You think I'm not going to marry you because Martin's father didn't."

"Oh! . . ." cried Joanna.

She pulled away her hand, but the next moment his arms were round her. He was kneeling beside her chair, holding her closely to him, drawing her down against his shoulder.

[177]

"My dear," he murmured, "my own dear."

She was shaken with sobs. She was amazed and frightened. How had it happened? How did he know? Her secret was out at last, and without her telling it. She was more shocked than relieved.

"I can't bear it," she sobbed. "I'd have done anything rather than you should know. Oh, I shall die . . . of shame."

"But, my dearie, it makes no difference."

Even in that moment her moral sense rose indignantly.

"Then it should ought to."

"Why?"

"Because . . . because . . ."

"I don't see why I should let a dead man spoil our lives."

"How did you know that he was dead?"

"I didn't know, though I may have guessed. All I mean is that he's dead to you. I know that."

Joanna's head shot up mournfully.

"It queers me. I can't understand how you know anything. Who told you?"

"Well, you, my darling, for one."

"Me! . . . I never!"

"Yes, you, darling, your own self. It was plain to see you had a secret. Why, you wouldn't tell me where you'd come from, and then one day without knowing you let out that it was Rye; and my sister had been asking me if you came from those parts."

"Your sister? Why should she ask?"

"Because she used to live there once, and seemingly there'd been some talk about you."

"I never heard of anyone of that name in Rye."

"You wouldn't. Her husband was only there for a bit on the shipbuilding. It must have been the year you left. When she came and saw you here, she told me she wondered if you were the same Joanna Godden that used to have a farm on Walland Marsh."

"What—what did she tell you about me?"

"Do you want to hear?"

[179]

"Yes—I do, and you've got to tell."

"Well, she said as this Joanna Godden got engaged to a young chap and was going to be married, and then the next thing people heard was that the engagement was broken off, though it was plain to all there was a child coming."

Joanna breathed angrily.

"She said that this Joanna Godden sold up her farm and cleared out, though she'd been in the place ever since she was born. No one knew where she went, though some guessed it wasn't far. Others said she went to Scotland—oh, there was all sorts of tales. Some folk spoke unaccountable hard of Joanna, others said she showed a proper spirit, and the man ought to be horsewhipped for the way he'd treated her."

"He didn't treat me any way. It wasn't his doing. It was I who broke off the engagement, and he never knew about the child."

"Why didn't you tell him?"

"Because I didn't want to marry him. I saw as he didn't really love me, and it ud be bad for

[180]

the child if we married and had an unhappy home. . . ."

The old struggle pulled at her heart, and her tears fell. He drew her closer.

"Don't cry, my Nannie—don't cry."

It was rather queer and sweet to be called "Nannie" instead of "Jo"—to have the woman's end of her name used in tenderness instead of the man's. It seemed to give her a new softness, a sense of protection that she had never experienced till now. She huddled against him, shedding her tears into the comfortable roughness of his sleeve.

Then suddenly she remembered that all this could never be. This was not the way she had chosen when long ago she had made her choice. It was not right that she should find happiness who deserved it so little. It was not right that this man should forgive her. It only showed him up as loose in his ideas, without respect for the Ten Commandments. The fact that he had loved her and sought her while knowing all about her was no excuse for surrender but another reason for renunciation. She pulled herself upright.

"It won't do," she said savagely; "it ain't seemly. You should ought to know better than love a woman who's done so bad."

"Don't tell me we're still talking about that."

"Yes, we are, and we're going on."

"I'm not. I don't want to hear another word."

"For shame! You don't seem to take in how bad it was."

"It was better than I thought."

"What do you mean?"

"I didn't know you'd been so brave—so brave in getting shut of the man yourself. I thought he'd jilted you."

"He didn't. But I don't see how that makes it any different."

"Then you'd better not think any more about it. It shows you're no fit judge."

"I'm a better judge than you. Oh, you can't think how it shocks me when I hear you treating it all so light."

"I don't treat it light. Really, my dear, I shall be angry in a minute."

A new roughness in his voice startled her.

"Yes," he continued, "if you're shocked at me, I'm shocked at you—living among the dead like that. Don't you know what it says in the Bible—'the living, the living, he shall praise thee'?—and you're spoiling the life of a living man for the sake of a man that's dead."

"Oh, but it isn't that. It's not that I care about Bertie any more. It's myself, and what I did."

"But that's dead too. Oh, my Nannie, don't you think I know how good you are, how good and straight and honest? Haven't I seen it day by day? And here you are talking about a thing you did once . . . as if it mattered now . . . as if there wasn't a lot of things *I* did once. If I started talking about them, then we'd be a pair."

He pulled up his sleeve, and she saw the girls' names—Milly, Connie, and Maude, and the pierced hearts.

"There! Look at 'em. Look at Milly—look at the rest. Reckon I haven't always been the man I should ought, but I don't go thinking of it now, or letting it stop me being the man I'd like to be."

"It's different for you—different ror a man."

"Oh, is it, ma'am? So that's your moral ideas, is it? That's the way you're going to bring up young Martin. It's plain to see you need me to look after you both, then."

He drew her close once more.

"Don't fight me, my dear, for you can't. Reckon I'm bound to win, since your own heart's taking my part against you. Now let's talk sober for a minute. I'm no lighter than you, and I don't like to see neither a man nor a woman breaking God's commandments. But you'll never make me believe that what's broken can't be mended, nor what's past can't be ended. I love you for what you are, and nothing you'd done five years ago can alter that. I want to marry the woman I see before me, the woman I know now; and I know, my dear, as you're more strict and virtuous than many a woman who's never had your story. Folks are harder on a woman than a man— that's all the difference. Maybe if there's a kiddie, a man don't care for bringing up another fellow's child. But you know I don't feel that way about Martin. I'm fond of the little chap, and I'd like to help you make a man of him."

"He won't mind me," mourned Joanna. "I can't do nothing with him. But he'll mind a man. That's why if ever I changed my mind —Oh, there's no sense a woman bringing up a child alone."

"And that's the first sense you've spoken to-day," he said, kissing her astonished mouth.

XXVII

HE WAS gone, and the dusk was upon the sea. The voices of the guns were still. In the new silence it almost seemed as if War itself had ceased. Joanna stood by the window, looking out on the tide that flowed over King Harry's ground. From the lamplit room behind her came Ellen's voice.

"Yes, it'll be an excellent thing for him to come and live here. He can do his job and you can do yours, and you'll neither of you get in each other's way. Perhaps for some reasons it would be better if you went somewhere else, but since you're so fond of the place . . . anyhow people will stop talking once you're married."

"Were they talking—here?"

"Naturally—since you wouldn't talk yourself."

"How do you know?"

"Simply because when I'm down here I hear what people say. That's all, and it doesn't matter now. It'll be done with and forgotten a month after you're Mrs. Carpenter."

Joanna did not speak. What a lot of "done with" and "forgotten" there had been to-day—more about ending the old life than beginning the new. Both Jim and Ellen had been quite angry with her for the way she had treated the past—and yet she never could think but that she had been right to treat it so. Perhaps she had been right till now; but now was wrong— now it was time to change and make a new beginning—for Martin's sake, for Jim's sake, and maybe for her own. He'd told her that she owed herself a happy marriage after all the unkind things she'd done to herself in the last twenty years. That was after she had told him about the first Martin. She had told him everything, about Martin and about the other men whom she'd almost forgotten. He had let her do it, he said, just so that she might get it all out of her life for ever. It did you good to tell things, to let everything come out of the narrow, aching places of your heart—then you really could forget and get on with the business of life.

She remembered some words he had said just before he left her, when the sunset hung like a furnace over the sea, and they stood together by the window, as she stood now, looking out on the drowned woods.

"What's over and done with, Nannie, is no more than those woods you've so often told me about, that are lying under the sea where you hear the dead King's horn. . . . We don't trouble about them, all we think of is the living country of the Marsh—where the cattle feed, and the corn grows and the spring comes every year. You tell yourself that—your whole life up till now is drowned."

Oh, drowned land. . . . She suddenly saw it would be good to start again from now—to walk in a land of growth and spring, to meet no more the past years that for so long had commanded her . . . except now and then for a ghost upon the road or the faint note of a horn.

Mrs. Adis

IN NORTHEAST Sussex a great tongue of
land runs into Kent by Scotney Castle. It is
a land of woods—the old hammer woods of the
Sussex iron industry—and among the woods
gleam the hammerponds, holding in their mir-
rors the sunsets and sunrises. Owing to the
thickness of the woods—great masses of oak
and beech in a dense undergrowth of hazel and
chestnut and frail sallow—the road that passes
Mrs. Adis's cottage is dark before the twilight
has crept away from the fields beyond. That
night there was no twilight and no moon, only
a few pricks of fire in the black sky above the
trees. But what the darkness hid the silence
revealed. In the absolute stillness of the night,
windless and clear with the first frost of October, every sound was distinct, intensified. The
distant bark of a dog at Delmonden sounded

close at hand, and the man who walked on the road could hear the echo of his own footsteps following him like a knell.

Every now and then he made an effort to go more quietly, but the roadside was a mass of brambles, and their crackling and rustling were nearly as loud as the thud of his feet on the marl. Besides, they made him go slowly, and he had no time for that.

When he came to Mrs. Adis's cottage he paused a moment. Only a small patch of grass lay between it and the road. He went stealthily across it and looked in at the lighted, uncurtained window. He could see Mrs. Adis stooping over the fire, taking some pot or kettle off it. He hesitated and seemed to wonder. He was a big, hulking man, with reddish hair and freckled face, evidently of the laboring class, but not successful, judging by the vague grime and poverty of his appearance. For a moment he made as if he would open the window, then he changed his mind and went to the door instead.

He did not knock, but walked straight in. The woman at the fire turned quickly round.

"What, you, Peter Crouch?" she said. "I didn't hear you knock."

"I didn't knock, ma'am. I didn't want anybody to hear."

"How's that?"

"I'm in trouble." His hands were shaking a little.

"What you done?"

"I shot a man, Mrs. Adis."

"You?"

"Yes—I shot him."

"You killed him?"

"I dunno."

For a moment there was silence in the small, stuffy kitchen. Then the kettle boiled over, and Mrs. Adis sprang for it, mechanically putting it at the side of the fire.

She was a small, frail-looking woman, with a brown, hard face on which the skin had dried in innumerable small, hair-like wrinkles. She was probably not more than forty-two; but life treats some women hard in the agricultural districts of Sussex, and Mrs. Adis's life had been harder than most.

"What do you want me to do for you, Peter Crouch?" she said, a little sourly.

"Let me stay here a bit. Is there nowhere you can put me till they've gone?"

"Who's they?"

"The keepers."

"Oh, you've had a shine with the keepers, have you?"

"Yes. I was down by Cinder Wood, seeing if I could pick up anything, and the keepers found me. There was four to one, so I used my gun. Then I ran for it. They're after me; reckon they aren't far off now."

Mrs. Adis did not speak for a moment.

Crouch looked at her searchingly, beseechingly.

"You might do it for Tom's sake," he said.

"You haven't been an over-good friend to Tom," snapped Mrs. Adis.

"But Tom's been an unaccountable good

friend to me; reckon he would want you to stand by me to-night."

"Well, I won't say he wouldn't, seeing as Tom always thought better of you than you deserved. Maybe you can stay till he comes home to-night, then we can hear what he says about it."

"That'll serve my turn, I reckon. He'll be up at Ironlatch for an hour yet, and the coast will be clear by then. I can get away out of the country."

"Where'll you go?"

"I dunno. There's time to think of that."

"Well, you can think of it in here," she said, dryly, opening a door which led from the kitchen into the small lean-to of the cottage. "They'll never guess you're there, specially if I tell them I ain't seen you to-night."

"You're a good woman, Mrs. Adis. I know I'm not worth your standing by me, but maybe I'd ha' been different if I'd had a mother like Tom's."

She did not speak, but shut the door, and he

was in darkness save for a small ray of light
that filtered through one of the cracks. By
this light he could see her moving to and fro,
preparing Tom's supper. In another hour Tom
would be home from Ironlatch Farm, where
he worked every day. Peter Crouch trusted
Tom not to revoke his mother's kindness, for
they had been friends when they went together
to the Council School at Lamberhurst, and since
then the friendship had not been broken by
their very different characters and careers.

Peter Crouch huddled down upon the sacks
that filled one corner of the lean-to and gave
himself up to the dreary and anxious game of
waiting. A delicious smell of cooking began
to filter through from the kitchen, and he
hoped Mrs. Adis would not deny him a share
of the supper when Tom came home, for he
was very hungry and he had a long way to go.

He had fallen into a kind of helpless doze,
haunted by the memories of the last two hours,
recast in the form of dreams, when he was
roused by the sound of footsteps on the road.

For a moment his poor heart nearly choked him with its beating. They were the keepers. They had guessed for a cert where he was—with Mrs. Adis, his old pal's mother. He had been a fool to come to the cottage. Nearly losing his self-control, he shrank into the corner, shivering, half sobbing. But the footsteps went by. They did not even hesitate at the door. He heard them ring away into the frosty stillness. The next minute Mrs. Adis stuck her head into the lean-to.

"That was them," she said, shortly. "A party from the Castle. I saw them go by. They had lanterns, and I saw old Crotch and the two Boormans. Maybe it ud be better if you slipped out now and went towards Cansiron. You'd miss them that way and get over to Kent. There's a London train comes from Tunbridge Wells at ten to-night."

"That'd be a fine thing for me, ma'am, but I haven't the price of a ticket on me."

She went to one of the kitchen drawers.

"Here's seven shillun. It'll be your fare to London and a bit over."

For a moment he did not speak. Then he said, "I don't know how to thank you, ma'am."

"Oh, you needn't thank me. I am doing it for Tom. I know how unaccountable set he is on you and always was."

"I hope you won't get into trouble because of this."

"There ain't much fear. No one's ever likely to know you've been in this cottage. That's why I'd sooner you went before Tom came back, for maybe he'd bring a pal with him, and that'd make trouble. I won't say I shan't have it on my conscience for having helped you to escape the law; but shooting a keeper ain't the same as shooting an ordinary sort of man, as we all know, and maybe he ain't so much the worse, so I won't think no more about it."

She opened the door for him, but on the threshold they both stood still, for again footsteps could be heard approaching, this time from the far south.

[197]

"Maybe it's Tom," said Mrs. Adis.

"There's more than one man there, and I can hear voices."

"You'd better go back," she said, shortly. "Wait till they've passed, anyway."

With an unwilling shrug he went back into the little dusty lean-to, which he had come to hate, and she locked the door upon him.

The footsteps drew nearer. They came more slowly and heavily this time. For a moment he thought they would pass also, but their momentary dulling was only the crossing of the strip of grass outside the door. The next minute there was a knock. It was not Tom, then.

Trembling with anxiety and curiosity, Peter Crouch put his eye to one of the numerous cracks in the lean-to door and looked through into the kitchen. He saw Mrs. Adis go to the cottage door, but before she could open it a man came quickly in and shut it behind him.

Crouch recognized Vidler, one of the keepers of Scotney Castle, and he felt his hands and feet grow leaden cold. They knew where he was, then. They had followed him. They had guessed that he had taken refuge with Mrs. Adis. It was all up. He was not really hidden; there was no place for him to hide. Directly they opened the inner door they would see him. Why couldn't he think of things better? Why wasn't he cleverer at looking after himself—like other men? His legs suddenly refused to support him, and he sat down on the pile of sacks.

The man in the kitchen seemed to have some difficulty in saying what he wanted to Mrs. Adis. He stood before her silently, twisting his cap.

"Well, what is it?" she asked.

"I want to speak to you, ma'am."

Peter Crouch listened, straining his ears, for his thudding heart nearly drowned the voices in the next room. Oh no, he was sure she would not give him away. If only for Tom's sake. . . . She was a game sort, Mrs. Adis.

"Well?" she said, sharply, as the man remained tongue-tied.

"I have brought you bad news, Mrs. Adis."
Her expression changed.

"What? It ain't Tom, is it?"

"He's outside," said the keeper.

"What do you mean?" said Mrs. Adis, and she moved toward the door.

"Don't, ma'am—not till I've told you."

"Told me what? Oh, be quick, man, for mercy's sake!" And she tried to push past him to the door.

"There's been a row," he said, "down by Cinder Wood. There was a chap there snaring rabbits, and Tom was walking with the Boormans and me and old Crotch down from the Castle. We heard a noise in the Eighteen-pounder Spinney, and there . . . It was too dark to see who it was, and directly he saw us he made off; but we'd scared him, and he let fly with his gun."

He stopped speaking and looked at her, as if beseeching her to fill in the gaps of his story. In his corner of the lean-to Peter Crouch was as a man of wood and sawdust.

"Tom——" said Mrs. Adis.

The keeper had forgotten his guard, and before he could prevent her she had flung open the door.

The men outside had evidently been waiting for the signal, and they came in, carrying something on a hurdle, which they put down in the middle of the kitchen floor.

"Is he dead?" asked Mrs. Adis without tears.

The men nodded. They could not find a dry voice like hers.

In the lean-to Peter Crouch had ceased to sweat and tremble. Strength had come with despair, for he knew he must despair now. Besides, he no longer wanted to escape from this thing that he had done. Oh, Tom!—and I was thinking it was one of them damned keepers. Oh, Tom! And it was you that got it—got it from me! Reckon I don't want to live!

And yet life was sweet, for there was a woman at Ticehurst, a woman as stanch to him as Tom, who would go with him to the world's end even now. But he must not think of her.

He had no right: his life was forfeit to Mrs. Adis.

She was sitting in the old basket armchair by the fire. One of the men had helped her into it. Another man with rough kindness had poured her out something from a flask he carried in his pocket. "Here, ma'am, take a drop of this. It'll give you strength."

"We'll go round to Ironlatch cottage and ask Mrs. Gain to come down to you."

"Reckon this is a turble thing to have come to you, but it's the will o' Providence, as some folks say; and as for the man who did it, we've a middling-good guess who he is, and he shall swing."

"We didn't see his face, but we've got his gun. He threw it into an alder when he bolted, and I swear that gun belongs to Peter Crouch, who's been up to no good since the day when Mus' Scales sacked him for stealing his corn."

"Reckon, though, he didn't know it was Tom when he did it, he and Tom always being better friends than he deserved."

Peter Crouch was standing upright now, looking through the crack of the door. He saw Mrs. Adis struggle to her feet and stand by the table, looking down on the dead man's face. A whole eternity seemed to roll by as she stood there. He saw her put her hand into her apron pocket, where she had thrust the key of the lean-to.

"The Boormans have gone after Crouch," said Vidler, nervously breaking the silence. "They'd a notion as he'd broken through the woods Ironlatch way. There's no chance of his having been by here? You haven't seen him to-night, ma'am?"

There was a pause.

"No," said Mrs. Adis, "I haven't seen him. Not since Tuesday." She took her hand out of her apron pocket.

"Well, we'll be getting around and fetch Mrs. Gain. Reckon you'll be glad to have her."

Mrs. Adis nodded.

"Will you carry him in there first?" And she pointed to the bedroom door.

The men picked up the hurdle and carried it into the next room. Then silently each wrung the mother by the hand and went away.

She waited until they had shut the door, then she came toward the lean-to. Crouch once more fell a-shivering. He couldn't bear it. No, he'd rather swing than face Mrs. Adis. He heard the key turn in the lock, and he nearly screamed.

But she did not come in. She merely unlocked the door, then crossed the kitchen with a heavy, dragging footstep and shut herself into the room where Tom was.

Peter Crouch knew what he must do—the only thing she wanted him to do, the only thing he could possibly do. He opened the door and silently went out.

Good Wits Jump

ROSIE PONT had been chicken-girl at Wait's Farm for a little over five years, which meant, as anyone who saw her round, sweet, childish face would know, that she had started her career at an early age. Mrs. Pont was a believer in early beginnings—a wise and practical belief in the mother of eleven children. All the little Ponts had been sent early to school to be out of her way in her mornings of cooking and scrubbing and washing; they had been taken away from school at the earliest possible moment so that they might look after still younger Ponts, and then had gone early to work to take their share of the burden which had grown too heavy for their parents' backs.

Rosie had not liked going to school. She had not liked leaving school when she was thirteen and looking after her little brother Leslie, and she had not liked, when Leslie grew old enough to go to school himself, being packed off by her mother to Wait's Farm to clean the fowl-houses, collect eggs, mix chicken food, scrub the dairy floor, and make herself generally useful for five shillings a week.

"You don't know your own luck, Rosie," her friend Emma Brown had said to her just as she was starting. "Now you might be having to go away into the Shires, just as I am. That's hard. I'd give anything to be stopping here among them all, but there isn't much work in these parts, and you're lucky to get it."

Emma Brown was quite four years older than Rosie. She had been a pupil-teacher at Rosie's school in the days when Rosie was still on the safe side of twelve. Then things had gone wrong with Emma. Her father and mother had died within a few weeks of each other, no money had been left, and she had been obliged to give up her ambitions in the way of education and turn to farm work like other girls in Oxhurst village. She had worked for some time at the Loose Farm, a mile from Wait's, but they had had bad luck at the Loose, and had turned away several hands, and now Emma could not get work in the neighborhood, so had been obliged to take a post as dairy-girl on a big farm in Shropshire.

Rosie was very sorry that she should have to go, for she was fond of Emma. But she could not feel that her friend was so unlucky as she made out, for it was possible that away in the big world of the Shires Emma might come to glories beyond the reach of chicken-girls in Sussex.

They wrote to each other for nearly a year. Emma did not like Shropshire ways, and she found her work hard and perplexing, owing to unaccustomed methods of farming. Botvyl, the farm in Shropshire, could have swallowed up two or three Waits and Looses in its acres. "And all the work there is to do, and the ways they have of doing it you'd never guess, Rosie."

Rosie wrote in her turn and gave news of Ox-hurst and the Ponts, and the Orpingtons and

[207]

Wyandottes at Wait's, but naturally letter-writing did not fulfill the same need for her as it did for the exiled Emma, nor had she Emma's pen of a ready pupil-teacher. Letters were a "tar'ble gurt trouble," as she told her mother, and after a time hers grew farther and farther apart, till there would be two of Emma's between two of hers. Then when summer came with the long evenings, Tom Boorner, the plowman's son, asked her to go out with him into the twilight fields and lanes. They would go down the Bostal Lane, to where the gate looks over the fields toward Udiam and the Rother marshes, full of the cold mists of the twilight east, with the stars hanging dim and still above them, and there they would stand for half an hour, perhaps. They had not much to say to each other, but somehow it used to fill their evening, and what was more, it filled Rosie's thoughts, so that at last she seemed to forget all about Emma Brown. Emma grew tired of writing and getting no answer, and after a time the letters ceased.

Two months after she received the last, when the summer was gone and the gold corn stubble had been plowed out of the autumn fields, it was known at Wait's and through Oxhurst that Tom Boorner and Rosie Pont would marry as soon as they were old enough and had the money. This did not plunge the neighborhood into any very great excitement, for it was not expected that the marriage would take place for five or six years at least. The couple were extremely young and their prospects were not very bright. Besides, a courtship which did not run into years was not considered "seemly" in the country round Oxhurst.

"Now don't you go thinking above yourself, Rosie," said her mother. "You'll have to work harder than ever with a marriage ahead of you. Tom's a good boy, but he ain't making more than fifteen shillings a week, and your father and me can't do nothing for you, so you'll have to put by a bit every week for buying your clothes and sheets and things, and then maybe, by the time Tom's ready to marry, you'll have enough money to set up housekeeping."

Rosie took her mother's words to heart. Under her rather stolid exterior was a very lively desire for the little home that Tom had promised, and she was anxious that it should materialize as quickly as possible. Not only did she do her usual work with more than usual thoroughness, but she occasionally helped Mrs. Bream, of Wait's, in the house when she was short of girls, and on Saturday afternoons, which were supposed to be holidays, she occasionally put in half a day's charing at the Vicarage or at the week-end cottage the artist people had taken in Bostal Lane. These extra shillings were carefully put away in a wooden money-box, bought by her father for that very purpose at Battle Fair.

Thus it happened that at the end of five years Rosie had saved nearly fifteen pounds. She was now nineteen and Tom was twenty-two. His fifteen shillings a week had been made a pound, and there was no reason why they should not be married in the spring. Tom was very proud of her; he said she had been a good girl to have worked so hard and saved so much, and that it spoke well for her success as housewife in the little cottage which on his marriage would be added to his wages from Tileman's Farm.

Rosie was proud of herself and inclined to boast a bit. She would be married in a white dress made by the dressmaker at Battle. She would have a coat and skirt in her favorite saxe blue, a felt hat with a quill in it, and a bit of fur to go round her neck. She had already begun to buy one or two little things—bargains that were brought to her notice by other girls or friends of her mother. She had a silk blouse and a pair of artificial-silk stockings and a belt with a silver buckle.

Then one day a peddler came to Wait's Farm with lace collars and hat ribbons and jeweled combs for the hair. He said that he had been told down in the village that one of the young ladies up at Wait's was going to be married, and he promised her that she would find nothing better or cheaper than what he carried on his tray.

"I've been all over England, miss," he said to her in the queer "furrin" voice which she and the other girls sometimes found difficult to understand; "I've been in Scotland, where the lasses never wear shoes to their feet—no good me taking my fine silk stockings there! I've been in Ireland, where the girls wear shawls over their heads—no use have they for my fine hat ribbons. And I've been in Norfolk and Suffolk and Yorkshire and Cheshire and Shropshire and every shire, but," said he, with a roving brown eye for all the young faces crowded in the doorway, "I like Sussex girls the best!"

Rosie stood silent, fingering a lace-edged handkerchief. "Did you say you'd been in Shropshire?" she asked after a bit.

"Shropshire? Why, yes, my lady. I've been to Salop and Ludlow and Stretton and Bridgenorth—a fine place, Shropshire, with the Wrekin and the Welsh hills that you see from the river, and the big jail in Salop where a murderer was hung three months ago."

"Did you ever meet anyone called Emma Brown?" asked Rosie. "She went to live in Shropshire at a farm called Botvyl."

"That'll be near Stretton, won't it?" said the peddler.

"Church Stretton, Shropshire, is the address, though it's four years since I got a letter from her. But maybe you've met her, knowing those parts?"

The peddler looked reflective. "Now I come to think of it," he said, "I did run across a young lady of the name of Emma Brown. But she was in the hospital in Salop where I went to see a cousin of mine who had been taken ill with the rheumatic fever. Yes, I remember it was Emma Brown from Botvyl in the bed next to hers. That's queer now, ain't it, miss? It's what they call a coincidence! Was this Emma Brown a friend of yours?"

"Reckon she was, but I haven't heard from her these four years."

[213]

"Well, poor girl, she must have fallen on bad times. There she lay in bed and could scarce speak to my cousin Polly. Now I remember, Poll told me she was down on her luck—all she'd saved gone on paying for being ill, which is a poor way of spending. Now, miss, which will you have? The lace border or the embroidery?"

"I don't think I'll have neither, thank you," said Rosie in a crushed voice.

"What, neither? But you'll never be married without a lace handkerchief!"

"I don't like to go spending my money when poor Emma Brown's in want."

"Now, don't you be silly, Rose," said one of the girls. "Your spending or not spending won't make no difference to Emma Brown."

"You can't keep the gentleman all this while talking and then buy nothing," said another girl.

They all wanted to see Rosie spend her money—it gave them a thrill of extravagance.

Rosie gave way and bought the embroidered

handkerchief, which was sixpence cheaper than the lace one. Then she went indoors quietly and rather sadly.

The peddler's visit had been a shock to her: it had made her think; it had made her a little ashamed of herself. How wicked she had been to forget poor Emma . . . poor Emma who had not liked going away from home! She had forgotten her because she had been happy with Tom, and now she was going to be married and would never have thought of Emma at all if it had not been for the peddler. And poor Emma was ill—she had not been happy, her journey to foreign parts had not been a success. It didn't seem fair.

That night at home she was very thoughtful, and as soon as supper was over she went upstairs to the bedroom where she slept with two little sisters. They were already asleep, for their mother had put them to bed early to get them out of the way. They did not hear Rosie go to her chest of drawers and take out her money-box. She counted the money that was inside—

twelve pounds. She had saved fifteen pounds in five years. Probably Emma had done as well as that, for Emma was a hard-working girl, a better worker than Rosie. But now all Emma's savings had been swallowed up in a long illness, so the peddler said, while Rosie was spending hers on clothes and linen for her marriage— as if marrying Tom was not good enough in itself, without the extra pleasures of silk and lace! Emma had spent her money on doctors and physic and all the hardships of a sick-bed— as if illness wasn't bad enough in itself without having to spend one's savings on it. It didn't seem fair.

The tears ran down Rosie's cheeks. She felt that she had treated Emma badly, and now she couldn't bear to think of spending all this money on herself. She must send it to Emma—it would help her if she was out of work because of her illness, or if she was still poorly it would allow her to go away for a change to the seaside, perhaps. She would not let herself think of all she must give up in the way of a white wedding dress and the saxe-blue coat and skirt and the hat with the quill. . . . Her marriage would be a poor affair indeed. Still, the chief thing about the marriage was Tom. She would have him, whatever happened, while poor Emma had nobody. They said she had been sweet on young Reg Vidler before she left Oxhurst, but it had come to nothing—perhaps because she had had to go away. Poor Emma!

The next morning Rosie asked her mistress for an hour off at dinner-time. Thinking she wanted to run down and see the peddler, who was still in the village, Mrs. Bream agreed, and Rosie went off. She carried her purse, not in her pocket, but in the front of her dress, inside her stays, for her purse this morning held more money than it had ever held in its over-long life.

"I want a postal order for twelve pounds, please," said Rosie to the postmistress. Her face was very pale and a little drawn.

"You can't get a postal order for all that,"

replied Miss Smith; "it'll have to be a money order."

She wanted to ask the girl some questions, but she took her office seriously and maintained a professional aloofness.

"Then give me a money order, please," said Rosie.

The postmistress produced one. "Sign your name here," she directed.

"But I don't want her to know who it's from."

"Then you can't send a money order."

Rosie's face fell. "What am I to do?" she said. "Reckon I don't want the person it's for to know it's from me."

"If you like I will change your money for notes, and you can send them by registered post."

"Then I'll do that. But I don't want to post it here."

"You can take the envelope and post it any-where you like," said Miss Smith. "But re-member, Rosie," she added, gravely, "it's a lot of money. I hope you're not doing anything rash, my dear?"

"No," replied Rosie, "it's something that must be done, I reckon. But don't tell anyone about it, Miss Smith."

"No, I won't tell. You've always been a sensible girl and I trust you not to do anything silly."

Rosie escaped with the registered envelope in her hand. She had not guessed that the matter would involve such difficulties, but she hoped they were now nearly over. She went next to the George Inn, where she found the peddler just setting out for the next county.

"I want you to post this letter for me," she said, "from some big town away from here. It's to Emma Brown, but I don't want her to know it's from me . . . she'd think I shouldn't ought to send it . . . or maybe she'd be angry and send it back, seeing the way I've treated her. So I've done the address in printing hand, and if you post it from a place like Lewes or Horsham she'll never know who sent it."

The peddler smiled. "I'll post it from Lewes," he said.

Of course Rosie Pont was a little fool, and deserved to lose her money after intrusting it to an unknown peddler to post at his discretion, but as a matter of fact her folly was quite successful. The peddler was honest, and in due course the letter arrived at Botvyl Farm in Shropshire.

" 'Miss Emma Brown, c/o Mr. and Mrs. Tudor.' That'll be for me," said the farmer's wife. "Who is sending me a registered letter, I wonder?"

She tore it open and in surprise counted twelve treasury notes for one pound each.

"Good gracious! Now who in the name of wonder can have sent me that?"

"Someone who doesn't know you're Emma Tudor," said her husband.

"Well, it's not six months since I was Emma Brown, and this comes right away from Lewes. Maybe some one from the old place has sent it

to me, thinking I'm still poor as I used to be.
There was old Mr. Prescott, the vicar, he was
a kind old man, and I think ud have done
more for me when I left if he'd been able, but
he was in a poor way himself. Maybe he's
luckier now and thinks to do me a good turn."

"But don't the folk down there know you're
married? Why didn't you write and tell 'em?"
asked her husband with reproachful fondness.

"Why should I? They'd all forgotten about
me. Rosie Pont, who was the last one to keep
up with me, hadn't written for over three years,
so why should I remember who had forgotten
me?"

"Well, some one's remembered you, as you
see. Can't you think who it is?"

"No, I can't—unless it's Mr. Prescott. I
don't know anyone round there who'd be worth
twelve pounds. Stay, it might be Mrs. Gain
of the Loose. She was sorry enough to turn me
away, and said she'd do something for me if
ever she found she could."

"Well, no matter who sent it, here it is! And

you can't send it back, seeing there's no address. We'll take it as a piece of luck and go into Salop to buy you a gown."

"I don't like to do that," said Mrs. Tudor. "I've got everything I want. I've been a lucky woman. I've had my ups and downs, but I've come through safe and happy at last. It isn't everyone who's had such luck. I'd like to give it to some girl who hasn't done so well. Now there's that girl Rosie Pont at home—I was middling fond of her once, and I don't suppose she's done much for herself, poor child. One of a family of eleven children, and a silly little thing. I'll tell you, Owen! I've a mind to put that money straight into an envelope and send it to her. You can post it at Ludlow Market, and she'll never know where it comes from. I reckon she'll find it useful, for these are hard times for those that haven't had my luck."

The Mockbeggar

MR. AND Mrs. Reginald Dalrymple were walking along the highroad that leads from Iden to Wittersham across the Isle of Oxney. They were very particular about being given their full name of "Reginald" Dalrymple to distinguish them from Mr. and Mrs. Charley Dalrymple, who were in Northampton workhouse; from the Peter Dalrymple, who tramped in Wales; from the Stanley Dalrymples, who were in prison; and from Serena Dalrymple, who had put herself outside the pale of decent society on the roads by marrying a "nigger."

Mr. Reginald Dalrymple was about sixty-five years old and his back was bent. Otherwise he looked hale enough, and his face, at least as much as could be seen of it through a thatch of brown whiskers, was red as an autumn pear.

He wore a frock coat, gray-flannel trousers, a pair of brown beach shoes with rather inadequate uppers, and a bowler hat.

Mrs. Reginald Dalrymple was about three years younger than her husband and inclined to stoutness, though she looked an able-bodied woman. She wore a very handsome cape trimmed with jet, a woolen muffler that might have been gray, but to which she referred as "me white scarf," and a man's cap set at a rakish angle. She wheeled a perambulator, which did not, however, contain a baby, but the Reginald Dalrymples' luggage—indeed, it may be said, their complete household equipment, which at a first glance would appear to consist entirely of old rags. However, a more sympathetic inspection would reveal a really excellent kettle (the leak was only just below the spout), a suspicious-looking rug, an assortment of cups, a tin plate, a screw driver, an ancient copy of *Tit-Bits*, a photograph of a robust young woman with a hat full of feathers, and another photograph of a sailor.

"I'm beginning to feel me feet," said Mrs. Reginald Dalrymple to her husband.

"And I'm thinking it's coming on to rain," said he, with a look up at the lowering sky.

It was autumn, and the red leaves were shaking against soft clouds of October gray which the wind brought down from Benenden in the west.

"Where's our next chance of a doss?" asked Mrs. Dalrymple.

"There's the Throws up at Potman's Heath," replied her husband, "but I reckon they'll be —— damp to-night."

"Reg! Don't use such words," said Mrs. Dalrymple, with dignity. "You forget my mother was a Stanley."

"I'm never likely to forget it, the way you goes on about it. Anyone ud think she'd been Queen Victoria on her throne, to hear you talk! But what I say is, it's coming on to rain and there ain't no union within fifteen miles. Besides, you're feeling your feet," he added, kindly.

"I've walked twelve miles since dinner, Reg," said Mrs. Dalrymple, with a little plaintive sigh.

"Hook on, then," said he, extending a ragged elbow.

She hooked, and for some moments they walked in silence. Then he said:

"It'll be awkward for you pushing the pram with one hand," and took it from her—though Mr. Reginald Dalrymple had often boasted that he had never come down to wheeling a perambulator, and never would.

"I've been thinking," said she, a few minutes later, by which time the rain was spattering freely in the dust—"I've been thinking we must have come near that mockbeggar place by the Stocks. The house was standing there five year ago when we was on the roads with Sue and her lot, and if it hasn't tumbled down since there's one good room in it, anyway, with the ceiling tight, and there's water in the well at the bottom of the yard."

Mr. Dalrymple reflected. "You're right,

Hannah!—I believe you're right this once.
We should be coming to that mockbeggar in
half an hour. It'll be raining the —— skies
down by that time, so we might go in and light
a fire and not trouble about getting farther to-
night. It's a good way from the nearest place
and we're not like to be meddled with."

Mrs. Dalrymple was feeling her feet more
and more, in spite of the supporting elbow and
the removal of the pram. She was also beginning to get wet, though this did not worry her,
being of custom. She was far more preoccupied
with the thought that she could not walk a
twelve-mile stretch without getting tired—and
she'd been able to walk twice that as a girl,
when she and Reginald had tramped all round
the country by Chichester. She had had the
children then, as well—one slung at her breast
and the other hanging on her skirt when his dad
did not carry him. She was glad when she saw
three sharp gables suddenly draw themselves
against the sky, which sagged low over the
fields, squirting rain.

"That's it," she said; "that's the mockbeggar. I knew it was somewhere in these parts, though we haven't been here since Sue was on the roads with her man. D'you remember that time we dossed under the stack at Wassall?"

Mr. Dalrymple grunted. He was looking for a gap in the hedge, for it struck him that it would be best to go straight across the fields to shelter instead of walking round by the road. He soon found what he thought was a proper opening, and proceeded to enlarge it to meet the ample requirements of his wife by pushing the perambulator through. He then gallantly offered a hand to Mrs. Dalrymple and, after much gasping and effort and crackling of twigs, she was at his side in the paddock which belonged to the mockbeggar.

A "mockbeggar house" in Kent is any large-sized house which stands empty close to a high-road, and seems to mock the beggar who plods along, thinking he will find charity at those doors which, on his close arrival, are found to be either swinging on their hinges or barred on

[228]

emptiness. The mockbeggar at Wittersham was an especially large house, which, owing to want of repairs, a poor landlord, and a defective water supply, had stood empty for some time. It was probably about fifty years old and was built in comfortable Victorian style, but neglect and the misty weather of the Isle of Oxney—that cone round which steam all the mists of the Rother levels and Shirley brooks—had eaten holes in its solid fabric of roof and wall and made its shelter doubtful even to the Reginald Dalrymples, to whom uncracked walls and fair slated roofs were only the occasional experience of the workhouse.

"A downstairs room ud be best," said Mrs. Reginald.

They went into one next the passage on the ground floor. It was full of dead leaves and bits of glass from a broken window, but there was a grate in it where a fire might possibly burn, and the rain was confined to a small pool under the window sill.

"You unpack here, Hannah, and I'll go and get some water for the kettle."

Mrs. Dalrymple extracted the kettle from the pram, carefully wrapped in a piece of news-paper, and while her husband went off she pro-ceeded to arrange her various belongings. The sinister-looking rug she put in the corner with a nice comfortable bit of sacking; that was the bedroom. The cups, the plate, and a broken knife she put on the remains of a shelf; that was the kitchen; while the two photographs she set proudly among the dust and cobwebs on the mantelpiece; that was the parlor. She was then, according to custom, going on to make herself comfortable by taking off her shoes, when she was startled by a noise overhead.

An empty house is full of noises, and Mrs. Dalrymple had a wide experience of empty houses. Mere scuttlings of rats or hootings of owls or rustlings of crickets or howlings of wind in chimneys could not alarm her, but this sound she knew at once was none of these. It was a footstep, a human footstep, which moved in the room overhead, and she held her breath to listen. The next minute she heard more and worse—that murmur coming to her through the boards was a human voice. She stuck her head out of the window (no need to open it first) and made a sign to Reginald, who was coming up the yard with the kettle. The sign urged both silence and attention, also haste. His response was immediate; they had often been together in these emergencies, demanding a quick stealth. He did not speak a word till he was back beside her in the room.

"It's people!" said Mrs. Dalrymple, in a hoarse whisper; "there's people here!"

"How d'you know? Where are they?"

"They're up above. I heard 'em talking. Listen!"

They both listened. The sounds in the upper room continued—voices and footsteps.

"There's two," said Mr. Dalrymple. "I can tell by the feet. Who can it be? It's road people like ourselves, most like; no one else ud ever come here."

"I wonder if it's anyone we know. It might be the Lovells—you know Lance and Aurelia Lovell are walking in Kent."

"I hope it ain't folk in the house after repairs," said Mr. Dalrymple, struck by a sudden thought. "You never know your luck, and some one may have bought the place."

"I hope it's not that stuck-up Eleanor Ripley and her husband," said Mrs. Dalrymple. "We had enough of their airs when we met them at Maidstone. She's got saucers to all her cups."

"Well, I'd sooner it was her than gaujos," returned Mr. Dalrymple; "it ud never do for us to get found here, and it ud mean a-spoiling of the place for visitors."

"You go and have a look," suggested his wife. "Take off your shoes."

Mr. Dalrymple shuffled them off without undoing the laces, and left the room with extreme caution. His progress upstairs and along the passage was as silent as only his kind know how to make it.

Mrs. Dalrymple strained her ears, which

were as quick as they were when she was seven-teen. The voices continued, but she detected more than conversation—she thought she heard a sound of sobbing. Time went on. Reginald was evidently maneuvering with his usual dis-cretion, for the flow of talk above remained un-interrupted. Indeed, so velvet-footed was he that he was back at her side before she expected him, and, old stager though she was, nearly made her jump.

"It's gaujos," he said, in a low voice. "There's two of 'em, mighty queer . . ."

"How queer?"

"Oh, the girl's got short hair like a boy, and the boy he's soft-looking. They're only a boy and girl. Maybe we could scare 'em out."

"I don't want to scare them," said Mrs. Dalrymple. "The night ain't fit for a dog and I'd be sorry to turn 'em out in it. But if they ain't road people, what are they doing here?"

"They're quarreling," said Mr. Dalrymple —"quarreling and crying."

"I thought I heard crying."

[233]

"It's the girl's crying, into a handkerchief. She's got a white handkerchief with a blue border."

"Are they gentry?"

"Fine gentry, I should say, by their clothes, but I don't think they're after repairs or taking the house or anything."

"What are they doing, then?"

"Sheltering from the rain, like us, and I don't think they've got much money, for they're talking a lot of words about the price of a ticket to London."

"Is that what the trouble's about?"

"No, I don't know as it is. I can't make out a lot of their foolish words, but it seems as either he wants to marry her and she won't, or else as they are married and she wants to get shut of him and he won't have it."

"I should think not!" said Mrs. Dalrymple. "I'm for sticking to your lawful certificated husband, and that's why I'd never go to the workhouse except just now and again for a rest. You know that Eleanor she says a woman

[234]

should be able to get rid of her husband if she wants to, and take a new one, which you can't do in a workhouse, but I was always brought up to strict notions as to marriage. My mother was a married woman, and so is my daughter after me."

"Well, maybe they ain't married. I don't rightly know. They had too many words for me to be able to make out the lot of them. But hold your tongue, Hannah; they're coming down."

Steps sounded on the rickety stairs of the mockbeggar—unskillful, gaujo steps that made every stair creak.

Mrs. Dalrymple made a hasty movement as if to gather up her possessions and thrust them back under the rags in the perambulator, stirred, perhaps, by some dim instinct of far-off ancestors who must not let the stranger look upon their household gods.

Her husband laid hold of her arm. "Don't be scared; they're nothing—hardly cut their teeth yet!"

[235]

At the same moment a young man appeared in the doorway. He was tall and loosely knit, with a heavy coltishness about him, as of one not yet full grown. Behind him a girl's face stood out of the shadows, framed in a queer little stiff mane of cropped hair. Her eyes were bright and resolute, but at the same time frightened.

"Hullo!" said the youth, truculently, to Mr. Dalrymple. "What are you doing here?"

Mr. Dalrymple looked the aggressor up and down. "This place belongs to us as much as you."

"*More* than you," said Mrs. Dalrymple, "seeing as we're road people and you're house people who have no business here!"

"Well, I might ask what your business is."

"Our business is to have supper and a doss on a wet night, and if you keeps clear and don't come round talking foolishness we won't meddle with you, and there's room enough for the lot of us."

"It's all right, Bob," said the girl. "Let's

go back." Her face was flushed, and her eyes were a little swollen under the straight line of her fringe.

Mrs. Dalrymple suddenly became professional.

"I'm not the one to interfere with a real lady and gentleman," she whined, putting on the manner which she kept for well-dressed strangers. "I'm sure you're a real fine lady and gentleman, and if the lady will only cross my hand with silver I'll tell her some gorgeous things about herself, and maybe about the gentleman, too. I can see a lot of money coming to you, lady—even more than the price of a ticket to London!"

The girl darted a surprised look at her companion.

"Come, lady," wheedled Mrs. Dalrymple, "I'll tell you a high-class tale about husbands."

The girl turned away with a heightening of her flush. "I can't bear this nonsense," she said, in a low voice to the young man. "These

[237]

people needn't interfere with us, nor we with them. Let's go upstairs."

The youth looked sulky. "It's all very well," he said, "but they've got the only decent room; the rain's coming through all the ceilings above."

"You should have put your traps in here," said Mr. Dalrymple, "then we should have kept out of it; but as we're here we mean to stick. My old woman's wet through, and she's going to have a dry doss, I'm blowed if she ain't."

"Oh, well, come on," said the young man. "It may clear up before night, and then we'll start again."

He turned away, following the girl upstairs, and the Reginald Dalrymples were left in peace.

"There's queer things you meets on the roads," said Mrs. Dalrymple, "and it isn't so much the people you meet as the places where you meets 'em. Now what are those two doing here? I'm beat."

"You're curious," retorted Mr. Dalrymple,

"fair eat up with curiosity, because you're a woman. Now I don't think twice about 'em as long as they leaves me alone, and nor won't you, Hannah, if you've got sense. Here, let's have a fire and get ourselves dry."

He turned to the all-providing pram and from its depths drew forth its last treasures— some blocks of woods and a bundle of sticks. The Dalrymples always carried a supply of dry firewood about with them, for they were getting old and considered themselves entitled to a certain amount of luxury in their old age.

A fire was soon lit and the kettle put on to boil; once it was blazing, the addition of a few damp sticks gathered outside no longer mattered. The room grew warm and Mrs. Dalrymple's clothes began to steam. Her husband took off his coat and put it over her shoulders.

"There you are, Hannah," he said. "I don't want it. This weather makes me sweat, but you've got to take care of your bones."

They made tea, which they drank in great comfort, with half a stale loaf and a lump of lard. Outside, the rain was hissing down, while the wind howled in the chimney.

"It'll be wet upstairs," said Mrs. Dalrymple, pleasantly.

The fire was beginning to die down, and Mr. Dalrymple did not fancy going outside to get in more sticks.

"I'll go and have a look at the banisters," he said, "and maybe there's a bit of a cupboard door."

The banisters looked satisfactory as fuel, and he was in the act of wrenching a couple of them out when he saw the young man on the staircase above him.

"Hi!" said the latter, dejectedly, "we're half flooded out upstairs. I was going to suggest that we come in with you till it stops raining. We'll clear out as soon as the weather lets us."

"We're poor people," said Mr. Dalrymple—"Mrs. Reginald Dalrymple and I are poor people, and we can't afford to take lodgers at our fire without a bit of silver."

"We aren't asking you to take us as lodgers,

damn it! I'm just asking you to let the young lady come and sit in a dry place. It's what you wouldn't refuse a dog."

"I would certainly refuse a dog," returned Mr. Dalrymple, with dignity. "My wife and I never allows no dogs to sit with us, it being well known as dogs have fleas, and my wife being a lady as 'll have nothing to do with fleas!"

The young man surveyed Mr. Dalrymple as if he himself belonged to that species.

"Well, if you want money," he said, "I suppose you must have it. Will a shilling do you?"

"A shilling will do me very well," said Mr. Dalrymple, loftily, "and it includes the fire. We have a very excellent fire!"

"So I gather," said the young man as he coughed in the smoke that was eddying upstairs.

But even the Dalrymple quarters, full of smoke and the smell of ancient rags, were better than the leaking, dripping rooms where he and Meave Anstey had been struggling in vain to keep warm and dry. Meave was shivering now, and her face was no longer flushed, but blue, as she sat down gingerly beside Mrs. Dalrymple's fire.

"Cross my hand with silver, lady," said that good woman, returning unabashed to the attack, "and I'll tell you the prettiest fortune that ever was spoke."

"I don't want your lies," said the girl, angrily, with a sudden gulp.

"Lies, lady! I never tells lies! May I be struck dead if I does."

"My wife is well known as a truth-telling woman," said Mr. Dalrymple, "and I'll thank you not to miscall her!"

For some reason Meave felt rebuked, though she believed neither of them.

"I'm sorry," she said. "Well, you may tell my fortune if you like, but I've only got sixpence."

"Thank you, lady. Thank you kindly, lady. Sixpence will buy me a packet of tea at the next village, lady. And I'll drink your very good health in it, for I never drinks nothing stronger than tea, which is well known."

Meave held out a soft, artistic-looking hand, which was by this time more than a little grimy.

"I likes dirt on the hand," remarked Mrs. Dalrymple; "it helps me to see the lines better. Now what I see is this: I see a railway line, with a train on it going to London, and you and a gentleman are in that train, and when you get to London I sees a church, and a priest, and a great crowd of people, and rice, and slippers. I see all that, and you in the middle of it, beautiful as an angel, and beside you a tall, handsome young gentleman with light hair and brown eyes."

The girl angrily pulled her hand away. "Don't talk such nonsense, please! I can't stand it."

"You don't want to get married?"

"No, I don't. As if I'd—— Rice! . . . Slippers! . . . White veil . . . !" The scorn grew in her voice.

[243]

"There's a wedding cake," encouraged Mrs. Dalrymple, "with sugar all over it!"

"I don't want to hear any more. Look here, you're a fortune teller, aren't you? I suppose I'm the first girl you've ever met who hasn't wanted to hear about marriage?"

"You would be the first if I believed you," said Mrs. Dalrymple, who had dropped her company manner in the familiarity of the scene.

"Well, you can believe it. I don't want to get married—I don't believe in marriage," and she threw a defiant glance not at Mrs. Dalrymple, but at the young man.

"But a girl can't never live by herself. It ain't natural."

"And it ain't safe," said Mr. Dalrymple. "I've known more than one time when my wife here might have got copped if it hadn't been for having me handy to show her the right trick."

"I don't mean to be alone," said the girl. "I don't believe in that, either. What I hate is the hypocrisy and the slavery of marriage." Her

voice rose and warmed; she became a little lec-
turer. "It's the idea of losing my freedom
which I can't bear. If women hadn't been
slaves for centuries none of them could bear it.
When I choose my mate we shall both of us be
free—free to love and free to part. There
shall be no keeping of the outer husk when the
kernel has rotted."

Mr. and Mrs. Dalrymple stared silently with
their mouths open, and the young man looked
uneasy.

"You see me and my friend here, now,"
continued Meave, "and even you, a woman outside the ordinary conventions of society, immediately form the idea that we're going to be
married. I tell you you're utterly wrong. If
we were going to be married we shouldn't be
running away; we should be sitting at home, un-
packing wedding presents. We are going to
join our lives together, but in freedom, not in
bondage. We shall be free to part whenever
we choose, free to work, free to go our own

[245]

ways . . ." She had almost forgotten that she had not got her debating society before her.

"Well," said Mrs. Dalrymple, "I don't want to part and I don't want to work and I don't want to go any different ways from Mr. Dalrymple, so I can't see the sense of what you're saying. Mr. Dalrymple and me has been married close on forty years, and we've got a daughter Sue who's been married twenty years to a fine feller in the osier trade. She has a caravan with brass rods on the door and lace curtains in the windows, and five of the dearest little children you could think of; leastways, the eldest's nearly grown up now. And we've got a son Jerome who's a sailor and has had two wives one after the other. The wife he's got now lives in a house and has a china tea service. We're proud of our children, but they've gone away from us now and I don't know what we'd do if we hadn't got each other."

"She's uncommon set on her children," said Mr. Dalrymple. "That's their likenesses up there on the shelf, what we carries about with us everywhere. My daughter Sue ud have us stay with her, and once we went and stopped with my son and daughter at Portsmouth and slept in a bed. But we'd just as soon be along of each other here."

"Reckon you wants your husband more when you're old than when you're young," said Mrs. Dalrymple. "I'm getting too old to do most of the things I used, and I don't know what I'd do if it wasn't for Mr. Dalrymple, who does them for me. Our idea is to keep on the roads till we're old enough to go into the married quarters at the workhouse. It ud break our hearts if we was to be separated after all this time. . . . I don't hold with being parted from your certificated husband."

"You gets used to each other like," said Mr. Dalrymple. "If I was to go on the roads with anyone else I'd be so bothered and vexed I shouldn't know what to do."

"If I was ever to see you on the roads with

anyone else . . ." said Mrs. Dalrymple, menacingly.

"Not likely, old lady," said he, pushing her cap over one eye in playful affection.

"Now, now," said she, "none of your larks." But she looked pleased and a little proud of him.

The rain had become a storm, with a rush of wind in the chimneys of the mockbeggar. Dead leaves flew rustling round the yard, and the pool under the window was a little lake. But beside the fire it was warm and dry, though the smoke, as it eddied and waved under the low ceiling, made Meave choke a little, and strange tears come into her eyes—of course that was the smoke. She felt proud and happy. She had broken free at last . . . and she was saving Bob, who otherwise would have become a slave, having all the instincts of one. . . .

"Ooo—ooo . . . yah!" A loud yawn from Mr. Dalrymple made her start. "I'm —— sleepy," he added, conversationally.

"Now don't you start using words again," said his wife. "I'm not accustomed to them, being a Stanley, and I reckon the young lady ain't, either, for all her uncertificated ideas. If you wants to go to sleep—go."

"I'm going," said Mr. Dalrymple.

"Then take back your coat. I've dried under it nicely."

"I don't want any coat. I'm warm as a bug."

"You want it, and you'll take it. Here now."

An amiable tussle followed, which ended in Mr. Dalrymple putting on his coat, while his wife had the piece of sacking in addition to her share of the rug. They took no more notice of Meave Anstey and Bob Pettigrew, but were soon asleep, with the queer, stiff, silent sleep of animals who rest among foes.

"Rum old pair," said Bob, under his breath. "I'm sorry you've been let in for this, Meave, but it's better than being swamped up stairs."

"Oh, they're all right! I rather like them, though of course they're frauds. They're de-

cent to each other, which is odd. I rather
thought that type of man always bullied his
wife."

"Men aren't quite such rotters as you think—
even tramps."

He spoke irritably, for the sordid side of the
adventure was unpleasantly obvious on this
night of wind and rain without, and stuffiness
and teasing smoke within. To his surprise, she
did not take up his challenge. She sat watching
the old couple as they lay huddled in the corner, a confused blot of rags and shadows.

"It's love that holds them together," she said,
in her debating-society voice, hushed down to a
whisper, "not the mere fact of marriage."

"I dunno," said he, truculently. "I don't believe they'd be together now if they weren't
married—anyhow, not together like this."

"Why not? Why shouldn't lovers be faithful?"

"It's different, as I've told you a hundred
times. Especially when you're old. I'd think

nothing of it if they were young or middle-aged. But they're old, and there must have been lots of times when they were tired of loving and tired of life, and would never have gone on if they hadn't belonged to each other."

"That's just it—they were tied."

"And the tie kept them together over the bad places. It's like being roped on a climb; when one or another of them went down, there was always the rope, and as soon as they were on their legs again they didn't notice it. I believe people who aren't married—no matter how they love each other—somehow they're hardly ever in together at the finish. . . . You generally find that if the going's rough they drift apart. Why you, yourself, say you'd hate to belong to a man all your life; you want the one great Moment, and then not to spoil it by going on together. I think there's a good deal to be said for that, though, as I've told you dozens of times, I want to marry you."

He looked very young as he sat there beside her in the dying firelight. He was only a boy or he wouldn't have come with her—he wouldn't have let her force her adventure on him like that. He was very young—but he would grow old, like Mr. Dalrymple. That soft brown lick of hair on his forehead would be gray—his face a little worn, perhaps. Should she see it then, or would they have gone their separate ways? She wondered what he would look like when he was old—what he would be like—kind, protective, unselfish, like Mr. Dalrymple—a strong arm to lean on when she needed it most? . . . Growing old together . . . together not only at the start, but at the journey's end . . . but tied . . . as Mr. and Mrs. Dalrymple were tied . . . by the memories of struggles and toils together, by adventures and hardships shared, by long years of companionship in wayfaring, by the love of their children. . . .

She bowed her head suddenly over her lap and tears fell into her hands.

"Meave—darling—what is it? Tell me."

His arm was round her, his shoulder under her cheek.

"Bob . . . Bob . . . will you always love me —when we're old?"

"Of course I shall always love you."

"As much as that?" and she waved her hand toward the indefinite mass of Mr. and Mrs. Dalrymple.

"I should hope so," with a little contempt.

"Then . . . Bob . . . let's go back."

"Go back where?"

"Home. I want us to get married."

"My little Meave! . . . But you said——"

"It's seeing them. They're so happy— they're so true. They're dirty, terrible, shameless old things, but they're happy; they've got something that we haven't got—that we can't ever have, unless we're married."

He had wisdom to be silent, hugging her without a word.

"Let's go back home. It's not ten o'clock yet, and we can tell mother we were caught in the rain and waited to see if it would stop. She need never know."

"And we'll get married?"

"Yes, though you know she'll make us go in for everything—bridesmaids and rice and church bells and all that."

"Never mind; it'll make Mrs. Dalrymple's fortune come true."

They both laughed a little.

"When shall we start?" he asked her.

"Oh, soon—now."

"But it's coming down in buckets."

"Never mind; we're only an hour from home. We haven't got to face all that walk into Rye and then the journey to London."

She shivered a little, and he drew her close in sudden, fierce protection.

"I shouldn't have let you come. I've been a fool about all this. I didn't believe in it, and yet I gave way because I was afraid of losing you. I should have had sense enough for both of us, and made you go my way instead of yours."

"Is that what you're going to do in future?"

"Yes—when you're a silly little thing."

She laughed, and their lips came together.

It was he who remembered the need for quick action.

"Come, we must be getting off, or we sha'n't be home till it's too late to explain. Are you ready?"

"Quite. I'm glad we didn't bring any luggage, except in our ulster pockets. It would have been difficult to explain why we'd gone for a walk with two suitcases."

They giggled light-heartedly, and went out on tiptoe.

They were off. But just as they were leaving the mockbeggar she remembered something that had been left undone.

"Bob, we ought to tell them. I want them to know."

"For Heaven's sake don't go back and wake them up! What d'you want them to know?"

"That we're going to be married."

"What on earth has that got to do with them?"

"Oh, nothing, of course . . . but I thought . . . Give me a leaf out of your pocket book, there's a darling."

He gave it, and she scribbled on it, "We are going to be married," and, creeping back into the room, put it on the mantelpiece beside the pictures of the blowsy girl and the sailor.

"And look here," she added, "as we're not going to London, we might just leave the price of our tickets with them. It may help them a lot."

"They'll probably spend it on drink."

"Well, let them. I don't care. I can't bear to think of people without proper boots on their feet."

The firelight was playing reproachfully on the toe of Mr. Dalrymple's shoe.

"Nor can I. Well, here's the money. It'll be a surprise for them when they wake up."

He put it beside the paper on the mantelpiece, and they went out.

It was daylight when Mr. and Mrs. Dalrymple woke. The storm had ceased.

"Hullo! They've gone," said he.

"Not taken any of our things with them, have they, Reg?" asked his wife, looking anxiously round.

"Not they. They're gentry. Gentry don't take poor people's things without a lawyer."

"You never know. Besides, they was queer gentry. All that talk she had about marriage . . . it was shocking. If I'd heard my Sue using such words I'd have——"

"Wot's this?"

Her husband had found the treasure on the mantelpiece.

"I'm blowed if they haven't left their money behind 'em! Ten bob if it's a tanner! Well, I'm blowed!"

"That's luck for us, anyway, if it ain't exactly luck for them."

"Oh, I reckon they done it on purpose. They'd never have put their dough just there by our Jack's likeness. It's Christian charity, that's what it is."

"I don't believe it's Christian charity—that ud be tuppence. Ten bob's nothing but an accident. Howsumever, it makes no difference to me what it is so long as it's there. I could do with a plate o' ham."

"A plate o' ham and a cup o' coffee, and a bottle o' whiskey to come along with us to Tonbridge."

"That's it. But look there, Reg—there's writing on the paper."

"So there is. Pity we ain't scollards."

"Maybe it's a word for us."

"That's what it is, I reckon."

She picked up the paper and inspected it solemnly, then passed it on to her husband, who did the same.

"Pity we never got no school learning, Reg."

"I've never felt the want."

"But I'd like to be able to read the word they've left us."

[258]

"That's because you're a woman and made of curiosity. I, being a man, says let's take the money and be thankful. And now, old lady, pack up your traps, for, thanks to this bit of luck, we'll have our breakfast at the Blue Boar."

A Day in a Woman's Life

I—MORNING

THE first colorless light of dawn crept slowly up from the east, over the meadows of Padgeham and Dorngate. It left the Rother marshes in shadow, touching only the tops of the hills, making them stand out as pale islands above the valleys of the little streams. It shimmered on the windows of Pipsden, that cluster of tiny cottages on the road from Hawkhurst to Rye. The cottages were beginning to wake—blinds were drawn, windows opened, columns of blue, wood-scented smoke rose out of their chimneys into the windless air. It was time for the men to go to work—on the Tong Wood estate, or on the Manor farm—and the women were busy preparing breakfast. Only a house rather larger than the rest, standing a little way back from the road among some barns, was still asleep.

For some time Joyce Armstrong had been conscious of the disturbing light. She had thrust her face into the pillow and tried to shut it away. But she was aware of it spilling itself about the room, over her shoulders, into the mirror, and she knew when the moment came that it filled itself with sunshine and she could ignore it no longer.

She sat up in bed, shaking back the long hair from her face, stretching out her arms slowly. She was a beautiful woman, of slow movement and heavy though not ungraceful build—at the beginning of her thirties, but bearing their trace not in any aging of her features or her skin so much as in an indefinite weight of experience shown in her somber eyes. The first spring sun had tanned her lightly, and her extended throat and arms showed a warm yellowish brown against her white muslin nightdress.

She yawned . . . carelessly flinging the back

of one large hand to her mouth . . . then a deep shiver went through her. . . .

Time to get up. It must be quite seven o'clock, and she had a lot to do before she started. Started . . . should she go? Why, of course she'd go! She must know for certain—understand the meaning of all this. Anything would be better than the past week with its uncertainty, its hope deferred.

There might be a letter this morning. Of course it wasn't likely that he'd write at the last minute—unless he put her off. He'd done that before—put her off at the last minute. He probably did it like that to avoid any protest or entreaty from her. Bah! It was horrible thinking of him like this—seeing his faults so clearly, preparing for his little treacheries. But after three years one couldn't help it—if only one could help going on in spite of his faults. That was what humiliated her—forgive, forgive, forgive. Angry tears flowed into her eyes and she jumped out of bed.

She pulled up the blind, and the sunshine

filled the room. A soft blue sky lay over the fields, over the woods that roughened the piling ridges of Kent. Near at hand was the smoke of the Pipsden breakfast fires, the red roofs slanting to windward, the busyness of the little back yards, the stillness of a pond. Her throat tightened, and the tears of anger became tears of blinding sorrow. Oh those soft blue and golden days that had been in the beginning, when every day some token of his love and tenderness came up to her from the marsh— either a letter or a little gift, or he himself in his big Sunbeam car. . . . She remembered how once she had heard its throbbing in her dreams, and waked at seven to find him already there. Those were the days before he was sure of her.

She turned quickly from the window, back into the sun-filled room, and shrugged on a kimono which lay over a chair, thrusting at the same time her bare feet into mules. Clap, clap went her heels on the carpet of the room, and then a louder clap on the polished boards that surrounded it. It would wake mother if she went clapping downstairs like that—mules were no good if your heels were slim—better have got moccasins. . . . But Laurie had loved the way they used to hang from her toes when she dangled her legs. . . . She must not think of Laurie—already she could feel the tears coming back. She made a vow to herself not to think of Laurie till she had made the tea.

The kitchen was dark. The blinds were down and the sun was at the other side of the house. She hoped there were no black beetles about. Oh, what was that?—only Perkins the cat, rubbing against her legs in an ecstasy of joy. His tail waved like a pine tree above his arched back, his hair stood out, all his body quivered with the organ-music of his song. The lovely, lovely thing. She picked him up and buried her face in the humming softness of his flank.

"Oh, Perkins, love me—don't kick—don't go away."

But Perkins was on the floor, still vibrant, but aloof. His love was strictly practical, with a view to the morning's milk—it was not to be squandered on anything merely human. He stepped daintily beside her to the door as she went to take in the jug. Then he led the way back to his saucer. She filled it with new milk.

"You don't deserve it, you naughty Perkins. You don't really love me—it's only cupboard love."

"Lap-lap-lap-smack," said Perkins.

"After all, why should you love me more disinterestedly than— No, I haven't made the tea."

She leaped to the stove. What a nuisance it was, being unable to get a girl to sleep in the house. One had to do all the morning's work oneself. In summer it wasn't so bad, but in the winter · . . . ugh! Thank Heaven, winter was over. But next winter . . . what would that be like? Not like last winter—no, it couldn't be. It must be different. But would it be? She mustn't think of it. "If winter comes, can spring be far behind?" . . . A tear fell hissing on the stove. "Some more milk, Perkins? Don't put your head in the jug."

A loud rat-tat sounded in the front of the house. Joyce jerked herself upright, and the blood ebbed out of her cheeks. That was the post. For a moment she felt as if she could not move. Was there a letter from him lying on the door mat, where she had so often seen it?—his black, vigorous handwriting distinguishing it from the other letters, even at a distance. But if there was, it could mean nothing good—it would be putting her off; otherwise he'd never leave her ten days without a letter and then write on the morning he was expecting to see her. It would be better if there was no letter—and yet, would it? Would the fact that he had not written tell her anything?—wouldn't it leave her more hopelessly in the dark than ever? At least, if he wrote, she would know definitely if he expected to see her, and if he did not, why not. Lord! what a coward she was! She had it in her power to put an end to

[266]

all this questioning by going to the door. But she could not move.

Rat-tat. Again! That meant the postman was waiting. She would have to go.

"Good morning—a registered parcel to be signed for"—that must be from Laurie—who else? . . . No, it was her mother's tortoise-shell spectacles, sent back from repair. . . . "Thanks. And the letters? Thanks. Good morning."

A circular, her mother's weekly letter from her aunt—that was all.

Then suddenly she knew that she had wanted desperately to hear, even if it meant the destruction of her one faint hope of seeing him. Anything was better than this uncertainty. He had not written for ten days, not since their last meeting. He had never been so long before without writing—and she had written twice, the last letter imploring him to write to her, if it was only a line. What had happened? Something must have happened to account for his silence. Had he gone away suddenly, and in his

[267]

hurry forgotten to post the letter that told her of it—or had he given the letter to some one else who had forgotten to post it? All the explanations which could possibly leave her a good opinion of him rushed through her mind as she took the kettle off the stove, filled the teapot, and set the teacups on the bedroom tray. By the time she was carrying the tray upstairs others more disquieting had arrived. Perhaps he was wanting to choke her off and had chosen this way of doing it; perhaps he had found some one else he liked. . . . Oh, no, he had been so sweet when she had seen him last and they had planned this day. . . . He could not have changed. Perhaps he was ill, too ill to write—perhaps he was dead.

"Good morning, mother dear. I hope you had a good night."

She set down the tray by her mother's bed and kissed her.

"Here are your spectacles come back—and Aunt Milly's letter."

"I heard you go downstairs a great while ago."

"Yes—I'm afraid my heels flopped and woke you. I must get some new slippers."

"No, no; I was awake. I've been awake since five. I wish I could get some one to help you in the mornings, dear; it's a shame for you to have to get up and make my tea."

"Oh, I don't mind it a bit. I like getting up early on these fine mornings."

So they prattled to each other—about the house and the weather and the tea and the cat; and all the time Joyce was saying to her mother in her heart—"Oh, mother, I'm in anguish because my lover doesn't write to me, because he's getting casual about me, getting tired. Soon he'll want a change, and I love him as much as I ever did, though I see all his faults as I never did. Oh, mother, help me! But you can't."

No, her mother could not help her because her mother had never known anything like this. Love had come to her, as it seemed to have come to so many of her generation, as an ex-

panding flower instead of a devouring flame.
Love for her had meant marriage, protection,
children. . . . Why must it mean something so
different to her daughter, who needed all these
things as much as she?—oh, why, why, why?
. . . "If Laurie really loved me, he would
marry me," she said in her heart. "It is all
nonsense what he says about being unable to.
He has a comfortable home and lots of money
to spend on things like cars and trips to London. If he really loved me, he'd let the mort-
gage rip, and be poor with me. Then why do
I love him? Because I can't help it, I suppose."

As she was carrying the tray out of the door
a new thought flashed upon her—"I won't go."
She suddenly made up her mind not to go to
see him at Warehorne. If he was calmly expecting her to come, though he hadn't written
to her since their last meeting, it would serve
him right if she failed to appear, and perhaps it
would make him appreciate her a little more.
If he had been untrue to her, it would save her
face—if he had merely gone away. . . . It

would be horrible turning up at the farm and having to ask, "Where is Mr. Holt?" and be answered, "He's not here, ma'am; he's in London." No, she had much better not go, and for quite an hour she really thought she wouldn't.

During that hour she dressed, let in the daily girl who prepared the breakfast, and helped her mother over the last stages of her toilet. Perkins came up, voluptuous with the thought of fish, rubbing against Joyce as she knelt to fasten her mother's frock, with little hoarse cries in his throat. Joyce thought: "If I don't go, it will mean more uncertainty. To-day's Saturday. I can't hear from him till Monday—perhaps I shan't hear then. I can't bear this for another three days. I must go and find out what's happened, however bad it is."

"What are you doing to-day, my dear?" asked her mother, when they were at breakfast.

"I'm going over in the car to Warehorne to see the Holts—don't you remember my telling you?"

"Yes, of course I do—and Lilian Smith is coming to spend the day with me."

That was another reason why she must go—she'd asked Lilian Smith to come in and spend the day with her mother. "So good of you, Lilian dear; you know I can't leave mother alone all day, and I simply must go to see some people at Warehorne." What a fool she'd look if she stayed at home!

"Has Mrs. Holt come back from Italy?" continued her mother.

"Yes—she came back last week"—no need to tell that Mrs. Holt had gone to stop with a sister at Brighton.

"Well, give her my very kind remembrances. Tell her I'm so sorry I'm not equal to calling upon her. Mr. Laurie Holt is at home, I suppose?"

"Yes, mother," said Joyce, and blushed heavily. It was dreadful having to deceive her mother like this—mother who was so understanding, and so young in spite of her age—so much younger than her daughter.

Mrs. Armstrong saw the blush and the droop of the head.

"Well, you be wise and careful, my dear. He's paid you a great deal of attention, but young men seem to be so queer nowadays. You mustn't let him play with you."

Joyce laughed.

"Darling, I'm not what you'd exactly call in my first youth, and if I'm not able to look after myself, I ought to be."

That was true, anyhow.

When breakfast was over, she went out to get her car. It was kept in one of the sheds at the back of the house—sheds which did not belong to the Armstrongs, but to the small-holder who rented the steading. The car was a small Humber; she had bought it second-hand in a fit of extravagance and daring with some money left her by an uncle. Those were the days when the big Sunbeam could no longer be depended on, as in the beginning, to bridge the gulf between Pipsden and Warehorne, and she had become terribly conscious of the looping miles of the marsh road. Moreover, the driving lessons had given her a less plaintive excuse for her demands on Laurie's time and company. She would never be a good driver—she was not capable or resourceful enough—but she had the right amount of timidity, neither so much as to make her nervous nor so little as to make her presumptuous, and had come through her first six months without any mishap, though her speedometer recorded over two thousand miles, most of which had been run to and fro between Hawkhurst and the marsh.

The Humber was difficult to start. She flooded the carburetor, advanced the spark, cranked furiously and in vain. This was when one wanted a man—when one saw the preposterousness of a woman living alone. Living alone . . . and she and Laurie were what she supposed was called "living together" . . . living together fifteen miles apart.

There! it had started at last. Chug-chug-chug. She brought it round to the door, and ran in to fetch her hat and driving gloves and say good-by to her mother.

"When will you be back, dear?"

"I don't know. They may ask me to stay to tea. But you'll be all right with Lilian, won't you?"

"Oh, perfectly. Enjoy yourself, my dear. You've got a lovely day."

Suppose Laurie wasn't there. What would she do about lunch? Suppose her conjectures were right as to his being away? She couldn't come home and tell them she'd found nobody at Warehorne. She'd have to get lunch at the inn—she must take enough money with her. Lord! what a fool she was, setting out on a wild-goose chase like this.

SHE backed out of the gate—a process she hated—and was on the great ridge road that flows like a ribbon from Hawkhurst to Rye. Craunch!—that was an ugly gear-change—how careless she was—Craunch—the second was just as bad. Now the little car was running smoothly, the speedometer climbing into the twenties. She leaned back, giving herself up to the soothing of speed. It soothed her thoughts into a queer rhythm—they no longer fluttered to and fro like the needle on the accumulator dial—but went resolutely and rhythmically forward like the wheels. They told her that she was a fool to make this journey, and just because she was a fool to make it, it must not be made in vain. When she came home some useful purpose must have been accomplished: she must somehow have retrieved

[276]

her life out of this miserable uncertainty, either by a fresh start in happiness or by a decided end. Her journey would definitely show her what had happened and what was going to be. She dared not think of joy, so she thought of sorrow.

She was going to break off with Laurie. She could bear no more of his treatment, of his neglect, of the slow, selfish dying of his love. Better end it all and find herself free again as she had been once. Free . . . it seemed a hundred years since she had been free, since she had woke in the morning feeling that the day belonged to her. Some words floated into her mind—*"union libre"* . . . that meant "free union"—free when you are bound in body, mind, and heart. . . . But soon she would be really free, so free that she would forget that once she had found her slavery sweet.

Free. . . . She remembered some words she had read in a novel, about how at the beginning of a love affair the man is the seeker, the maker of occasions, and how at the end it is the woman.

That was true. At the beginning it had all been Laurie's pursuit, his delicious pursuit—now it was hers, her sorrowful, humiliating pursuit. Why, it was she who had fixed to-day's meeting —he would have trusted to something more fortuitous bringing them together. Why couldn't she let him go?

But she would let him go—more, she would send him away. "Laurie, I have endured enough—I can endure no more." "Oh, Joyce . . ." he would plead. But she would be firm. "No, I'm going. You must learn that a woman can't be treated like this." Oh, she almost hoped that he would give her the opportunity —that he would not have a reasonable excuse for his conduct. . . . Of course, he might. He might have gone away—he must have gone away—he couldn't have received both her last letters and not answered them. . . . Perhaps he had been away, and for some reason the letters had not been forwarded, and he had come back either last night or early this morning, and had found them there, and was now waiting for

her full of anxiety, full of regret and tenderness. . . . "Oh, my darling little Joyce—how
dreadful for you! I'm so terribly sorry. But
I was sent for suddenly up to town, and those
idiots never forwarded anything. How can I
make things up to you? It's difficult now, but
when we are married . . ." The color had
mounted on her cheeks and her lips parted joy-
fully—she almost forgot it was a dream.

She came out of it the next moment as a flock
of sheep met her in Sandhurst. She stopped
the car, and her thoughts seemed to stop with
it. She saw only the dusty, panting sheep, and
her heart was full of pity—the poor things!—
many of them had lambs running along beside
them, bleating too, but in shriller voices. They
were past now, and she set forward again,
through the trim, wide street of Sandhurst,
quickening her pace towards Linkhill.

How well she knew the road—the sign of
the running greyhound outside the inn, the
throws where one road went into Sussex and
the other into Kent. She had hardly ever been

along that Kentish road, though she had often wanted to. She had used the car almost entirely for her visits to Warehorne. But when she was free she would drive a lot about the country, she would take her mother out for drives—her mother had often seemed as if she wanted to come and wondered why her daughter drove off without her. She would make up to her mother for a lot of things when she was free. . . . She knew now that she would be free—that momentary softness of hope was but a dream. Laurie would have no reasonable excuse to offer, and short of a clear, convincing, reasonable excuse she would not forgive. If he had been unfaithful (she had forgiven him for that once) or remiss (she had forgiven him for that a hundred times) or had got into another of his queer, selfish muddles, her mind was made up as to what she would do. "I can bear no more. You don't really love me, or you couldn't treat me like this. No—it really is ended now."

"Let us agree to give up love
And root up the infernal grove,
Then shall we return and see
The worlds of happy Eternity"—

sang the car, as she ran across the Rother
marshes into Sussex—where the villages of
Northiam and Beckley and Peasmarsh were
threaded on the road like beads on a string.

Well, she had lived through three years of
it, and only the first had been worth living. The
others had been hell. However, they had done
her this service in showing her the kind of husband he would have made—weak, selfish, un-
reliable—how dreadful it sounded!—but it was
true. It was true, too, that she had loved him
in spite of it all. He was so attractive. . . .
But she was glad she had not married him . . .
though she would never forget the day he had
told her he could not marry her, bringing forward long strings of figures and talks of mort-
gages and his plans for the farm, and other
things which she could not understand. What
a fool she had been not to finish it all that day

[281]

. . . that was when she ought to have broken with him and spared herself all this. What had made her stick to him?—love or hope? Had she hoped that her love would make him change his mind, change his fate, and marry her, after all? Hadn't she all along been hoping that he would marry her in the end?—didn't she hope it still? O, God!—what it is to have a patient, indestructible hope . . . and wouldn't it be degrading as well as foolish to marry him after all that had happened? . . . Hang it all, he had treated her badly from the start . . . a woman like herself, desirable, well connected, who had been sought by others . . . to condemn her to this unutterable life, just so he could be free and spend money and buy land . . . it was monstrous!—she owed it to her dignity to end things at once.

> "And throughout all eternity
> I forgive you, you forgive me—
> As our dear Redeemer said,
> This the wine and this the bread"—

sang the car, taking her through Peasmarsh.

She would soon be in Rye. Already the fields were falling away to the southeast. She saw the blue line of the sea . . . and then the green vastness of the marsh spreading away into veiled distances. From the ridge it looked like a huge map, marked out with roads and watercourses, with dots of roofs and steeples. She saw the foot of the Isle of Oxney—she saw the abrupt hillock of Stone with its square church tower. When she was free she would go to church again. . . . Now she was entering Rye, and for a few relieving moments her mind was fixed on maneuvering the car through the narrow streets. . . . Now she was out of the town, rushing along the straight mile—zip-zap . . . let her out . . . open the throttle wide . . . zip-zip . . . thirty coming round on the speedometer tape . . . thirty-five . . . oh, if only I can get her up to forty, Laurie will have a reasonable excuse that I can accept . . . zip-zip . . . Guldeford corner . . . I must slow down . . . and of course I won't accept any excuse . . . I'm going to be free.

Now she was nearing Warehorne she began to feel afraid. It would be a very terrible meeting—it would make her sick. And suppose he had taken the matter out of her hands and had decided to get rid of her; suppose she found a message from him telling her all was over . . . it would be a cruel way of doing things, but then men were often cruel when they were frightened . . . or angry . . . angry with themselves. Besides, what else could have happened? What else could account for his silence, except a definite determination to break with her? . . . Unless he was dead. O, God, Laurie dead!

Then a new fear attacked her. What should she say to the parlor maid when she arrived? If he was away from home, she didn't want the girl to think that she had come to lunch. She must put on speed and arrive well before the luncheon hour—she must put on a careless and haphazard manner, as if she'd called in on the chance. Yet, if he was expecting her and had

[284]

told the servants, it would look queer if she seemed undecided herself.

Both these fears—the big that made her feel sick and the little that made her feel silly— went with her all the way to Warehorne. Her hand on the steering-wheel was clammy, her foot shook on the accelerator. What a pitiful spectacle is a woman driving a motor-car when she's in love!

By the time she had reached the house she had made up her mind to be casual—better that the maid should think her foolish than disappointed. Agney House stood just outside the village—it was really a glorified farm—in the midst of its steading—a red, comfortable, seventeenth-century house, with staring, white-rimmed windows. It looked prosperous—exceedingly prosperous for a man who professed himself too poor to marry; but of course the prosperity was in the house only, and the penury was in the land, the land which Laurie refused to give up for her sake.

She was on the doorstep; her tongue was

thick and her mouth was dry. In a minute now she would know.

"Is Mr. Laurence Holt at Warehorne?"

"Yes, ma'am. But he's gone over to Brenzett on business."

"When will he be back?"

"He said about three o'clock."

"Then he's not lunching at home."

"No, ma'am; he's lunching at Mr. Staples'."

"I see. But he'll be back at three."

"Yes, ma'am. Shall I give him any message?"

"No—that's to say—yes, tell him Miss Armstrong called, and that she'll call again later in the afternoon. Tell him it's on urgent business."

"Very well, ma'am."

The girl was a new importation—she suspected nothing. Joyce had saved her face, but nothing else.

She mechanically got into the car—as part of her program of casualness she had left the engine running—and drove round the little

[286]

sweep and out of the gate. Mechanically she turned to the right, into the village. Everything she did was mechanical. Her brain felt rigid, frozen—ossified—she could not think.

Then suddenly she began to feel, in furious throes. She felt anger, bewilderment, grief, despair—so violently that she had to bring the car to a standstill. She was trembling all over. This was worse than anything she had expected. Laurie was at home, but had gone out to lunch with some one else on the day he had invited her to come to him. He could not have forgotten their arrangement—no, that was impossible—he must have meant to slight her, to show her in this incredibly male, clumsy way that all was over between them. What should she do?—for nothing was certain. How should she act? For the first time she knew the meaning of the expression "at your wits' end."

Should she go home? No; that was impossible. What explanation could she make to her mother or Lilian Smith? Besides, she would be condemning herself to long days of uncertainty.

She could not endure that. Should she drive to Mr. Staples' and demand to see Laurie?— in her desperation, she felt inclined to do that —she had a right to make a fuss, to make things hot for him—he mustn't expect her always to take everything lying down. But something at the bottom of her heart restrained her from exposing herself; better far wait till he came home, and see him there. She could manage to fill in the time somehow till three o'clock.

What should she do? Lunch was out of the question; she could not eat. Neither could she sit still. A terrible restlessness was in all her limbs—her anxiety translated into terms of motion. She would drive out somewhere in the car—drive really far and really fast—fill up all the hours with speed.

There was a wide space to turn in outside the church, and she swung round, the nose of her car pointing toward the sea. A long, white, flat road ran out into flat distances. It was the road to New Romney, so she was told by the sign-post, and she set out along it, with the throttle well open. Oh, she was thankful she had got the car, that she could fill her waiting-time with fierce activity and the lull of motion, and yet was not required to support herself on legs that were weak and shaking. Her speedometer showed her that she had already come twenty-five miles, and there would of course be twenty-five miles home. By driving out seaward she would probably add thirty miles to her day's tally, and fifty was quite enough for her un-skilled driving. But she did not care. She must go—she could not live through time with-out the help of space.

She had never been out on the seaward side of the marsh, knowing only the road between Rye and Warehorne. Soon a toll-gate pulled her up. "Sixpence . . . thank you"— . . . craunch another noisy change—and how her leg was shaking as she put out the clutch!

> "How many miles to New Romney?
>   Scarcely more than ten.
>   Shall I get there by three o'clock?
>   Yes, and back again."

[289]

She mustn't be later than three, or he might have gone out again. She had better be there at a quarter to three. She could contrive to sit still for a quarter of an hour.

The marsh felt very huge, lying there all around her, misty, flat, and green. It was foreign—unlike the country round Hawkhurst, which was all little hills covered with spinneys and fields, and farms with fairy names. Here the farms were set far apart among sheep-dotted miles of pasture—their roofs were immensely steep and high, and yellowed over with sea-lichen, and their ricks were thatched with osiers. She passed an enormous church standing between two farms; a few miles farther on she passed another, standing among some tiny cottages which could easily have been packed into its aisles. She thought of Brookland church, and the color left her face.

It was in Brookland tower, all among the salt-riddled oak beams, that he had first told her that he loved her, holding her to him in the darkness. She had not been surprised—for

[290]

several days she had been expecting, hoping he
would speak, and now at last he had spoken
. . . at least, he had not spoken—his lips had
given her kisses instead of words. But she had
understood—or rather, she had not understood.
She had thought he had wanted to marry her—
it was not till quite a week later that she discovered he did not.

> "O stop your ringing and let me be—
>   Let be, O Brookland bells—
> You'll ring Old Goodman out of the sea
>   Before I wed one else.
>
> "Old Goodman's farm is rank sea sand
>   And was this thousand year.
> But it shall turn to rich plough-land
>   Before I change my dear."

That was the way her little car, rushing and
humming along, always set her thoughts to
music. But this was a silly song—because she
was going to change her dear that very evening.
She had made up her mind. Weakness hitherto
had been her fault, but now she would be firm.
She could bear no more. How many times had

she told herself that since the beginning? The
first year had been beautiful, full of happiness,
in spite of some twinges of conscience and the
stinging of the lies she had to tell. By the
second year he had grown casual and remiss, but
she had borne with him, knowing that it was his
nature, and having always understood that men
don't bother about little things the way women
do. In the third year he had been unfaithful
to her, but she had forgiven him, because she
had always understood that men were liable to
these attacks. Besides, she could not do without him. . . . What had happened that she
could do without him now? A lot had happened—her heart was dead. He had slowly
killed her heart. She did not love him any
more. No, she didn't, she didn't, she didn't.

The flat horizon was growing rough. A great
shaggy wood spread across it, out of which a
tower rose. Here was New Romney and the
marsh's edge. Should she turn before going
into the town? What time was it?—nearly two.
She had better turn. It would be too dreadful

if she were late and missed him—she would turn at the next cross-roads.

A sign-post said—to New Romney: to Ivy-church: to Lydd. She stopped the car and backed up the Lydd road. She did it clumsily and blocked the way. A little boy on a bicycle squeezed past. He turned round and smiled at her—not mockingly, but encouragingly and kindly. The smile at once comforted and melted her—she felt grateful for this unknown being's token of good will.

BACK again . . . back over the same road she had come. The bonnet of her car running before her was like the nose of a living thing—the top of the radiator was like a funny little inquiring snout. If only her car was alive and loved her, how happy she would be! She was a big fool . . . but, oh, she did want a little love—a little affectionate, tender love—love that never demanded anything. . . . She did not think she had ever had it. Of course there was her mother. She would love her mother when she was free. Well, to-day wouldn't be wasted now, for all its anguish—at the end of it she would be free. No longer would she have to tell lies, no longer would she have to wrestle with circumstances, no longer would she have to run after Laurie, either drawn by his whims or driven by her longings. Free . . . free . . . he

[294]

had set her free at last—kicked her out, put her on the pavement—but she was free. "There's no good, Laurie—it really is done—finished this time. You don't love me. You wouldn't treat me like this if you did."

Ah, here was the toll-gate. How much quicker she seemed to have come back. Another sixpence. . . . The girl said, "If I'd seen who it was, I'd have let you through. We're not supposed to, but . . ." Another kind creature. Joyce wanted to thank her, but instead she said in her heart to Laurie: "No, this time I really will not pass it over. It's nothing to me if you care for this woman or not. You can take her, or nobody; you're not going to have me. Of course, I will always be your friend." No—she was done with him—for good—till she was fifty, at any rate . . . then perhaps. . . . No, not even then . . .

Lord! There he was in the road in front of her. She recognized his jaunty step, his familiar tweed suit, the way he flourished his stick instead of walking with it like other men. He must have left Mr. Staples earlier than he had intended. What should she do? Pass him carelessly by? . . . that might hurt. . . . No, she must speak to him, otherwise the break would not be definite. She would leave no raw edges. She would cut—clean.

She sounded her horn as she drew even with him, ran on a few yards ahead, and then stopped. Without getting out of the car she turned and faced him—she saw the recognition dawn in his eyes, without reproach or fear.

"Dearest child . . ."

He came up to her, and was in the car beside her before she could speak.

"Laurie . . ." she said, faintly.

"Start away, dear, and drive me home. You'll come in for a few minutes, won't you?"

"Laurie—didn't you know I was coming to-day? Weren't you expecting me? You'd asked me to lunch."

She saw his face grow blank—his brown, speckled eyes looked vacantly into hers. It was only for a second, but in that second such an agony of realization rushed over her as almost to deprive her of consciousness. She knew that he had forgotten. All her wild conjectures of unfaithfulness, urgent business, or determined slight were beside the mark. He had made no effort to shake her off, to break bad news; his absence had been no part of a plan either cruel or compassionate. He had simply forgotten all about her.

"My dear," he was saying, "how absolutely dreadful!—how perfectly awful of me! But surely we didn't fix anything definite. I said I'd let you know."

"No, you didn't"—she spoke gruffly; "it was fixed. Don't you remember? You said your people would be away and we'd have a whole lovely day together. We'd go over to St. Mary's . . ." Her voice broke.

"Yes, of course . . ." He was beginning to be embarrassed. "Mind the gate-post"—she nearly struck it as she swung the car into the sweep. . . . "I'm awfully sorry, Joyce—you came all this way and I was out. You make me feel dreadful."

He got out and opened the door for her. She followed him into the familiar room, half office, half study. She sank down in an arm-chair and burst into tears.

"Joyce—darling—don't. Don't be so upset about it—it's only a little thing."

"A little thing! . . . Oh! . . . and I've been thinking all sorts of things about you—that you'd thrown me over—that you were dead, even—but this is worse, worse than anything I'd imagined . . ."

"Worse!—my dear girl, don't be hysterical."

He came over to her and tried to pull her hands down from her eyes.

"Don't. You don't love me, or you couldn't have forgotten me. And you haven't written, either—not for ten days."

"I'd nothing to write about . . . and I was waiting till I was sure about to-day . . ." He was tying two lies together.

"Laurie, don't tell me you'd have forgotten

about me if you loved me as much as you used to."

"But I do love you just as much." Again he tried to pull away her hands.

"You don't."

"I do."

"You don't." This wasn't what she had meant to say, how she had intended the interview to go off. He slipped his arm round her, and in spite of her resistance drew her head to his shoulder as he knelt beside her.

"Oh, Joyce, darling, don't be angry. Don't let's quarrel over this. Surely we know each other well enough not to be upset by an accident."

"An accident! Oh, Laurie, if you knew what I've suffered—what I've thought . . ."

"But it's all over now. Oh, do be generous and forgive me."

"But it will happen again—something like it. . . . Laurie, I can't bear any more . . . and I mean, what am I bearing it for?—where is all this leading us?"

"What d'you mean, dear?"

"I mean—are—are we just going on like this until one of us marries some one else?"

"My dear child, I've told you that I can't marry you. Don't let's go over all that again."

"But I don't understand . . ."

He had risen and was walking about the room.

"Dearest, can't you let that alone? Can't we love each other as we used to do, without worrying about what may happen years ahead?"

"But we don't love each other as we used to do. Oh, Laurie, I won't say you love me less, but you love me differently. You forget me. I could bear it if I thought it was . . . I mean if we were going to be . . . if I'd something to look forward to . . . but if I have to bear it in vain——"

"In vain! So this is 'in vain,' Joyce—all our love, all our friendship, all the heavenly moments we've had together?—it's all in vain if you haven't something material to look forward to. Is that what you mean?"

"Oh, no, no!"

"Then what in God's name do you mean?"

She wished she knew. She wished she had said the things she had meant to say—done what she had meant to do. His sin against her was even worse than she had imagined, and yet . . . free . . . the things she had meant to do when she was free. . . . But she would be free— even the sight of him there before her in all his alert and lovely strength should not cheat her of her freedom. She sprang to her feet.

"Laurie . . . I'm not going on with it—I can't . . . I can't bear . . . I'm going to be free."

His arms were round her—her words were choked out against his breast . . . the smell of his tweed coat seemed to stifle her. She felt his warmth and strength, his arm upholding her. His lips were warm against her ear, murmuring tenderly and reproachfully.

"Oh, you silly little thing—you don't know what you're saying. You're going to forgive me and love me more than ever. Of course you are. You're upset with the heat."

Then her spirit fainted. She did not know whether she despaired more of him or of herself. He tilted back her unresisting head, and his lips came down upon hers, the seal of her bondage. "Lord, how oft shall my brother sin against me and I forgive him—until seven times?" . . . "Not until seven times, but unto seventy times seven . . . unto seven hundred and seventy times seven . . . unto the bitter end . . ."

Tired . . . tired . . . that was the only refrain her car had for her on the journey home . . . no more furious thinking . . . no more furious rhymes . . . only tired . . . tired . . . exhausted, eighty-seven miles on the speedometer . . . tired . . . tired.

Home at last.

"Well, dear, have you had a nice day?"

"Yes, mother, thank you—a lovely day."

The Fear of Streets

I

THE old man had ridden round his fields and the end of the day was near. The last sad, solemn rays rested on the steep roofs of his barns, and his pond was a red eye, gleaming under the stacks. The sun hung just above the sea, and the path of its glory swept across the gray waters and across the gray town—over the roofs and through the smoke, till it reached the old man's farm, high up on the Totty Lands, above All Holland Hill.

He had gone out after tea on his white horse, to ride round his land, as was his custom once a week. But he had never ridden quite as he rode to-day, with quite the same silly fondness in his heart, that feeling which came only when he remembered much. There were many memories belonging to his fields—after sixty years' ownership it would be strange if there were not —but he generally recalled only one thing at a time, going back one week, perhaps, to the years of his childhood, another to the time of his marriage; another to the year he bought the big stallion—or the year Jem went to sea—or the year the Tories lost the seat—or the year they built the waterworks just outside his gate, as you might say, and the trouble began.

But to-day there was in his mind the clamor of many years. They seemed to say: "So many, so many behind, so few ahead." Yes, there could be only a few years ahead now. He scarcely knew whether he was glad or sorry about that.

He rode down to the southern boundary, where a weatherworn fence, broken and leaning, divided his land from Mildred Road, a street of workmen's dwellings. The inhabitants had been pretty generous in the matter of tin cans— he saw them lying all along inside the fence, but to-day he had not the energy to dismount and throw them out. He just rode on, staring in front between old Daisy's ears, over the climbing roofs that thronged his boundaries, toward the sea, where the town could never spread.

Why wasn't his farm on the cliff edge, so that at least he could have one boundary clear of streets? Now they lay all round him, a close threat. The town was hidden for a few minutes as he rode through his tiny, skew-blown wood, with a stream tinkling down the midst; but on the other side it was upon him again, with a new tin church and a corner shop; and here were the waterworks, crowding on him from the northeast, with a great belching chimney which sent down smoke into his apple trees. He almost laughed. Yes, it was funny when you came to think of it—a hundred-acre farm in the middle of a town.

Of course, up at the house you did not notice it so much—you could potter about up there and forget that huge, threatening, spreading town which was surging round Fryman's Farm as the tide surges round a rock. Up by the house were his barns, his orchard, the little paddock where he kept his half-dozen cows, his five acres of wheat. He would like never to go beyond them; but was it not his duty to ride round his farm every week, as he had ridden for sixty years?

At last he had done with the circumference, with its penance of tin cans and imminent walls, and could turn toward the center, toward the heart of his dear place. But before he left the borders, he halted in a field which lay just by the waterworks road—a rough, hummocky, sea-bitten field, where nothing much would grow, and in the corner of which a brown tent stood beside the smoky column of a fire.

They had come again, and it was only two weeks that they had been away. They were fond of his place and the quiet camping ground that it gave them; that was another thing the Corporation had against him, that made them doubly anxious to buy him up. People complained of having gypsies encamped in the middle of the town. Yet they were unaccountable good folk, these Lovells, unaccountable quiet and well-behaved—better behaved than the trippers, anyway, that the Corporation set such store by.

A man came stooping out of the mouth of the tent and hailed him.

"Good evening, Mr. Gain."

"Good evenun."

"A fine evening."

"Surelye."

"Maybe you're surprised to see us poor people back so soon. But both Mrs. Lovell and I have business in this town, and we often says to each other: 'Where is a better camping-ground than the Farthing field at Fryman's Farm? Where else would you be able to pitch a tent in the middle of a gorgeous town like Marlingate, where we can send our children to school and do genteel trade with the residents?' "

Mr. Gain did not speak for a moment; then he said, stiffly: "What ull you do when you can't come here any more?"

[307]

"Any more?—but you'd never turn the poor people away, Mr. Gain?"

"I reckon you know what I mean—I mean when I'm dead."

"That won't be for a great while yet," said Mr. Lovell, politely.

"Maybe it ull be middling soon—I'm eighty-two, and it ain't natural to live much longer; and when I'm dead the Town Council ull buy up all this farm and build streets over it and turn you away. They'd like to buy it now—and they'd give me more money for it than they'll ever give those that come after me, who'll be as willing to sell as I've been unwilling. I could get five thousand for this farm any day—but I woan't, because it's my fancy to die like a yeoman on my own place."

"Indeed it's a good fancy and a fine place," said Mr. Lovell.

"Sixty year it's been mine and thirty-eight year my father's, and I pray God I don't see what becomes of it after I'm dead. Sometimes my heart aches to think of its going—to think of those rotten streets going over my plows, and my good house coming down and all the bad houses going up. I remember the day when Fryman's Farm stood out on the open hill, looking down toward the sea. Those were the days your dad and uncle used to camp here in the Farthing; there was naught but woods before us then, right away to the Slough, but they cut the woods down, and the town came up the hill, and it's all around us now, and when I'm gone it will be over us."

He talked on in the slow, monotonous voice of the very old. He felt the relief of pouring out his grievance for the hundredth time to Mr. Lovell, whom he remembered from the shock-headed days of his boyhood. He had not many people to talk to now—his stockman was nearly deaf, his boy stupid, and the girl at the house was just a girl and unworthy of being taken into his confidence.

"I was born here," he continued, "and married here and widowed here. My children were born here, and two of them married from here and one of them died here. My boy Jem ran away to sea—he liked the sea better than the land, though the land was his. If he'd stopped at home and cared for the place he could have fought the Town Council after I'm gone—but he cared for the sea, and the sea drowned him."

A woman had come out of the tent while he was speaking, and stood beside Mr. Lovell, staring up with her inscrutable eyes at the white, agitated old face.

"I've made you a cup of tea, Mr. Gain—it's down on the cloth outside the tent door. Maybe you'll rest a bit before you go on to the house."

"Thank you, ma'am—thank you kindly." He was beginning to feel tired—of late his weekly round had grown more and more of a labor.

II

THE old man died as he had wished—like a yeoman on his own place. He died swiftly on one of his evening rides round his land, down by the broken fence of Mildred Road. They found him there as he had fallen, his horse cropping the grass beside him. It is true that there were tin cans lying round his head, and it was the children playing in the street who found him, when one of them squeezed through the fence to pick up what she thought was an old hat flung among the rubbish. "Mum! mum—there's a gentleman asleep, and his hat's fallen off."

He could not be buried in what used to be his village churchyard, where his father and mother and wife and son had been laid, for the town had swallowed up the little church with its Norman rusticity, and the graveyard was closed for burial. He was laid in new ground in the Borough Cemetery, and his two married daughters dressed in new black stood beside the grave. Afterward they went back to the farm with their husbands.

"It won't be long now before we're finished," said Mrs. Wright.

"But I'm going to stand out for the full price," said Mrs. Pearse. "I won't take less from the Council than what they offered dad."

"Oh, dad was tough and wouldn't sell! The price they offered him went up every year. But they know we could do nothing with the farm, so they're trying to get it cheap."

"It ud have been better for us," said Mrs. Wright, "if he'd sold for the top price in his lifetime."

"Yes—but he was that obstinate, you'd never believe. He was dead set on the place, as you might say, and yet he never made much out of it."

"That's the trouble," said Mrs. Pearse. "If only we could have shown 'em a fine dairy busi-

[312]

ness, or the vegetable and fruit trade he might have done, living in the middle of a town, with no transport to pay . . ."

"While all they see is a few old fields with nothing growing in them; just a camping-ground for gypsies."

Mrs. Wright shuddered.

"That's why I wouldn't sleep here in the house, with those people around. We ought to be getting off now, Lucy, if we're to call in at Pole's about the auction."

They went, and the gypsies saw them go.

III

"NOW there is time for us," said Mr. Lovell.

"Shall we take the children?" said Mrs. Lovell.

"Yes," said Mr. Lovell. "He was kind to the children, and it's right that they should see how things are done Romanly."

So the Lovell family walked up to the deserted house—husband and wife, followed by a tail of little Lovells—Synfye, Aurora, Jasper, Ryley, and Rhoda, the eldest girl, carrying the baby, little Pyramus. The old stockman was making tea at his cottage, and regretting the old days when a generous tea was part of the funeral rite; dreaming of the teas he had eaten for Mus' Gain's missus and his boy Ernie, teas that were really breakfast and dinner and supper rolled into one, so rich were they, so various in meat.

The boy had gone out with his sweetheart, and the young servant-girl had gone home to her mother, for she was afraid to be left alone in the empty house, where for four years she had ministered to the queer old man who seemed so remote from her day of cinemas and cheap silk stockings.

So no one saw the gypsies as they crept through the orchard and the yard, nor heard Mr. Lovell break a pane of one of the lower windows, that he might undo the catch and let his family in.

"It's the first time I've been in this house," said Mrs. Lovell.

"Houses are not for us—anyway, I'm not for houses," said Mr. Lovell. "This is the first time our younger children have been in a house."

"There's not many like us."

"Too few—the Lovells and the Lees and the Ripleys take up with houses and forget themselves. Maybe we shouldn't have brought the children into the house."

[315]

"They don't like it, anyway—which is a comfort" (for young Ryley Lovell had burst into tears).

"He thinks it's a school," said his big sister Rhoda, "he thinks every big place with rooms and stairs is a school. He doesn't like houses."

"May he never do so," said his father, "but I have a feeling that the houses will eat up the Roman people, just as they will eat up the old man's farm."

Mrs. Lovell shivered.

"We shall not have our camping-ground here next winter. It will be cold out in the free country. Perhaps we shall think of houses then."

"Silence, woman!" cried Mr. Lovell.

"It would be nice to live in a caravan with a big bed and brass doors, like our Cousin Bella Carew," said Rhoda Lovell.

Her father turned on her furiously.

"If you speak like that I shall forget I am your father and shall strike you. Oh, but that's the way we're all going—the free people the same as the old people. Some day there won't be any tents by the wayside, same as there won't be any farms in the fields. It'll be all houses, houses, houses. The caravans are only halfway to the houses, and I'd rather die and see my children die——"

"Oh, hush, Mr. Lovell. It's bad to be talking of death in the house of the dead. And here's his room."

"Are you sure it's his?"

"Yes—I've seen him many times at the window—and there's the picture of Mrs. Gain, and other pictures of fine people. But look in the drawers, Synfye, and see if his coats and clothes are there—then we'll know for certain."

"Oh!" cried Synfye, at the strange smell of mingled camphor and moth-killer that poured out of the drawer.

"That is a genteel perfume, my dear, the same as the good folks use in church. Years ago when I went to the Good Place, before it was a town place and I could not breathe in it, I used to smell that smell. It is a good smell—

a church smell. Those are his clothes in the drawer—but it's many years since I saw him wear that coat with the blue tails."

"He said it was his father's coat," said Mrs. Lovell.

"Yes—but the gorgeous brats of the town used to laugh at him when he went out in it, so he gave up putting it on. Some day they will start mocking at our tents and little carts, and we will give them up, too—and that will be the end of the Roman people."

Mrs. Lovell and the children were pulling garments out of the drawers and cupboards, and cramming them into sheets and dusters they had brought. Then they tore the bedding off the bed, while Mr. Lovell rolled up the mattress and heaved it on to his shoulder.

"There's the cups and saucers, too," he panted, as they staggered out of the room with their loads—even the baby Pyramus was hugging a pair of carpet slippers. "We must have the cups and saucers if he's to be buried Romanly."

"Of course we'll have the cups and saucers, Mr. Lovell. They're downstairs in the kitchen, and we'll take the lot. Ho! Ho! I'd like to see the faces of those women who gave him such a mean funeral—the ten-pound hearse and only one carriage to follow. That big one who wore her teeth outside her face, I heard her say she wasn't going to give him a fine funeral because he ought to have sold the farm before he died and got more money for it. She was angry because she wanted more money. I wonder what she will say when she finds out what we've done. She'll wish she'd buried him like a lord."

"He's going to be buried better than a lord," said Mr. Lovell, "he's going to be buried like a Roman."

"I hope he knows what the poor people are doing for him."

"Of course he knows. His spirit is in the house."

Synfye lifted up a wail.

"Be quiet, girl!" cried her mother, "the old

[319]

man's spirit is a good spirit. He was kind to our people and now our people shall bury him."

"But he's buried already—he's under the ground."

"His body may be," said Mrs. Lovell, grimly, "but his spirit ain't. His spirit could never rest after the miserable ten-pound funeral he's had. He won't rest till we've done it Romanly."

They were in the kitchen now, and had shot their burdens to the brick floor. The room was full of dust, through which the plates and cups on the dresser gleamed in faint, white patches.

"Which were the ones he used?" asked Mr. Lovell.

"I don't know—the ringed ones, I think, but I'm not sure, never having sat down to table with him."

"We'd better take the lot."

"Yes—then the woman with the dog's teeth won't have none."

They began to take the crockery off the dresser and throw it to the ground. Synfye and

Aurora and baby Pyramus cried at the first crash of broken china—the other children laughed; the room was full of sound—footsteps, laughter and crying, and the tinkling crashes of broken chinaware.

"Don't cry, children," said Mr. Lovell, "and don't laugh. This is a Roman funeral—it is what I did for my father and what I hope you will do for me."

"Then why do you do it for a Gentile, father?"

"Because he was a good friend to my father and a good friend to me. He let us camp on his ground, and everyone knows that a pitch near a town is good for the poor people. The poor people have grown rich through camping on his ground, and he has been kind to us in sickness. You haven't heard, Jasper and Rhoda and Ryley, how he brought the clever doctor to your mother when she was sick, and how he sent down gentlemen's food from the house till she was well again.

"Now the good farmer is dead, and the big

[321]

town will eat up his farm, and the poor people, who have grown rich in the big town, will now have to go out into the roads again, and perhaps once more become poor. Who knows? But before we go we will perform for him the good customs of our fathers, so that his spirit may rest, and forget the ten-pound funeral, and never see the houses eat up his farm—and so that you, children, may see how we bury Romanly, and bury your father and mother so, when their time comes, and most likely everyone but yourselves has forgotten how a Roman is buried."

"How is a Roman buried?" asked Aurora.

"A Roman is buried in the ground like other folk; but in the old times he was laid in his good horse-fair clothes on his clean bedding, with his drinking-cup in his hand, and his tent above him, and he was burned with fire from his own hearth. But these days he must be put in the ground like other folk; yet we burn his tent and his bedding and we break his cup, or his spirit would never rest."

"And since we don't know which was the old man's cup, we break the lot," said Mrs. Lovell.

The crockery, the clothes and the bedding were now in a heap together in the midst of the floor. In the kitchen range a few red coals were still alight.

"Stand near the door, children," said Mrs. Lovell, "and run out when your father starts the fire, and burns bedding and tent together, as is Roman custom."

"But how can he burn the old man's tent," asked Jasper, "seeing as he never had one?"

"Isn't his house his tent—the house they would sell to the Mayor and Corporation? Why are we burning the things under his roof, instead of outside in the field? Stand near the door, children. Your father is carrying fire from the hearth."

Mr. Lovell had laid two red coals in the midst of the heap. Then he took the ancient bellows, which from the days of the old man's mother had hung beside the fire, and fanned the coals into a roaring flame. The flame caught the dry bedding, fed itself, and grew.   Mr. Lovell ran to the door.

"Outside!" he shouted.

The room filled itself with smoke.

They stood in the little square garden, filled with old-fashioned, neglected flowers, and watched red lights leap and flicker in the dusk.

"It'll be well alight before they can see it from the road," said Mr. Lovell, "and by that time we'll be gone.   We'll naturally take his white horse with us, and I will open the cow-shed door, though I expect the fire-engine will be here long before the fire gets there.   I will sell our old horse in the next town, and his white horse shall pull our cart and make us think of him and his good ways.   For he was a good man, and I rejoice that we have buried him Romanly.

"And I feel that he was one of us for all his Gentile blood, seeing that the houses will one day be the end of us the same as of him.   I'm thankful to have burned down one at least, for the houses will eat the roads the same as they have ate the fields, and the free people will go the way of the old people. And now, wife, I hope our stuff is packed, our tent is down, and our cart is ready, for we must leave to-night, seeing as we have done this Roman thing."

A Workingman's Wife

MR. REDWOOD surveyed his wife and family.

"Well," he said, "I'm off."

"Good-by, Jim," said Mrs. Redwood, "and I hope you'll enjoy your day."

Her husband looked at her unappreciatively.

"You sound stiff," he remarked; "you might put more heart into it."

"You know what I mean, Jim. I want you to enjoy yourself, but——"

"But what, Missus? Why don't you have it out?"

"But be careful what you spend—and mind how you come home."

She flushed deeply as she spoke and looked round uneasily at the children.

"You mean I'm sure to chuck my money away on dud horses and come home drunk. Well, you're a nice one."

His wife made no reply for a moment. Katie and Albert sat stolidly devouring their bread and jam, but she could not help feeling ashamed before them. At their age she had never even seen a drunken man, and she shrank from the thought that such farewells as these must be commonplace to them—as commonplace as the returns which succeeded the farewells.

"I'll go with you to the door," she said.

"Oh, you want to jaw me in the passage."

"I don't want to jaw you, Jim," when the door was closed between them and their offspring's reproachful stolidity—"it's simply that I want to remind you that they'll be needing new boots and coats and things for the winter, and we must be careful what we spend."

"Well, and how long is it since I had a spree?"

"It isn't your sprees I mind, Jim. Don't think that. I like you to enjoy yourself. But it's the way you do things—throwing your money about when we're short, and then taking a drop too much and coming home queer, and the children seeing you."

"That's it—the children. You think of nothing but those children—never of the children's father."

"It's not only for the children's sake I don't like to see you drunk."

"Drunk! I ain't drunk. They've never seen me drunk. I come back a bit sleepy after a long day and you call it drunk. You've no idea of things, brought up as you were."

"Well, take your coat, anyhow"—lifting it off the peg.

He grumbled to himself as he shrugged it on, and suddenly she pitied him—her children's father, with his pathetic futility and sorry pleasures.

"Enjoy yourself—I want you to enjoy yourself so long as you don't forget us."

Then she leaned forward and, moved by an impulse which for long had never stirred her, kissed his red, ruffled face.

"Good-by."

"Good-by, Missus."

He looked sheepishly gratified as he went out.

Mrs. Redwood turned back into the living room. Her next task was to get the children off to school.

"Now, Katie and Albert, it's a quarter to nine."

"We're just finishing, Mum."

They set their jaws to a brisker movement, but the mother noted with a sigh that their faces would have to be washed before they could leave the house.

"It's a marvel to me," she thought, "how they can't eat jam without getting it all over themselves." But she did not say it aloud, for she was already sick of fault-finding.

At last the bread and jam were finished and the last traces of the latter removed with a rag and a drop of hot water conveniently found in the kettle. Two tam-o'-shanters were crammed over the cropped head and the hair ribbon, and two pairs of nail-shod boots clattered down the stairs. Mrs. Redwood went back into the living room and cleared the breakfast table, taking the crockery to the sink in the corner, where she washed it up. Then she went upstairs, cleaned the two bedrooms and made the beds; then she peeled potatoes and put them on the fire to boil, and set on the remains of yesterday's stew for the children's dinner. A rice pudding was also prepared and put in the oven, a few clothes washed through, and a frock of Katie's ironed; then, at a quarter to twelve, she sat down to rest.

She wondered where Jim was now. At the races, of course—he must have got to Folkestone some time ago. It would take about an hour to run from Maidstone to Folkestone in the charabanc. She pictured the sweep of cool woods each side of the road, the sunny spreads of meadowland, the glimpses of the Medway, the views of rolling weald from the hill-tops, the first sight of the sea. And she knew that Jim would see nothing of all this. He wouldn't even look at it. He'd read his paper the first part of the way, and then he'd take out a pack of cards, and he and three other chaps would manage to play somehow with a board on their knees. It seemed a waste . . . a day in the country . . . that wasn't how she'd spend it.

It was overlong since she'd been in the country. Of course there was country all round Maidstone—beautiful country, too. But she didn't seem to have time to get even that far— if she was free she was too tired, and if she wasn't tired she wasn't free. She'd been born in the country, too—born and bred there—not just on the edge, but right in the heart of it, as you might say . . . Nineveh Farm, at the back of Benenden. . . . Her father, the cows, old Batup, the pond, Sam Crookall. . . She might have been out there now if she'd married Sam . . . at Sam's new little place between Yalding and Pleasant Hill. . . .

"Mum! Mum!"

Once more the clatter of nailed boots in the passage. She must be quick, or there wouldn't be time for them to eat their dinner properly before afternoon school. Queer how one didn't get time even for remembering. . . . She was dishing up the stew as they broke into the room.

"Mum! Mum!" from Katie. "Albert was naughty—he was stood on the form by Miss Williams."

"Telltale tit."

"Well, it's time. He would talk in the jography lesson."

"I never."

"Be quiet, children; you haven't time to quarrel and eat your dinners. See, you've got a pudding to-day."

"A milky one?"

"Yes, a milky one; but don't gobble up your meat. You've plenty of time if you don't get quarreling and talking."

All her conversation seemed nowadays to consist of directions and finding fault. She realized it with a wry smile at herself. That hadn't been the way at home—at Nineveh. But now, if she didn't speak sharp, there would never be anything done; life had taught her that her tongue

[332]

was her best weapon, so she used it, despising it.

The children ate their dinner heartily, and as she watched them she had a momentary feeling of content and gladness. It was worth the trouble of cooking to see them enjoy their food —her reward and her only thanks.

Soon the dinner was eaten, the little faces were wiped, and the noisy boots were in the street again. No more of them now till tea-time, for they each had threepence to go to the pictures; she was glad to think that so far they had never missed this weekly treat.

She would get through a bit more washing, and there was some mending to be done for Jim, and then she must go out and buy one or two little things for the house.

II

THE afternoon light was spreading up the High Street in a fan of clear gold. It gave a glamour to the pavements and the shop fronts, even to the people who moved to and fro, to the cars and carts that tore and jolted up and down the narrow thoroughfare. It made Mrs. Redwood think of the fields of Great Nineveh at tea-time—that hour just before the evening's milking. It was like the country coming to town, through the dingy suburbs and the brick-fields and all the spread web of the railway sidings—charging up the High Street like a golden horse . . . that was a funny way of thinking, but then she often thought queer things . . . even now . . . Jim used to say she was a rum one for thoughts. . . .

"Half a pound of the shilling cocoa, half a pound of the one-and-tenpenny tea, a penny

packet of custard powder, three soap squares
. . . " So she made her purchases at the
grocer's.

She had now to go to a side-street butcher
who sold sheeps' heads and bullock's hearts for
pence, and was preparing to cross the road, when
she saw a smart gig coming along toward her,
driven by a big round-shouldered man in a
square bowler.

It was strange that her heart could still
quicken at the sight of him, though it was now
twelve years since he had courted her under the
apple trees at Nineveh. She remembered that
time when . . . but she had better not remember. She hoped he would not see her. After
all, he couldn't have very pleasant thoughts of
the girl who had thrown him over for the
handsome Jim Redwood . . . though he had
always been kind and friendly and never forgot
the children at Christmas.

"Well, Bessie . . . "

He had seen her, after all.

He reined in his horse at the curb, and looked down at her. His face was red and weather-beaten, like a pippin, with thread-like lines all over it, and especially at the corners of the clear blue eyes. The lips were thin and kind. It was a kind face, an innocent face, a stedfast face. It suddenly went from her in a mist of sun-shine and tears.

"Hullo, Sam!"

"I haven't seen you for months. Have you been about as usual?"

"Oh, yes. I thought perhaps you hadn't come into the town."

"I've been in most market days. How are you? How's the children?"

"We're all well, thank you. Jim's gone to Folkestone races."

"Ah! Is he out of a job again?"

"No—he's in a job, though not a very good one, at Tunstall's works. He's got this day off to go to the races with his club."

"And the children are at school, I reckon."

"That's right. Though I expect now they're at the pictures. It's their day for going."

"They do love them pictures, don't they? I never could stand them before my eyes, though they're good enough, my eyes are—see any sort of bird at a distance, I mean. Look here, Bessie, since the children are out, what about you and me having a cup of tea together? I'd meant to stop for one at Masters', and I'd be proud and honored if you'd join me in it."

Mrs. Redwood hesitated. Ought she, Jim's wife, to feel so happy, so utterly cheerful and at rest, in Sam's company? Then suddenly she answered her own thought: "There's nothing wrong in being happy with him. I've got no other thoughts of him. I belong to Jim and the children, and this is only one afternoon . . . "

"Thank you kindly, Sam," she said; "I'd be grateful."

He drove her round to Masters', and left his horse in charge of a loafing boy while they went in together. It was years since she had had tea in a shop, though the experience had been common on the market days of her youth, when she had driven in to Maidstone with her father, sometimes with Sam as a third, and they had had tea at Masters' or Overington's or sometimes in the parlor of the Lion. . . . Now she felt the thrill of novelty and adventure as she and Sam edged their way through the marble-topped tables to a little corner by the window, where they sat remote, with a patch of sunlight on the cloth between them.

Masters' was not one of the smarter shops in the town. It was mostly frequented by farmers on market days and their wives on shopping expeditions. But to Mrs. Redwood it seemed almost palatial, so much had the business of "a cup of tea, with roll and butter and watercress" developed in the course of the twelve years. She stared respectfully at the waitress, with her frilled cap and two bushes of hair over her ears, though mentally she catalogued her as a hussy. Her left hand with its wedding ring lay out on the table, and it suddenly struck her that the girl would think the wedding ring was worn for Sam. She felt her heart swelling with happy pride . . . then she thrust her hand guiltily under the table.

She had not forgotten whether Sam took sugar in his tea. Those far-off market days of her youth seemed to have been brought suddenly close to her. She could almost see the red-and-white-striped gown she used to wear that went so well with the cherries in her hat. She didn't dress much now—hadn't the time or the money—but she would never forget that gown. Then suddenly she had a thrill of nearly supernatural experience when she heard Sam say:

"Have you still got that hat with the cherries in it?"

"Got it!" She smiled with tender good will at masculine ignorance. "Why it's more than twelve years since I wore that hat!"

She had given it away at her marriage, she remembered, to Nell Vine, the chicken girl.

[339]

She had wanted to get rid of it . . . and Jim had given her so many nice new hats.

"Well, it's like old times, anyway," said Sam.

He beamed at her across the teapot. His face had no bitterness, even in the secret places of his eyes. But she, she knew, had secret places of bitterness, in her eyes and in her heart—places where lurked the slow disillusion of married life, disappointment, self-reproach, regret. She hoped Sam could not read those secrets in her eyes, and suddenly she hid them with tears.

That was silly of her, for of course he could see the tears, though probably he would never have read the sorrow that they hid. His own eyes brightened with a puzzled, anxious look; his kind lips parted——

"All well, Bessie? Children all well?—and Jim?"

"Oh, yes, thank you, all well."

She blew her nose and the tears were gone.

"The tea's a little too hot," she said, discovering an excuse, and poured some milk into her cup.

After that they did not talk much. The crust of the new rolls was tough and occupied their jaws. Sam had lost a great many teeth. Now she came to think of it, he must be past fifty. He was about sixteen years older than she was, whereas Jim was two years younger. Those two years meant a lot now, and the sixteen very little. She remembered a proverb she had heard in her youth—"Better an old man's darling than a young man's slave."

Well, she must make up her mind not to see Sam again after this—at least not to see him again in the regretful intimacy of a meal. It wasn't right. She belonged to Jim and the children. For better or for worse she had chosen Jim, and it wasn't right to wish she had chosen Sam. It wasn't fair to Sam, either, she felt more indefinitely. She must just be a bit stand-offish when she met him next time in the street—and that wouldn't be sooner than she could help. She would try and avoid the shops on market day. But she would always be thank-

[341]

ful for this afternoon; she would put it carefully away into her memory; it should belong to her memory only. If she did that, it could not be wrong to enjoy the few minutes that were left. . . .

III

"MUM! Mum! There was a lady fell through the bottom of the train, and you saw her knickers."

"Mum! There was real lions."

"Oh, Mum! Can't we have jam for supper?"

"Not with your nice pudding—it doesn't want it. (Oh how she wanted to give them jam! but she had had to make a rule about the pot lasting a week, and new . . .) So you enjoyed the pictures?" she said, as she helped them to the remains of the milk pudding.

"Yes, but there was no Charlie. They said there'd be a Charlie next week. We can go in the first half, can't we, Mum? He comes on Monday."

"Yes, you can go in the first half, I expect. I'll ask your dad."

She said the last words on principle. She had always wanted to show the children their father as a responsible being.

"When will Dad be home?" asked Katie.

"Not till after you're in bed."

"I'd like to see him come in," said Albert.

Something in his tone made his mother ask sharply, "Why?"

"Oh, I'd just like to—that's all."

He put his hand up to his mouth and hid a reminiscent smile. Mrs. Redwood felt the color in her cheeks as a burning dye. So this was what it had come to . . . Jim actually amused the children . . . they liked to be awake when he came in because he was funny when he was drunk. . . . Was that better or worse than being frightened of him . . . his threats, his blows? It was worse, a hundred times worse. . . . No, it wasn't. Poor little kids! Why should they be frightened? Why shouldn't they be amused? . . . they hadn't much to amuse them. Something like Charlie —Charlie Chaplin on the pictures. . . . Drunk

. . . funny . . . yes, it was funny . . . ha! ha!

"What you laughing at, Mum?"

"She didn't laugh," said Katie; "she choked. A crumb went down the wrong way."

She thumped her mother conscientiously between the shoulders.

"It's all right, dear," said Mrs. Redwood; "the bread *is* dry. Now, run away, both of you, since you've finished, and undress. I can't get about my evening's work till you're in bed."

When they were gone she went up to the window and pressed her face against the dark pane. The street was in darkness, but, now she had blotted out the dim lights of the room, she could see the pavements, wet in a slight shower. There was no traffic now. The place seemed empty—dead. Then suddenly a man stepped out of the shadows beyond the street lamp and knocked at her door.

As she went to open it she wondered what anybody could want at that time. It was half-past seven. She didn't expect her husband for

[345]

another two hours. Perhaps it was some pal come round to see him, not knowing he had gone out—some one come round to fetch him to the public house, she reflected bitterly, on the chance that he hadn't gone there already.

True enough, on the doorstep stood a man called Porter, whom she knew distantly and disapprovingly as a friend of her husband's.

"Good evening, Mrs. Redwood. May I come in for a minute?"

"Jim's not at home; he's gone to Folkestone for the day with his club."

"Yes, I know. That's what I came to talk about."

He looked nervously over his shoulder, and she saw that he was in a state of extreme agitation. She shut the door, and they stood facing each other in the little dimly lit passage.

"I had Tim Buffard come along with me," he said, uneasily, "but he cut and run. I've got a hard thing to tell you, Mrs. Redwood."

"About Jim?"

"Yes—about Jim. We called in at your

minister's, but he was out, else I'd have brought him along to do it."

"You mean you've got bad news?"

"Yes, ma'am, bad news. I tell you I don't know how to begin."

He took out a spotted handkerchief and wiped his forehead.

"There's been an accident."

For a few seconds her mind had reviewed all possibilities and decided that it was either accident or prison.

"Yes, ma'am—an accident—they was in a churrabong, yer know."

"Is he badly hurt?"

He nodded.

"Dead?" Her lips moved silently round the word, and again he nodded.

For a moment neither of them spoke. Both stood against the opposite walls, which did not hold them more than three feet apart. Then in the light that came through the open door of the living room she first saw his features, like a child beginning to cry.

[347]

The next minute the bell rang again, and, as if released from immobility by a spring, she ran to answer it. There were two men and a woman on the doorstep.

"I've brought Mrs. Kemp," said a man's voice, "and here's the Reverend Shales."

"Well, I've broke it—she knows now—I've broke it," said Porter. "You was a tick to leave me, Tim."

"I thought better fetch Mrs. Kemp and the Reverend. Come along, Mike. Women and ministers are best at this sort of job."

"But I want to know how it happened," cried Mrs. Redwood.

"The vehicle, ma'am," said Mr. Buffard, pompous with sympathy—"the vehicle unfortunately overturned."

"And—and where is he?" She wondered if some mangled form on a stretcher waited outside in the darkness, and thought anxiously of the children.

"Well, ma'am, unfortunately they all went into the Medway at the bottom of Megrim's

[348]

hill. You know how the road turns before the bridge, and seemingly the driver missed it in the dark and sent the car over. There's ten foot of mud at the bottom and they haven't got your poor old man out yet. Only Carter and Pont and two lads managed to save themselves, and there's six other poor chaps and the driver with your husband at the bottom—turned turtle on 'em."

The house seemed quite full of people, and she suddenly knew she was doing all the things that were expected of her—she was crying, she was swinging her hands, she was fainting. . . . Mrs. Kemp and the minister were helping her upstairs.

IV

SHE sat in the children's bedroom, with her arms round Albert and Katie, as they sobbed against her knee in their nightgowns. Her own eyes were dry now, though her lips still quivered. Jim . . . husband . . . father . . . dead; she could hardly realize it. Mrs. Kemp was putting away the teapot after the inevitable cup of tea; the others had gone. Once more there was a ring at the bell.

From force of habit Mrs. Redwood rose to answer it, but her neighbor had a better sense of what was fitting.

"Don't you go, dear. I'll see who it is."

She disappeared. A man's voice sounded in the passage, and soon there was a double set of footsteps on the stairs.

Mrs. Kemp came hurrying into the room.

"Here's Mr. Sam Crookall of Pigeon Hoo

Farm came to see you, dear. I said you was prostrated with grief, but he seemed to think you might like to see him, so I said I'd ask you."

"Yes, let him come in."

Sam came in, holding his hat in red, embarrassed fingers.

"Bessie, my dear, I've heard, and I've come to see if there's anything I can do."

She suddenly realized that he was afraid of her sorrow. Nothing but his passionate longing for service could have forced him thus to venture into the sanctuary of her grief. His eyes pleaded like those of a dog which has strayed into a church and is terrified.

"Come and sit down, Sam. I'm glad to see you. It was a kind thought made you come."

"Till I got here I didn't know that you'd heard, and I thought maybe you'd hear it easier from a—a—an old friend. I drove back within a mile of Megrim's, and there was chaps all hurrying up from Harrietsham with ropes to drag the river."

"Have they found anything?"

"Not that I know of—but I came straight here. It—it was a quick death, Bessie."

"I hope to heaven it was."

"Oh, it must have been—overturn sudden in the dark—deep water there—and it's all over—easier than what many a man has in his bed."

She shuddered.

"Some of the chaps were saved. Have they told how it happened?"

"I haven't seen anyone myself, but their drover at Megrim's Farm says as nobody's got a clear story yet. Seemingly all old Pont's done since he was pulled out has been to ask for his hat."

"Terrible shock to everyone," said Mrs. Kemp, feelingly.

"Turr'ble," he echoed in his Kentish drawl.

"It was kind of you to come, Sam," said Mrs. Redwood. At the bottom of her heart a spring was welling—a clear spring, in which, as in a mirror, she saw reflected the tearoom at the back of Masters' shop, sunshine lying on the tablecloth, and in the midst of the sunshine her

[352]

hand with its wedding ring. . . . But it was too soon. She must not look yet. Her arms strained round the children—Jim's children— and the tears flowed again.

"Reckon I couldn't keep away from you when I knew you were in trouble," he said. "Poor little man! poor little woman!" And he touched the children's faces.

"You're tired, my dear," said Mrs. Kemp— "wore out. What you want is a good night's rest—and sorrow makes sleep."

Sam Crookall took the hint.

"Well, maybe I'd better go. But you'll let me know, Bessie, if I can be useful to you in any way. The coroner will be sitting—at Megrim's. I could drive you over . . . "

"Come again—soon."

"Reckon I will, my dear. Pleased to help you in any way, I'm sure. God bless you."

It struck her that he walked out more erect than usual.

"An old friend, dear?" said Mrs. Kemp.

"My father's friend," said Mrs. Redwood,

and hid the blush that was burning under her tears.

"Well, it's good to have friends and neighbors round us in our trouble. I'll get your poor little fatherless lambs to bed if you'd like to start undressing. Come along, my poor dears."

V

IN the familiar room, where she and Jim had slept together for so many years, the sense of him almost overwhelmed her. There were traces of him everywhere—there lay his razor; there lay his brush, with its pathetic deficiency of bristles; there was his second coat hanging over the back of a chair for her to mend when she had time. His pillow was still beside hers on the bed, which twelve years of his weight had given a definite drop toward the right. Her nostrils seemed almost to inhale the customary smell of liquor with which he came to rest. . . . She shuddered. No more of that—no more drunkenness—no more shame. . . . But it was cruel to remember him so. She must remember him as he had been in the days of his courtship—young, handsome, clean-limbed, both sweet and free of tongue. Oh, he had been splendid, her Jimmy! It wasn't fair to think of him as what the years and drink had made of him. She ought to think of him as in the days when he had really been her Jim—her lover, her husband, the proud young father of her children. This other man—who loved her no more than of habit, who was less husband to her than troublesome child, whose children considered him less as a father than as a comic interest in the house—this other man was not Jim, and she must not think of him as Jim. He was dead now, and Jim had come back.

Long after Mrs. Kemp had left her, with tearful sniffs and promises of an early-morning return, Mrs. Redwood lay awake in the darkness which a street lamp made freakish with golden bars. She was thinking of Jim, recapturing his memory, bringing him back, walking with him through the lanes at the back of Benenden, taking from him a rapture that all Sam Crookall's tenderness had been unable to impart. Yes, she must remember that, for she had forgotten it until now. Jim had given her once the real ecstasy of love—she must remember that. Sam had given her a dog-love, humble, faithful devotion, which, unlike Jim's rapture, had survived the years—and of course, now that she was getting on, faithful devotion counted for more than rapture which was dead. . . . But she must not forget that once, and not so long ago, she had been young, and Jim had given her then what faithful Sam had never, and could have never, given.

No doubt in time she would marry Sam, and his devotion would go down with her into old age. She would have for the rest of her life the solid, comfortable happiness the first of it had lacked. But could she really, now she lay in the darkness, face to face with these strange thoughts, could she really wish the past any different, wish she had foregone those wonderful moments for the sake of a humbler but less short-lived happiness? No, she must honestly face the answer—she did not wish it. She was glad she had known such happiness, such a springtime joy, in spite of all that had come after. She must never forget that Jim had given it to her, as he had given the other, the sweet as well as the bitter, and she must be grateful to him always. . . .

Then suddenly her thoughts changed, or rather seemed to pass on. The handsome, glowing youth was gone, and in his place stood Jim as she had last seen him—red-faced, shame-faced, fumbling, degraded—and yet with the old Jim, the vanished youth, looking at her out of his eyes. She seemed to hear him say, "Don't despise me. I'm the same as him—that Jim Redwood who courted you at Nineveh. If you loved him you can love me; if you're grateful to him you can be grateful to me. For there aren't two of us—we're one, really. I walked beside you in the lanes and gave you that rapture you can't forget. *He* was the man you helped to bed drunk the other night. The man who gave you the joy is the same as the man who gave you the sorrow, so when you think kindly of him won't you think the same of me, too?"

She felt the tears running out of her eyes on to the pillow. Poor Jim! with the loose mouth and ruffled hair . . . that bright, keen eye and hair swept back like a starling's wing. . . . Poor Jim! how hard the years must have been that had made him so different! Of course he'd never been a strong character and he'd always had a taste for drink—and he'd had a lot of trouble . . . Poor Jim! She saw now that she must take him as a whole—not divide the romantic lover from the common, sodden husband. They were the same and she must always think of them as the same. It was his dying that had enabled her to get away from him like this and see him whole. While he was alive she had lost all he used to be in the darkness of what he was. But now she could see him more clearly—in a light of kindliness and gratitude—she could build him up again into the lover she had lost; and all through the happy quiet years ahead with Sam she would be able to think gratefully of her children's father. That was something good.

[359]

. . . She must have dozed a little, for the next sensation was one of sudden waking, definitely prepared. She lifted herself on her elbow and listened. What was it? . . . Yes, a knock; there it was again. Some one was knocking at the front door.

It was still night, for the light of the street lamp still lay on the floor in a pale pool of gold. It was still night—night gripped with the chill of coming dawn. Shivering, she crept out of bed and wrapped the quilt round her; she had long foregone the luxury of a dressing gown. Her head was heavy with sleep, and she scarcely thought as she went downstairs, or feared the darkness. The door was unbolted, for Mrs. Kemp had naturally been unable to do more than shut it after her. It struck her that she ought to have gone down and seen after the bolts. . . .

She opened a cautious crack and looked out. A man leaned up against the post of the door, the dazzle of the street lamp spilling over him. Mrs. Redwood's heaviness seemed to fall suddenly from her head to her heart. Her head became astonishingly clear and awake, but her heart felt numb.

"Jim!"

She trembled all over, but she knew it was not a ghost.

"Hullo!" he mumbled.

"Jim—why?—what's happened? . . . Haven't you heard? . . . I mean, the car. . . ."

"I lost the b—— car. They wouldn't wait while I finished my drop." He cursed the car in symbolical language. "They went off without me and I've had to walk home—every b—— mile. I'm dog tired. Damn them for a lot of . . ." He finished the sentence in his familiar way.

"What you standing there for," he continued, "gaping like that? I wan'er go to bed."

VI

IT WAS not till the next morning that he realized how, by over-much drinking and dalliance with the barmaid at the Station Inn, he had saved himself from what he described as "a nasty, sticky end."

"There you see, Missus," he remarked goodhumoredly; "if I'd taken any notice of you and kept off the drink, I'd most likely now be lying at the bottom of Megrim's pond in nine feet of mud. Nice corpse I'd be if I'd gone on the teetotal lay. Put me down for five shillun toward the club wreath for the funeral, Mr. Kemp."

The house was once more full of people, but the atmosphere was no longer solemn and tearful. Mr. Redwood sat in the armchair, a child on each knee, for Father's return—as surprising as anything on the pictures, though not, of course, as exciting as the funeral would have been, had demanded a holiday from school for its fit celebration. Mrs. Kemp was back, sniffing hilariously as yesterday she had sniffed dolorously. She had also brought her husband, averse from scenes of woe, but by no means reluctant to share his neighbor's joy and the bottle of whisky which Mr. Porter had brought as appropriate to the occasion. Also present were Mr. Shales, the Wesleyan minister, Tim Buffard, and the young reporter from the *Courier*, at that very moment taking down the "story" from the hero's lips.

"I didn't take much notice o' the time. I'd made nearly a quid on the course, and I never thought they'd all be hurrying off like that. There was a lot of chaps in the bar and we all got talking of Dirby Street and the surprise he give us at the Selling Plate. . . ."

"Mr. Redwood, not realizing that the charabanc was to depart immediately, joined some friends at a hotel to discuss the fortunes of the day," wrote the eighteen-year-old reporter in shorthand.

"And when I got to the station, there wasn't a b—— train. Beg pardon, Mrs. Kemp—I was forgetting there was ladies present."

"On reaching the station, Mr. Redwood found that the last train had already departed," wrote the reporter. "Work in some stuff about the badness of the local service," he added in brackets.

"So I had to hoof it all the way, except for a bit cross-country between Shelve and Long Halden when a chap gave me a lift in his lorry."

"So Mr. Redwood applied himself to the arduous task of walking home. A timely lift in a lorry, from Shelve to Long Halden, allowed him a little rest, and was also the means both of his missing the site of the accident and of his being able to turn his unhappy wife's despair into delight at least two hours earlier than would otherwise have been the case."

Mrs. Redwood was busy making tea for those

who weren't taking whisky. She went to and fro from the table to the dresser, from the dresser to the stove, without speaking, almost like a machine. She was not thinking, she was not feeling, but in her head and in her heart something was saying itself over and over again.

"Don't despise me. I'm the same as him, that Jim Redwood who courted you at Nineveh. If you loved him you can love me; if you're grateful to him you can be grateful to me. For there aren't two of us—we're one really. The man who gave you joy is the same as the man who gave you sorrow. So when you think kindly of him won't you think kindly of me?"

Jim Redwood filled up his third tot of whisky.

"Here's your health, Missus," he cried, bowing to her over his glass—"your very good health. My! but I wish you could have seen your own face when you opened the door!"

At that moment there was a fresh sound of voices in the passage. The young reporter looked eager—there was something he wanted besides the story.

"That must be my camera man." He put his head out. "Yes. Hullo, Miller! . . . Yes, I'm just ready. . . . Mr. and Mrs. Redwood, may I trouble you to come to the front door, so that we can have a photograph of the reunited family? . . . Yes, the children too, of course. . . . That's right . . . just inside the doorway. A little more to the left, Mr. Redwood. . . . Place your hand on your wife's shoulder. . . . Mrs. Redwood might put her arm round the little girl. . . . Now—all smile, please. . . ."

The Redemption of Tintageu

A Christian Fairy Tale

I

TINTAGEU sat on one of the outlying rocks of the Dirouilles, chin propped on hand, gazing across the water to Sercque. He sighed, and his sigh was the sound of the sea when it withdraws itself over wet sand. His eyes were the color of the sea, and his hair was the color of the brown seaweed. The skin of his body was green, a translucent, aqueous green, like the skin of a drowned man. But it had not the same appearance of death, since its color was due, not to the withdrawal of the blood from its race, but to the color of the blood itself, which was greener than the sea can be even in the pools of Havre Gosselin.

[367]

For Tintageu belonged to the Green People, of whom the sea people are only a sub-nation. He did not belong to the human race, nor to the race of the Sons of God, nor to the race of the Evil Lords, but to the Intermediary Kingdom, where dwell those who took the side neither of good nor of evil in the great days when Michael and his angels fought the Dragon and his angels—who, when the Dragon was cast out, were also cast out, not into hell (since they deserved it no more than they deserved heaven) but down into the shadow of the earth, where as yet there was neither good nor evil, since as yet there was not life.

"What ails you, Tintageu, that you have sat all these days upon the rock, gazing over the water to Sercque?"

It was the voice of old Fano, a lord of the sea people. He was not really older than Tintageu, since all the Green People were created together shortly before the creation of the Morning Stars: but the title "old" is given to those among them who have traveled farther than the rest, who are wiser and more experienced. Fano had a wider knowledge of the earth than Tintageu, who had never been beyond the waters of the Norman Isles since days when those waters first broke in between the lands which are now England and France.

"What ails you, Tintageu?"

"Fano, I am athirst for the land."

"For the land? Would you join the land race of the Green People? If you would, you will have to swim to France, for we have driven them from the Isles."

"No, I do not wish to join any other race of the Green People. I am athirst for the kinship of Mankind."

Then Fano shouted, and at his shout a ship went aground on the Paternosters, and the waves swept over Alderney.

"Mankind! You thirst to become one of Mankind! Oh, oh, Tintageu, you must have drunk fresh water and be mad."

"No, I am not mad. Why is it so strange that I should wish to leave our people? I am not the first who has wished it—yes, and had his wish."

"It is true that some have abandoned our race, though more of us have taken the way of the birds than the way of men. Why do you wish to become man and share man's curse?"

"Because I have also seen his blessing. One day in Sercque I rose out of the sea between Port du Moulin and Pegane Bay, and, all being wet and fresh after rain, I went up the valley to the Moinerie, where the Monks of St. Magloire were chanting their Office. I sat outside for a while on a wet stone. Then I looked through the door, for their chanting had ended, and I saw that they had begun to show Life in a Mystery: and in the midst of the Mystery, place and time ceased, and He whom we may not know came down among them and they were caught up to Him. Then a great and terrible longing was born in my heart, and I stretched out my hands and cried to them, since I could not cry to Him. I cried, 'Oh, Mankind, let me share in this gift that you have—this gift that

[370]

makes you more blessed than we, though you suffer pain and sin and death, and know the dominion of the Evil Lords which we can never know.' But they could not hear me, nor could they hear me on the other days that I came— and the Mystery lay like a cloud in the sanctuary, though I knew that to them it was brightness and knowledge. So I have sat here for seven days, longing for the kinship of the human race, which has such sweetness offered to it in the midst of its sorrows."

Then Fano spoke:

"Listen, my son. Before time was, we were: and as you know, we were happy people, contented in the ways of heaven. So content were we that when war came, we would not take our part, either on the side of Michael or on the side of the Dragon. We chose rather to remain at peace in our own country, saying that such things should not touch us. We did not know that no created thing can ignore the issues of its creation. So when war ended, and the old Dragon was cast out, we found ourselves

[371]

cast out with him, into the shadow of the earth, which is known as the Meteoron. Here we have dwelt ever since—on the earth, in the air, in the fire, and in the water. But it has been our punishment that we should not know the joys and sorrows of that earth, in the midst of which we live.

"We have powers—we can do many things that the children of men cannot do, such as the changing of substances, and assuming new forms. We can do these by means of our power over the Meteoron. But though we have power we have not knowledge—we know not the things that men know. We know not love, we know not death, we know not birth, we know not sorrow, we know not joy, we know not the Evil Lords, we know not the Sons of God, and we know not, nor can we ever know, Him who made us and them. We have had no share in the growth around us. When life was first miraculously born of the virgin sea, we did not know it, since we are neither alive nor dead. When the New Life was miraculously born of

[372]

the Virgin Mary, we did not know it, since we are neither matter nor spirit. Also when death was born we knew it not, for we are neither good nor evil. Nor yet when death died, for we are neither men nor gods. If you become a man you will know all these things."

"I will gladly know them all for the sake of the One among them."

"You know, Tintageu, that there has always been one grace allowed us. Because we did not hate good, nor follow evil, but held aloof only because of our love of the quiet ways of heaven —our love of its appearances, which though imperfect, was not evil—we are allowed to escape from our neutrality under certain conditions. There are two ways—there is the way of the birds, which many have taken, and there is the way of mankind, which few have known. The birds are the nearest point at which the earth-spirit touches ours, and it is possible, without much danger, for one of us to become one of them. The birds feel love and sorrow and joy and death, but do not know them,

[373]

therefore they are wiser than we, though more ignorant than mankind. The beasts we cannot touch, for in them the earth-spirit does not come near us, but it approaches again in man. It is possible for us to enter direct the Kingdom of Mankind. But the venture is one of extreme peril, and has been rarely attempted—and has still more rarely succeeded."

"What does failure mean?"

Fano snapped his fingers.

"Out!—Gone! The spirit falls between two worlds and is lost. Even if it succeeds it will have sooner or later to face death, since all men must die. The bird also will die, but in that case the spirit comes back among us. The spirit who becomes a man never returns—the new Kingdom claims him."

"And what happens when he dies?"

"I do not know. Perhaps he too falls between two worlds. Or he may come into the power of the Evil Lords. . . . You have seen the Evil Lords riding over the floor of the sea, led by Ortac their Prince, and you know

[374]

that they have no power over us, but have power over men. If you become a man you will come under the sway of the Sons of God, but also under the sway of the Evil Lords and their Tetrarch. The Meteoron which kept you sundered from the one can now no longer save you from the other. Do you still wish to join the race of men?"

Tintageu lifted his head.

"I do."

"Then I will say no more," cried Fano. "You have drunk fresh water and are mad. But I will do my utmost to save you from the worst evils you have chosen. It is not in vain that I have traveled from coast to coast. I will take you to St. Magloire himself, as he sits on his rock, watching the deep. He will assist you to enter the Kingdom of Earth, and maybe protect you once you are therein, since he is a mighty man, a giant among men and spirits, and is feared even by Ortac, Prince of the Darkness under the Sea."

II

S T. MAGLOIRE sat upon a peak of the Ecrehos. His head was among the clouds and his feet were on the floor of the sea. Thus he had sat for seven years, meditating on the Two Natures of the Incarnate. His beard flowed over the rocks and the gulls nested in the shadow of it and brought up their young.

Fano and Tintageu came to him, swimming.

"Oh, great Magloire," cried Fano, "mighty ruler of these waters and of Brittany and of Cornwall, whom men know also as Malo and Mullion. Listen to us poor outcasts both of good and evil, and hear our prayer."

Now Magloire loved the sea people, and had helped many of them escape into the race of birds, for he said, "It is better to rejoice and to suffer and to mate and to bring forth young and to die in a few short years than to live forever without the gifts of joy and sorrow."

Said he that day:

"What can I do for you, my children?" He called the sea people his children, though they were not of his race.

"Lord," said Fano, "I bring here one of us who wishes to become a man."

"A man!"

"Yes, Lord. He wishes to pass into the race of mankind."

"But, my son, have you considered that it is easier and safer far for you to pass into the race of the birds, where you will find many beautiful things that you know not now, and will escape many evil things which may befall the children of men?"

"Lord Magloire," said Tintageu, "the race of the birds cannot satisfy my desire, for my desire is for that which even the race of mankind sees only in a glass."

St. Magloire looked at him fixedly, and his eyes were like two great pools of sea water, such as lie under Brenière.

"My son, what do you mean by that?"

"Father, I cannot tell you, for I know nothing of these things. All I can say is that I mean that which comes to your own monks in the Isle of Sercque when they shew forth Life in a Mystery."

Then St. Magloire cried out:

"My child, you have spoken. It shall be as you wish. What you desire cannot be desired except of God, nor can it be found except in God. You shall indeed become a man, for you desire that for which the whole creation groaneth and travaileth in pain together. I will not persuade you any more, but will tell you what you have chosen.

"Up to this day I have enabled six of your race to join the race of men. Of these three were lost in the translation and fell between two worlds. The three others safely passed over and obtained their desire. For this change is never made except at the urge of some desire, which can be satisfied only among men. In each of these spirits it was the desire for a maiden, and when she was won, the new man

[378]

died: for it is a condition of the change that it can last only as long as the desire which brought it about."

"And what happens when a man dies?"

"I do not know. None of the race of men knows what is after death. Even those who died and came back to life at the bidding of the Word, such as Lazarus who was four days dead, came back knowing nothing. If you die as a bird, I can tell you what will befall you; but if you die as a man, I cannot tell you, for I do not know."

"Still, I wish to become a man."

"I have set your danger before you. You may be lost in the change and fall between two worlds—and if you come safely to mankind, you will know the dominion of the Evil Lords, you will know fear, you will know sickness, you will know injuries and wounds, you will know death; and all these shall not be external to you as they are to the birds, but shall also have power within you."

[379]

"I will face all dangers in the hope that by facing them I may learn something of Him whom here we do not know."

Then St. Magloire praised the Trinity and the Undivided Unity, and he set Tintageu before him, while he sent Fano a great way off, and he lifted up his voice and cried:

"Whither shall I go then from Thy spirit; or whither shall I go then from Thy presence? If I climb up into Heaven Thou art there; if I go down to Hell, Thou art there also. If I take the wings of the morning and remain in the uttermost parts of the sea, even there also shall Thy hand lead me; and Thy right hand shall hold me."

Then he liberated Tintageu from the Meteoron. First he invoked the Holy Ghost the Lord, beseeching Him to divide the waters; and the waters of space were divided, and Tintageu felt no longer the influence of the planets and stars. Then Fano looked, and Tintageu was gone. Instead, a swallow flew wildly here and there over the deep. The spirit of Tintageu was in the swallow for safety, while the change was being made, but even so he was stricken with terror and wildness, for he felt no longer all those innumerable sweet influences of the Meteoron—the attraction of the stars, and of the tides, and the movements of the earth in space. But instead were strange, new, sinister attractions, calls of the spirit. Then he looked and saw Ortac sitting on a rock, opposite St. Magloire, and he knew that he fought with Magloire for his soul, which he could hurt at last. Then a great wind caught the swallow and flung him against the cliffs of the Ecrehos, and his soul was dashed out of his body. For what seemed untold ages it spun and whirled in the wind, tossed naked through space. He could feel himself falling—down—down—down—still spinning like a leaf in a gale—and as he suddenly looked into the space between two worlds, he heard Ortac laugh. . . .

But the next moment a great hand came

[381]

down and covered Tintageu, and a great voice said, "In the beginning was the Word and the Word was with God, and the Word was God." As it spoke, Ortac's laugh slowly died away, and the hand was lifted, and Tintageu looked up and saw a calm sea, in which Ortac's throne stood empty. Then he heard Magloire say:

"Rise up, oh man, my son."

He stood up on the rock, and he saw that his skin was white and his blood was red. And suddenly all a new language came to him and he understood his own heart, and standing there naked upon the rock, he lifted up his hands to heaven, and cried: "At last—at last!—my God!"

Then he turned to St. Magloire, and said:

"Holy Magloire, pray for me that I may attain my heart's desire, and receive the Lord's Body. It is for this that I have become a man."

"My son," said Magloire, "you shall not be disappointed of your hope. I myself will baptize you, so that once again you shall be born; and after that second birth I will take you to my own monastery in Sercque, where the prior shall give you the Bread of Life—and then, oh, Tintageu . . ."

"Then, Father, nothing matters—life or death."

III

SO ST. MAGLOIRE baptized Tintageu and clothed him, and brought him to his own monastery in the Isle of Sercque, saying to the prior—"You know our Saviour's words— 'Other sheep I have who are not of this fold.' Here is a young man who hath been redeemed by the grace of God from the Intermediary Kingdom. Teach him, that I may lay my hands upon him and anoint him when next I come."

Tintageu was now a man like other men. He ate and drank and slept and labored with his hands. He knew weariness and temptation and the happiness which comes from the love of God, and the love of men, and the love of earth. Every morning he joined with the monks in the offering of the Holy Sacrifice, and throughout the day he joined them in singing the Hours of the Passion. The prior found

[384]

him an eager pupil, thirsting for the truths of God, and his gayety commended him to the young monks. All saw his happiness, for indeed Tintageu was happy. He did not regret the people he had left, nor the powers he had lost. Though among men he met antagonisms, faults, and frets that he had never met among his former kin, who know not love nor hate, nevertheless he delighted in men's company as he could never have delighted in the company of the Green People. Though he could no longer take the form of bird or hare or fish, he now knew that he had a kinship with these which he had never had before, and a kinship with the earth and the winds and the sea, such as he had never known when he had the freedom of them all. This kinship was due partly to his birth among them as a man, made of their substance, and partly to his Second Birth in Baptism, without which he could only have loved them longingly. For man has in his own nature betrayed the earth, and cannot feel at ease with her till he has put on the New Creation and become her mediator.

Only sometimes Tintageu had moments of qualm—when he looked out to sea and saw Ortac sitting on his rock a great way off, and knew that the Tetrarch of the Evil Lords now had power over him as he had not over the Green People. But sometimes when the day was clear he could also see St. Magloire sitting on his rock, and then he would take comfort, knowing that the Sons of God are more powerful than the works of Darkness.

One morning toward Lammastide, Tintageu came out from the monastery just before Prime. The sea and the sky were fresh and blue, and a great soft wind blew over the island, cooling the sunshine. Then he saw that for the first time the valley of La Fregondée was not empty at this hour, for beyond the brook stood a young girl dressed in green. Now Tintageu had not seen a maiden since he became a man. He had of course seen many before his change, but they had not affected him in any way, for he was

unlike those of his people who have desired to
become man simply for the love of a maiden—
after the fashion of the Sons of God themselves, who saw the daughters of men that they
were fair.

But now that he looked on the maid as a man
he saw that she was lovely, and a strange power
drew him toward her. She came as if to meet
him through the tall ferns, but did not cross the
stream, which, however, ran so narrow at this
spot that he could see her eyes were like the
big green pools in the sea-gardens under Fontaine.

Tintageu did not know how to greet her, for
he had not learned the ways of greeting, save
those of the monastery.

"Peace be to you," he said, to which she made
no reply.

Then he looked on her again, and felt his
heart beating quickly under his habit. His heart
seemed full of songs, and there were wild songs,
too, in his head, so that he did not hear the
singing of the monks at their Office:

"Wherewithal shall a young man cleanse his way; even by ruling himself after thy word.

"With my whole heart have I sought thee: O let me not go wrong out of thy commandments."

Then suddenly the girl spoke, and her voice was like one of his songs.

"Oh, Tintageu, we of this island have heard your story. We have heard of the longings which brought you to earth out of the free, powerful sea, and the protecting Meteoron. We have heard that you are to dwell with St. Magloire's monks till you are fit to receive your heart's desire. But, Tintageu, has any told you that in seeking these things you are seeking that which, as a whole, the race of man seeks not, and passing by those things in which it takes delight? Oh, Tintageu, you are not truly man till you have known woman. These things they seek and teach in the cloister are not things of this world, but of another which may or may not be. Will you then turn away from your true manhood and lay down your life for that which may be but a dream?—for you know that when you have won your heart's desire and satisfied the hunger which brought you to earth, you will die."

Tintageu trembied, for he understood not these things.

Then the girl continued:

"Those of your people who before now have joined our race did so for the sake of that very love you are passing by. They attained their desire in the love of woman, and, having attained it, died. But it would not be so with you, since the love of a maiden was not your purpose in coming to earth."

"What is your meaning?" breathed Tintageu.

"I mean that the power which brought you to earth was desire, and when that desire is satisfied the power ceases, since you Green People have not, like us, life by inheritance from Adam, but life by the creation of desire. When the desire has ceased the life ceases with it. If you satisfy this desire of yours at the altar, at the altar you will die. But if you do not satisfy it, and turn instead to that which is better worth having, you will not die, but live. You will live—your unsatisfied desire will keep you alive—and yet you will live in the enjoyment of that which is sweeter than your desire."

"Lady," said Tintageu, "you are very learned, and speak words which trouble my simplicity."

The lady bit her lip and looked discomfited.

"Fear not," she said; "we shall meet again. My name is Platte Fougère, and I dwell over by Les Petites Côtes. I will meet you in three days under Fontaine, and perhaps by then you will have understood my words."

She turned away up the stream, and Tintageu went back to his Monastery.

IV

BUT for the next three days he was troubled;
for the first time since his coming to earth,
he was afraid to die. Till then he had not been
afraid of death, for he knew that though death
is unknown to man it is not unknown to Him
who tasted it for every man. But now he knew
that in death he would lose the joys of earth
—eating and drinking and toiling and dancing,
courtship, marriage, and fatherhood—lose them
without ever having had them. A sudden great
longing came over Tintageu, to have the common joys of earth. These were the joys he
should have come to seek, and not mere dreams,
which might or might not be true. The vision
for the sake of which he had come to earth did
not belong to earth but to realms which were
not the realms of men—and he was now a man.

He knew besides that he could have these

common joys—have them all the more securely
because for their sake he renounced the desire
that had brought him to earth. As long as that
desire lived unsatisfied he would live to satisfy
other desires. . . . Because he had been filled
with that desire he had powers which none other
of his people had had when they came among
men. Because he had desired heaven, he could
take earth. . . . Tintageu was afraid. He
shunned the Seven Hours of the Great Work,
and when the Sacrifice was offered he knelt in
fear, seeing not life but death. The third
morning found him on the shore under Les
Petites Côtes, gazing at the pinnacles of Moie
de la Fontaine; and as he gazed he saw Platte
Fougère standing on the Moie, and suddenly he
heard her voice—

"Tintageu—Tintageu. Here am I, waiting.
Will you not come to me and know that which
is better than any dream? Here am I, seizable
by your five senses. Will you sacrifice me to
that which your senses cannot know? Will you
refuse love and life for a shadow and death?"

The Moie de la Fontaine was covered with green seaweed, which poured over it like heavy green water, and Platte Fougère standing upon it was dressed in green, like the sea and the weed, and the water between him and her was of a deep, glaucous green. Then Tintageu realized that both times he had seen her there had been water between them, for at their first meeting she had stood beyond the brook.

"Platte Fougère, what are these waters which always lie between you and me?"

"Tintageu, they are the waters of your baptism. I cannot cross them to you, but you can cross them to me. Come quickly."

Then gazing upon her, his heart sick with love of her and the fear of death, Tintageu stepped down into the water. But at that moment a thunder rolled out over the sea, and the cliffs echoed, and the wind rose and swept the Roussel Channel as far as Guernsey. Ortac had laughed upon his rock. And at his laugh Tintageu was roused out of his sickness, and he knew that Platte Fougère was no human maid, but a fetch of Ortac, sent by him to take by craft what he could not have by strength. With a wild cry, he turned and raced over the sand, and clambered up the cliff path to La Moinerie, calling upon God. At the same moment the simulacrum which was Platte Fougère crumbled and dispersed, and became wind, and then seaweed, and then a cormorant upon the wing, and last of all an evil rock under the tides, with pinnacles athirst for the keels of ships.

Then another laugh rang out over the sea. St. Magloire laughed upon his rock, and at his laugh all the steeples in Normandy and the Isles were set ringing.

"Ha! Ha! Ortac—Ha! Ha! You laughed too soon. The great laugh is with me. Ha! Ha! Ha! Ha!"

And the bells rang all the afternoon.

V

IT WAS on the Sunday in the Octave of St. Peter's Chains that Tintageu knelt before the altar in the monastery chapel and received the Lord's Body. He had been shriven, blessed, and anointed, and now St. Magloire himself had said Mass and laid the Sacred Victim upon his tongue.

The bishop said the Communion and the Post Communion, gave the blessing, and recited the Principio from the Gospel horn, and still Tintageu knelt before the altar, his eyes closed, his hands folded upon his breast.

St. Magloire with his ministers and acolytes turned to leave the sanctuary, and seeing Tintageu still there on his knees, he asked:

"Why are you here, my son?"

And Tintageu prayed:

"Father, let me die here, kneeling where His

[395]

divinity has given me the fullness of my humanity."

"Tintageu, you seem to me more foolish than they who of old time sought the living among the dead—for you seek death at the throne of life."

"I have received that which my soul craved for, and by the laws of my translation I now must die. I shall not fear death if I may die here where I have received His life."

Then Magloire spoke very tenderly, and his voice was like the humming of great organ notes, or of the June wind passing over the Isles.

"Oh, Tintageu—oh, my son—do you not yet understand? Do not you yet know the meaning of life, that you wait for death where death can never come? True, you were to die when you had received your heart's desire. But do you imagine even now that you have received it, or can ever receive it? Do you imagine that your thirst for God is truly now sated, or can ever be sated? Do you not desire

[396]

Him with a desire that is immortal, since it can never fail and never be slaked? Who eats Him hungers still, who drinks of Him still thirsts. Those of your people who came among men moved only by earthly desires, satisfied them and are dead, as all that are satisfied shall die. But you who bear a desire which can never be satisfied shall never die. The more you have Him the more you shall desire Him, and as desire is life, you shall live forever. It is true that in time the manner of your desiring Him shall change, as you pass from His earthly to His heavenly kingdom, but your desire itself shall neither change nor fail nor be satisfied. Arise, Tintageu! You are immortal."

Then Tintageu arose, and laughed, and went to his work rejoicing, wondering why he had never before understood so simple a matter.

The Man Who Was Lost in the Animal Kingdom

A Christian Fairy Tale

I

WIDE from the train windows to the horizon swept the waste, the desolation of Caithness. Scotland, of the tidy farms and high castles, of Saxon stolidity and Celtic romance, had been left behind in Sutherland, Ross, and Cromartie, and now the train ran through the lost land of Norroway, a wilderness which had once been the hunting-ground of Scandinavian kings. Low hills swelled out of the green bog-like moor, with never a house in sight, only sometimes the white road running and dipping to John o' Groats—and always the wooden snow-screens beside the line, which

[398]

joined with the scattered spreads of unmelted white to remind the traveler of the days when the snow swept over the moorland from the coast and the hills of Morven.

In a third-class carriage at the rear of the train a clergyman read: "Oh that I had wings like a dove! for then would I flee away, and be at rest. Lo, then would I get me away afar off, and remain in the wilderness. I would make haste to escape, because of the stormy wind and tempest."

As he read, sometimes his eyes roved, and he watched the wilderness slip by, its colors ranging from green to brown under the low drift of the clouds. His spirit found a kind of refuge in the loneliness of it all, in its utter remoteness from life as he had known and lived it for the last ten years. When he shut his eyes he could still see that life, or rather the stage on which its struggles and futilities had been played out. He saw the walls of the houses, scratched and scribbled over by the children, just as the pavements were chalked out for their games—their

[399]

everlasting hopscotches on pavements either slimy with rain or baked with sun. He saw the faces of the houses, with the dirty gape of their windows and the darkness of their open doors in which the women sat, with the stairs ricketing up behind them. He smelled the stench that came from the open house-doors—the stench of cooking and washing and rotting—the stench of the gutters—of pavements hot and pavements wet. He heard the cries of the street-sellers, the oaths of the men outside the public house, the distant tinkle of his own churchbell, faint and resoundless, like a voice that has lost its meaning—and drowning all, the everlasting squeals and chatter of the children at their unending games, shrill, restless, meaningless, busy —like gulls.

He twisted in his seat, and groaned. His dog, sitting at his feet, whined at him, and his wife, sitting opposite, leaned over and touched his knee.

"What is it, dear?"

"Nothing. I'm all right."

[400]

He turned again to his Office Book, and she spoke no more. She knew that he would be better in time. His Office would quiet him and he would have a few hours' rest until—it all began over again. She closed her eyes, and her lips moved in prayer. She prayed that at last this curse which had lain over them for so long might find cure, that in these strange islands whither they were bound peace and healing might lie. At last they had left that other life far behind, the life of the crowds and the slums, which had slowly worn her husband's body and soul till at last they had refused to work together, and the doctor spoke of "a complete nervous breakdown."

For ten years he had worked single-handed in the slums of Paddington, himself scarcely better off than his parishioners, unable to pay for the rest and fresh air that might have saved him if they had been allowed to break the monotony of those grinding months. He had been beaten at last—rest and change had become such necessities that a kindly power had intervened and ordered him six months' holiday. At first she had been appalled at the thought of how they were going to manage, but apparently they would not lose the pittance of his wages as shepherd of ten thousand souls, and a friend who heard of their plight offered them the loan, rent free, for the whole summer, of his little place in the Orkney Islands.

The doctor had insisted on complete change, on utter remoteness from the old conditions and ties. The offer of Mist House almost seemed to come from God. They gladly accepted it, and here they were with their tickets bought by a kindly diocesan fund, and a night in the train behind them, and before them all the width and wilderness of the north—of strange, treeless islands, once the dowry of a Norse princess, of blue, cold seas, of slopes of bog and heather, of towering strata'd cliffs, worn by the waves and booming with sound. Nothing more remote from the slums of Lisson Grove could be imagined. She could not but think that in this new place her husband's spirit must revive; that his face would lose its harassed, pleading look; that his mind would lose its strange terrors, its wild half-formulated longings that terrified her both by their vagueness and by their violence.

" . . . O cast thy burden upon the Lord, and he shall nourish thee: and shall not suffer the righteous to fall for ever."

The clergyman had finished the psalms for the day, and already felt at rest. For twelve years now he had never failed to read his Office, day and night. Through distractions, excitements, hopes, fears, struggles, and weariness his share in the Great Work had gone on. And now he was beginning to experience the reward of those that are faithful. No matter how sick of soul he felt when he opened his book, how listless, fettered, confused, how close to the Ultimate Terror of all, which is madness, the reading of the Psalter never failed to bring him comfort and stability. It was as if a great voice spoke within him, the voice of all the men who have ever sought God, and that he had a share in their seeking and in their finding.

[403]

II

THE train ran through Georgemas to edges
of the waste. Thurso . . . Scrabster
. . . and the Pentland Firth, the old firth of
the Picts, lay spread before the clergyman and
his wife. Then, with a white wake of foam
behind her in the sea and a white wake of gulls
behind her in the air, the little ship *St. Olaf*
plowed her way through the crests of the waves,
toward dim, misty shapes that crouched in the
North.

"Who was St. Olaf?" asked the clergyman's
wife, seeking to interest and distract her husband, as he gazed brooding out to sea.

He shook his head.

"I dunno. At least, I've forgotten."

"We must find out. It's interesting to meet
the new saint names as we go north. In Glas-
gow it was St. Tenoc and St. Mungo—now

[404]

we're, so to speak, in Scandinavia, and we have
St. Olaf—and there's St. Magnus too, I believe,
actually buried in Kirkwall Cathedral."

He did not answer. He was staring at the
wake of gulls that followed them. He said,
"Oh that I had wings like a gull! for then
would I flee away and be at rest."

The little *St. Olaf* beat her way through the
tides and cross-currents of the firth. The misty
shapes on the horizon became clearer. The
great walls of Hoy stood out of the sea, sheer
and stern, towering up toward the low clouds
that hung on its mountain tops. South Ronaldshay appeared on their port side, and then they
were running into the midst of the Norse archi-
pelago, through peaceful, landlocked seas, till
at last the heartbeat of the *St. Olaf's* engines
ceased at Scapa pier.

The clergyman and his wife disembarked,
and were taken with their dog and their shabby
luggage to a farmhouse in the only inland
parish. Here a few trees managed to grow,
sheltered from the great winds that sped west-

ward from Tröndjem, and round the little place
were spread many great pools, on the waters of
which a thousand gulls were swimming like toy
ducks. The clergyman's wife was delighted.
Could there exist a place, she asked, more remote, more utterly different from their old life?
Here was quiet where there had been noise,
solitude where there had been crowds, peace
where there had been strife. Surely in this
gracious spot her husband must cast his burden.

The couple who were in charge of the house
welcomed them courteously, in slow, sedate
speech—very different from the broad Doric
of the Scots.

"We trust you will be very comfortable here.
We will do our best to make you so."

She felt sure they would be happy. Already
it seemed as if all middle age had slipped from
her shoulders. He still was listless and low, but
then he must still be tired after his journey.
He would feel better to-morrow.

But the next morning he still seemed ab-
stracted and cast down. After all, his sickness

had gone even farther than she knew. The years had eaten into him and were gnawing at his soul. He could not really see the happy new world in which he lived. It seemed to him something outside himself, something in a picture, something unreal. All that was real to him was the life of the slums he had left, with the peeling, crumbling houses and the children playing in the streets. Though his wife did not know it, it was there that he really lived, while she took him to the shore and they sat and watched the slow tides run among the rocks and the eider ducks guiding their chicks along the currents; while she took him to the Stones of Stinnes in their gaunt ring, or to the green slopes of Deerness, or to the top of the Ward Hill, whence forty-six islands are to be seen— Ronaldshay, and Copinsay, and Egglesay and Papa Estray and many others lying like emeralds in the green matrix of the sea. All the time he walked with her there his citizenship was in Paddington, among the railway arches where the homeless lie and sometimes die, and the public houses and the brothels and the smoke.

The place she liked best to visit was the Maeshowe, an ancient Pictish burial house, which in later years had been Christianized by the Celtic missionaries. In her quiet way she was sensitive to the influences of the Spiritual Kingdom, and when she was in the Maeshowe or Maiden's House, she felt specially close to the Mother of God, whose name the Celtic teachers had set up instead of the name of Frey.

Her husband did not care for the Maeshowe. He preferred the coasts, and especially a part of the north coast of the island, which terrified her a little. There was first of all a Gloup, or roofless cavern, akin to the Cornish blowhole and Breton *souffleur*, into which the sea rushed, and out of whose mouth, far inland, it cast itself up in spray. Beyond came a narrow bay known as Galtic, in the midst of which stood a great pillar of rock, the top grass-grown, the sides in strata, and giving shelter to an innumerable company of sea birds. On the top were the gulls, now at the beginning of their nesting time; beneath them came the city of the puffins, sitting like little aldermen in white waistcoats at the mouths of their holes; at the bottom dwelt the cormorants, mournful and apart from the others with their continual bustle and chatter. The clergyman loved to sit watching the birds at their business, his sad eyes never moving from them as they swooped and flew and strutted upon the rock.

Once she said to him:

"Oh, my dear! Can't you feel better here, away from the world—away from everything that has tried you? Surely, nothing in London need trouble us now."

But he shook his head.

"I'm far away, I know. But not far enough."

She wondered if he found the island too frequented. Remote and lonely as it was, it had on it two towns and several villages. If he really wished it she was ready to seek even a farther refuge—the lighthouse, perhaps, on Copinsay, which rose to eastward, a green mound battlemented with white, off the cold blue floor of the sea.

But he did not want that.

"No—if you took me away to Copinsay—to Shetland—to Faroe—to Iceland—it would all be no good. While I remain in this world I can never be far enough off. What I suffer has nothing to do with place—it's in myself, in my mind, in my memory. The only thing that could cure me would be if I ceased being a man. If I became like one of these gulls here, then could I really flee away and be at rest."

The clergyman's wife shuddered. Her husband's words struck a chill into her heart. They seemed to her, somehow, terrible and blasphemous, as of a man denying his heritage.

"Don't speak like that, my dear," she begged him; "you have an immortal soul and the gulls have not."

He laughed wildly.

"And if I have, what use is it to me except to make my sufferings more dreadful? The brutes don't suffer as we do—the birds, the animals, their lives are sorrowless compared with ours. We pay dearly for our immortal souls. I would willingly part with mine if I could live a life like those birds yonder on the rock—free from care and anxiety and memory. I would willingly——"

"Hush! Hush!" she cried, interrupting him. "You mustn't speak like that. You aren't yourself, dear one, or you wouldn't. Come home with me, and rest. It's getting late."

She longed to have him home so that he could read his Office, for then she knew he would find peace for a while.

III

SO THE days passed till the time of the summer solstice, and still the clergyman was no better. Then on the second day of the solstice, the day that is called St. John the Baptist's day, or midsummer, a terrible thing happened. He had gone out alone with Swaddy, the spaniel dog, as his wife had a headache, and having been out all the morning, felt unequal to another long tramp in the afternoon. She had never let him go out alone before, but he had seemed better these last days, with a happier air in his abstraction. Besides, the dog was always regarded as a companion by them both—no walk was solitary that he accompanied. It seemed to them as if his heart and mind must at least sometimes touch the edge of humanity, so really did he seem to love them and understand them.

At tea time he had not come back, and she

began to feel anxious. An hour passed, and she was really afraid. He had promised to be home early. She reproached herself bitterly for having let him go alone, and, though her head still ached, she started out in search of him. Intuition led her to Galtic, and there she found him, lying unconscious on the sheep-bitten turf between the Gloup and the bay, the dog crouching beside him and whining pitifully from time to time.

At first she thought he must have had an accident, but there was nothing which could have caused it, and, besides, he was unbruised and apparently unhurt. He must be in a swoon or trance, and as she gazed at him her fear deepened. His illness had taken a new turn—he had definitely passed beyond knowledge of the world that had used him so hardly, and in doing so had passed beyond knowledge of her presence and her love.

She rubbed his cold hands, and called his name, bidding him come back to her, telling him that she was here, that she loved him and would never leave him. After a time she was rewarded by a faint response. The color came back into his face and his eyes opened, but they stared at her unrecognizingly and he did not speak. She slipped her arm under his shoulders and raised him up, but still he did not seem to see her and his lips were dumb.

But she was able to make him rise to his feet and to lead him home, the little dog running sorrowfully behind them. When they reached Mist House, she sent one of the farm men into Kirkwall for the doctor, while she brought her husband into the sitting room and made him sit down by the hearth, where a small peat fire burned even in midsummer. Then she put his Office Book into his hands, prayed, trembled, and waited.

At first she thought he would not see it— that he was as far from his priesthood as from his daily life. For a moment or two he stared blindly, and the book nearly fell from his hands. But evidently the summit of his soul was still unclouded. After some preliminary listless-ness, followed by one or two tortured posturings of his body, he made the sign of the Cross and raised the book. She saw his lips move, and a sob of thankfulness broke from her. His mind was not entirely gone, and, though beyond her reach, could still be touched by the Grace of God. Cut off from the ordinary business of mankind, he was yet able to maintain his part in the Great Work. She knelt at his feet and watched his lips repeat the opening verses of the One Hundred and Nineteenth Psalm, as appointed for the twenty-fifth evening of the month.

"Blessed are those that are undefiled in the WAY: and walk in the LAW of the Lord."

The great psalm of Order and of Law was upon his lips, and she knew that the great power of Order and of Law had not forsaken him in his trouble, but that the Law and Commandments and Testimonies and Word and Statutes and Judgments of the Ruler of all would preserve him in the Way.

Trembling, she waited for him to finish,

[415]

hoping that, his Office said, he might come back to her as he had often come back from slighter wanderings; but this time there was no return. He sat on, holding the book, then let it slide from his fingers to the floor. Her comfort must lie not in that the prayer of his tortured soul was answered, but that it still had power to pray.

When the doctor arrived he was much as he had been when first she found him at Galtic. It was impossible to rouse him out of his abstraction. His eyes were open; he was able to walk without stumbling; he was able, they found, to eat; but he did not know anyone, he seemed unaware of his surroundings. The Kirkwall doctor, without experience of such ways, accustomed to the concrete and comparatively simple ills of fishermen and crofters, looked perplexed. He did not know what to advise. They must wait for any change that might take place.

IV

WHILE they waited for a change and his body sat in his chair by the hearth, the clergyman's soul shrank trembling into a cranny of the great rock of Galtic. The sea pounded against the rock with an incessant roar, but the noise of it was not so great in his ears as the smell of it was great in his nostrils. The whole world seemed a world of smell—of salt smells and fishy smells and strong strange living smells that he could not identify. They filled him with a peculiar horror and weariness, as if they attacked him, and he fought desperately to repel them, knowing that when his world passed from a world of sight and sound to a world of smell, something precious, something vital, would be lost. Already sight as well as sound was growing dim. His eyes seemed as good as ever, but everything was vague and unrelated to everything else. The picture before his eyes had no relation or meaning—it was a mere pattern, or rather a scrap heap of disconnected objects. He saw the sea, the sky, the rocks, the wheeling sea birds, but the meaning that they once had had was lost. He nearly screamed aloud in a new agony.

He could still remember how he had come there—how he had been walking on the cliff top, gazing out to sea, and repeating to himself the words that had sung in his head ever since he had come to Orkney.

"Oh that I had wings like a gull! for then would I flee away and be at rest."

He had envied the gulls their freedom, their remoteness from human life and care. He had felt that he would willingly sacrifice his prerogatives as a man—his priesthood and his immortal soul—in order to flee away and be as one of them.

Then suddenly he had found himself in their midst—out on the great rock in the bay of Galtic, looking back as on a picture of himself standing with his dog upon the coast. There had been an awful moment when his spirit had struggled, when two kingdoms had fought for him, and it had seemed as if he would be torn to pieces. But at last the strife had ended and he had fallen exhausted upon the turf that crowned the rock, while at the same time his body fell limply upon the turf at the top of the cliff.

He had done it. He had escaped. He had forsaken the Kingdom of Men, with its sufferings and its cares and its love and its service and its lien upon the Kingdom of God, and had entered the Kingdom of Animals, with its instincts and its fears and its behaviors and its blind unity within itself. At first he was like a man trying to breathe in water—he felt as if he must suffocate. It was a physical feeling. Though he had left his body on the shore, his feelings were, so to speak, more acutely physical than any he had experienced in his flesh. The whole of life seemed to have taken a heavier turn, to have become more concrete, more desperately a matter of sensation. Objects seemed to have lost something of themselves. The gulls were different. They had ceased to be lovely wheeling shapes of whiteness and freedom, but had become mere masses of feathers, flesh, and bone, making certain movements in the air. He was terrified. Something was broken—and suddenly he knew it was the Law.

He had broken the Law of his own being, the Law by virtue of which he lived and loved and suffered as a man. In order to escape from mental pain he had tried to escape from Mind and all that it is and means in the eternal Plan. He had separated himself from his fellows— he had separated himself from God. He had entered a strange land, which was not his, whose language he did not know, and with whose people he could never speak as brethren. He could not, as he had vainly imagined, flee away and be at rest, for the spirit of fear which had driven him was now closer than it had ever been before. Hitherto the laws of the universe and of his own being had protected him. But now the Law was broken. He was lost.

He looked round him wildly for help. But there was none to be found in images—in anything that he saw. The world was meaningless —a mere cloud of alien beings, none of which cared for him or for the other, but went its own way, obedient to the laws of the lower kingdom. In this world there were no souls, only the undefined group-soul of the Animal Kingdom which he saw brooding over it all, waiting to devour him, too. At present he stood outside it, but in time, if he continued here, it would absorb him and hold him as it held the rest. Cringing and weeping, he cowered upon the rock, fearing no longer his old fears, but held by the new fear of the bottomless abyss—the abyss of chaos and formless matter. . . .

Then suddenly he heard a voice speak:

"Blessed are those that are undefiled in the WAY: and walk in the LAW of the Lord.

"Blessed are they that keep his TESTIMONIES: and seek him with their whole heart."

[421]

He listened awestruck, looking round for a speaker. But none was to be seen. The voice continued, and as it spoke the broken mirror of life seemed to mend and once more reflect true Images—the scattered pieces of the world seemed to combine once more into a pattern, the broken music formed a rhythm.

"I will thank thee with an unfeigned heart: when I shall have learned the JUDGEMENTS of thy righteousness.

"I will keep thy CEREMONIES: O forsake me not utterly."

The voice, with its pause at the colon, seemed to be bringing the order of a great rhythm into his world. It rose and fell like the beating of a great heart. Indeed, in time it seemed less like a voice than a continual heartbeat, the pulse of a wonderful life.

"I am a stranger upon earth: O hide not thy COMMANDMENTS from me.

"My soul breaketh out for the very fervent desire: that it hath alway unto thy JUDGE-MENTS."

Then suddenly he realized the voice was his own, repeating the Divine Office as he had repeated it morning and evening for over twelve years. Once more his life was linked with the life of men and the life of God in the Great Work, in the beating of the great heart of prayer. The voice seemed to come from very far away, but it brought with it the comfort and strength of the unity and the law that he had broken.

"Take me from the way of lying: and cause thou me to make much of thy LAW. . . .

"I will run in the way of thy COMMANDMENTS: when thou hast set my heart at liberty."

V

WHEN night came the clergyman's wife could endure no more. All through these hours her husband had not moved or spoken, but had sat as one inconceivably remote, gazing blindly into an even greater remoteness. She felt that she must move and act, or his soul would be lost and he would never come back to her. This was no doctor's matter. What she wanted was a priest. But here in the land of Calvin was no priest, for it happened that the priest of St. Olaf's church in Kirkwall was ill, and the church was not served except on Sundays, when a priest came over from Thurso to say Mass. To-day was Wednesday, and she could not wait.

Deprived of earthly assistance, she must go straight for help to an invisible world. Linking herself to her husband by prayer, she put on a

[424]

wrap and went out into the cold, northern night. Cold, but not dark; for in those regions there is no darkness in summertime, and this midsummer night was light and clear as day.

She walked quickly on the road that winds under the slopes of the Ward, or Watch, Hill, till at last she came to the place she loved, the Maeshowe. It was fenced about, and the gate locked, but she was able to climb over and creep down the long tunneled entrance into the heart of the ancient place. There was darkness here, but no terror for her as she knelt down to pray. Here, she felt, help would come.

She prayed to the Creator of the World, the Maker of the Law, and the Father of Men; she prayed to the Saviour of the World, the Fulfiller of the Law, and the Redeemer of men; she prayed to the Spirit of the World, the Mediator of the Law, and the Comforter of Men. Next she called upon the great army of the Intercessors and begged them to join with her in moving the gates of prayer. Last of all she called upon the Scottish Saints—Andrew,

Evangelist, and Patron of the country, then Colomba and Aidan, Saints of the Culdee, who had first brought the Gospel to the North; then Tenoc and Mungo, whose city she had passed through on her way; then Margaret the Queen, who was also wife and mother; and in the end the two saints of Scandinavia who had lived and worked in these islands, Olaf the Bishop and Magnus the Earl.

Her prayer was ended, and she sank back on her heels, exhausted with the agony of it. At the same time a ray of sunlight shone directly into the Maeshowe. It had been so built as to receive the first ray of the rising sun every day during the summer solstice—it was part of a homely, sweet ritual of generation by which the men of old had sought to show the summer sun fertilizing the earth. This morning in that ray the clergyman's wife saw standing a goodly company—men and women, and one little child.

"Who are you?" she asked, happily and faintly. "Who are you—friends?"

A sweet voice answered:

"You do well to call us friends. We are the Scottish saints whom you have summoned to your aid."

A queen stood just inside the hall of the Maeshowe, wearing over her shoulders a woven mantle in shades of flame and gold.

"I am Margaret the Queen—whose name is in these islands. I have a township on South Ronaldshay. With me here is Tenoc, a mother like myself, and this is her little son. She died at his birth, and he was brought up by the sea gulls, so it is little Mungo who can best help you now."

"How is that, Lady Margaret?"

"Because he alone among the saints can speak their language, and he alone among human beings has ever known from them any love or kindness. He may be able to release your husband from their power."

"But, how is my husband in the power of the gulls?"

"You do not know it, but your husband is lost in the Animal Kingdom, which he entered

[427]

of his desire, thinking to escape from his sufferings as a man. He dwells at present with the gulls on the rock in the bay of Galtic. That is why his soul is far from you and his eyes gaze blindly. This evil is not unknown, when a man deliberately flies from experience and seeks rest in a dimmer life."

"Lady, my husband's mind was sick. It had broken down under a long strain of work for God. He cannot be said freely to have forsaken the world of men."

"No, and there his hope lies. It was his desire only that failed. His will was but indifferently in the matter, for the desire and the will are not the same. His will escaped and dwells in the summits with his priesthood. But he has placed himself in danger of the animal soul."

"Surely it has no power over the Image of God."

"Not of itself. But by your husband's turning down to beasts instead of up to God for his escape, the Law has been broken. He has reversed the process of life, which is to ascend.

He is now an outlaw. The universe cannot befriend him. That is why he stands in danger of the animal soul."

"Then for the sake of the Maker of the Law, help me, Queen."

"This child shall help you, and these two saints to whom the island belongs. Olaf and Magnus and Mungo shall work together for you. Though we dwell in a world more remote from the Animal Kingdom than the world of men, we have powers therein which men have not. The saints grow in knowledge as well as in love, and among other things we have learned to unite ourselves with different conditions and forms of life. We do not this by desire, for it is unthinkable for us to desire to be other than we are—but by the science of mathematics, which is both the purest and most mystical of sciences. I cannot explain the wisdom to you, but we have power to reach your husband, and the memories of this child Mungo—or Kentigern, as he is named in the South—will assist you in reaching the gulls, who once cared for him when his mother, Tenoc, died upon the shore."

As she spoke, Margaret vanished from the ray, and with her Andrew and Aidan and the Culdee missionaries, and Tenoc herself after a fond look at her son. There was left none but the boy Mungo, the Bishop Olaf, and the Earl Magnus, who stood praying in the golden light till with the climbing of the sun it passed from the Maeshowe.

VI

HE WAS back—back in the dreary streets of Paddington. The houses towered high —heeling against the sky like the cliffs of Galtic; their windows and doors were like the holes which the puffins made. The roar of distant traffic around the station had in it the roar and boom of the sea. The children played at the street corners, wheeling, chattering, crying, flapping, like gulls.

He watched them as it were from a great way off, and their game seemed to him meaningless —it was none of the hopskotches or prisoner's bases that he knew. It seemed to him more as if the children were fighting, not actually with blows, but moving to and fro in a perpetual warfare. He saw one swoop to the gutter and pick up some morsel. Immediately the others set upon it, fought and shrieked for the scrap of

[431]

putrefaction, wrested it from its finder, gobbled and scattered it. He sickened to see such un-human behavior—he waited for the robbed child to retaliate, or to run away weeping. But though at first it struggled to recover its own, when the treasure had finally disappeared it seemed to take no further heed. It seemed to experience neither resentment nor indignation. The interrupted game went on, the children once more wheeling, chattering, crying, and flapping, like gulls.

Then suddenly he knew that they were gulls. He was not back in Paddington, in what seemed to him now the dear familiar streets of the Canal and Lisson Grove, but sitting on the great rock of Galtic, watching the sea gulls wheeling, chattering, crying, and flapping over the sea. With his sight of the gulls had mingled in those last few minutes the death-struggle of his human memory.

He sprang up with a cry which seemed to be part of the ceaseless cry of the gulls. He saw now that he had gone even farther from the

Kingdom of Men—that he could not remember them as men, but must see them moving and thinking according to the laws of the Animal Kingdom. Gone were the human funninesses and kindnesses of the London gutter child—in their place was the animal soul seeking its own, blind, indifferent, obeying an urge which was neither good nor evil—pursuing equally a companionship without love and a warfare without hate.

But he knew that there were escapes from this limbo even for the animal soul. Love also dwells in the Animal Kingdom. The gull sits long hours upon its nest, patient, brave, devoted to the hope of its young. The idea of childhood was still with him, and thought seemed to have revived—" the animal parental instinct is the first seed of altruism and the beginning of all love." Then for a moment he seemed to see a child standing upon the rock some little way off. Once more his thought took courage: "the most selfless love among human beings has its origin in the instinct which makes a poor half-starved cat suckle her young. Men lay down their lives for one another as the cat lays down her life to save her kittens from the burning house."

Hope suddenly grew up in him, and he cried: "The child! The child shall save me."

Once more he seemed to be back in his Paddington slum, though it was still under a sea change, with houses like cliffs and alleys like creeks. The mothers sat with their babies in the doorways as the gulls sat upon their nests. There they sat, patient, devoted, selfless, blind. He shuddered in his dream—for human life was a dream to him now. He saw the mothers as he had seen the children, as gulls, and knew that in their hearts was neither hope nor love, merely a blind instinct that they did not understand. Nature, for her own prolific purposes, had ordered them to bear children, and they, powerless to do otherwise, had obeyed her. She had ordered them to care for the children till they were old enough to care for themselves, and they had obeyed her. It is not as mother,

[434]

but as servant, that the gull sits upon the rock, nor does the cat give her life for her kittens in the spirit of love, but in the spirit of bondage.

The glimmer of hope had passed—the hope that he might find love in the Animal Kingdom, and by virtue of it climb back to his humanity. There was no love in the Animal Kingdom, only Law—and he, who had once been under love, was now under the Law, the Law that he had broken. With an anguish that grew as his human memory failed, he realized that he had lost his power to see beasts as men, but must instead see men as beasts. Sinking upon the rock, he felt that the ultimate peril of all must seize him now, and the animal soul devour the last of the humanity he had forsaken.

But then, once again, a sound fell upon the air—a soft heart-beat, a throbbing that pulsed and grew. Once more the severed kingdoms were knit up in one, and lived in the unity of one law, to the beating of one heart.

"My soul hath longed for thy salvation: and I have a good hope because of thy WORD.

"Mine eyes long sore for thy WORD: saying, O when wilt thou comfort me?

"For I am become like a bottle in the smoke: yet do I not forget thy STATUTES.

"How many are the days of thy servant: when wilt thou be avenged of them that persecute me?

"The proud have digged pits for me: which are not after thy LAW.

"All thy COMMANDMENTS are true: they persecute me falsely; O be thou my help.

"They had almost made an end of me upon earth: but I forsook not thy COMMANDMENTS.

"O quicken me after thy loving-kindness: and so shall I keep the TESTIMONIES of thy mouth."

VII

THE second night had fallen in a pale
gleam of strangely lit whiteness, over the
cliffs of Hoy and over the Ward Hill. Once
more the clergyman's wife had come to the
Maeshowe, and knelt waiting for the midsummer ray that would bring the saints into her
company. Her heart was heavy with a hope
that was nearly dead. Away at Mist House her
husband still sat motionless, staring into a darkness she could not see. The hope that the child
Mungo, who had been brought up by the gulls,
and knew their thoughts, could reach his ban-
ished soul, was now extinct. Indeed, her husband seemed farther away this night than he
had seemed in the morning. For over an hour
she had waited and prayed before he had been
able to read his Office; and at times it had
seemed as if his memory was beginning to fail

him in the work and he stumbled in the ways of his priesthood. If memory failed him altogether and his soul slipped at last from prayer. . .

She moaned at the thought, and from the darkness beside her came an answering moan. She started, and then the next minute realized that Swaddy, the spaniel dog, was with her. He must have followed her from Mist House without her seeing him, and now lay crouched beside her in the dim chamber of the Maeshowe.

"Swaddy!" she cried, caressing his silken head, "I believe you know how we suffer. I believe you would help us if you could."

There was enough light for her to see his eyes liquid and mournful with love. His whole body quivered as if racked with the struggle for speech.

"Oh, little dog, I can't believe that you have any share in my dear one's agony. It is not the laws of your sweet soul that bind him—you seem to belong to us and to our kingdom."

[438]

She held him close to her, and suddenly the ray came, dazzling them both.

In the entrance to the Maeshowe, gleaming with the sun's gold, stood Olaf the Bishop and Magnus the Earl—rather taller than men, but otherwise as in the days of their pilgrimage, with mild, broad, Scandinavian faces, Olaf wearing his miter, and Magnus bearing the bloodless scar of his wounding.

"Oh, Saints, you have come!"

"We have come, friend and daughter. We are here to share your grief. You know without our telling that the child Mungo failed to reach this soul you love. He was too fast in prison for human thought to touch him. The child strove with his childhood, linking it with the love of the animals for their young, but the poor prisoner could not look up—he could only look down, and instead of being lifted up with the parental sacrifices which the beasts make daily before God, he dragged down the love of human parenthood to the level of the beasts."

[439]

"Then is it quite impossible to reach him? Is all hope gone?"

Magnus and Olaf looked down at her sadly and tenderly as she sat with the dog held close in her arms.

"It is very nearly impossible," said Magnus, and Olaf's words followed him swiftly:

"There is scarcely any hope."

"But there is some—there is still a chance of saving him? Oh, tell me. I will do anything, face anything. . . ."

"It is not you who have to do anything or to face anything."

"Who is it, then?"

"Your friend."

She glanced at the spaniel's brown muzzle, lying against her sleeve.

"He—the dog?"

"Yes. Only the dog can save you now."

She held him more closely as she looked up.

"Explain to me. I don't understand."

The spaniel whimpered, and once again she felt that emotion of struggling speech.

"There is one hope left to us," said Olaf, "and it is this. Your husband has gone too far into the Animal Kingdom to be helped from without, but he can be helped from within. The process of evolution consists in the eyes of the lower kingdoms being lifted up toward the higher, as the eyes of a maiden toward the hand of her mistress. Without humanity the Animal Kingdom is without purpose or meaning, a mere blind mass of instincts. In the beginning mankind was appointed as mediator between the Animal and Spiritual kingdoms. God brought all beasts to Adam that he might name them, and thus through him they might obtain their place in the world order. Man, as we know, failed God's high purpose, and the unity of creation was broken. Humanity as a whole has betrayed the Animal Kingdom; but separate men have been able to save and help separate beasts, such as your dog, who has received from you a special grace, and through you has learned the meaning of love, which he could not have known without you. The blind loyalty that in a natural state he would have given to the herd, has by your training and companionship been transformed into love. Your dog loves you. He loves you in the human sense of the word— he shares one of your human qualities. He stands in relation to the other animals as the saints stand in relation to the rest of humanity. By virtue of association with one higher than himself he has acquired that which by his own nature he could never have had. Yet he remains an animal, and part of the animal soul. Therefore—and this is the end of my words—he may be able to reach your husband in the Animal Kingdom and return to him the gift of human love which he has received from him. By means of this he may be able to lift up his eyes once more and escape, but I cannot allow you more than a faint hope, for the matter is uncertain, depending on many things—on the degree of your husband's loss, and on the degree to which the dog has risen in love. Say now, beast to whom man has given such grace, is your gift

[442]

great enough for you to be able to give it back, without hope of reparation or reward?"

He looked down into the spaniel's eyes, and Magnus looked, too, and their lips moved, and their hands, uttering numbers and forming measures. In the pure science and wisdom their soul met the dog's, and she knew that they spoke together, in quantities and combinations. The silence made her afraid, but suddenly it ceased as a noise ceases, and Olaf and Magnus spoke once more with human lips.

"The dog will venture. He will give himself in the hope of saving your husband's soul."

She clasped the spaniel to her more closely, and kissed his brown silk nose. She seemed to feel the power of this love that she herself had given him, burning in his heart like a flame.

"Oh, Saints—surely he will succeed? It cannot be possible that his good deed should fail."

"It is possible. We can give you hope, but not a promise. Take him—go back to your house, and wait there till your husband has read his morning Office. Then take him by the hand,

[443]

and carrying his Office Book with you, follow the dog to Galtic, down the cliff path to the shore of the sea. We do not know what will happen to you there, but meanwhile our prayers and works shall assist the divine mercy, and when evening comes, and the sunset makes us a path from Copinsay, we will be with you again."

VIII

THE world was dead. Its unsouled body lay round him like a corpse. The rocks of Galtic, the sea, the clouds, the gulls were mere forms of putrefaction. Death . . . the body unsouled . . . decaying . . . this was the world to him now—time ended, memory gone, hope and love departed. He was the body in the tomb, lying there helpless to await the final rot. Death!—It was not death, but hell! This was indeed "the place where all things are forgotten." This active, crushing death, which seemed to weigh down upon him and upon the world like lead, was not the gentle, natural death of the tomb, soothing the body's sleep while the soul keeps vigil in still sharper life, but the foul, unnatural death of the spirit, the corruption of the worm which never dies.

His consciousness was shriveled to a single

point. The three powers of the soul—memory, will, and understanding—were gone, just as the five senses of the body were gone. His loneliness was terrible—neither body nor spirit seemed to be with him now, neither animal, man, nor angel. All that was left seemed to be a consuming awareness of his plight—the knowledge that he was dead, that he was in hell, that he was alone—cut off. He had forgotten, and was forgotten.

Then suddenly he became aware of a memory, as of something outside himself, something not his own. It took symbolic form, the form of a little mouse, running to and fro over his body and gnawing at the cords that bound it. Then it became actual, and he remembered himself sitting in front of a sweet-scented peat fire, at the feet of somebody he loved. Who could it have been whom he had loved so, at whose feet he had sat, toward whom his eyes had looked as the eyes of a maiden toward the hand of her mistress?

Then, with a sudden expansion of his dwindling consciousness, he realized that it was the beloved and not the lover who was himself. It was he who had been loved so much. This memory was not his own, but another's. He had not ceased to forget, but some one had not forgotten him.

Another change came. He felt this outside memory linking with his own. Once again the process took symbolic form, and he saw a man breathing on a dead butterfly, which lay with spread drooping wings on the palm of his hand. After a while the beautiful thing stirred, then its wings began to flutter, and as the man breathed on, it spread them in all their glowing colors, and raised itself on them, and flew away . . . Psyche set free, and flying toward the sun on the many-colored wings of memory. The first power of his soul had revived.

His whole being was astir with memories, they came upon him from every side in fluttering iridescence. He realized vaguely that some of them were not his own—queer memories of hunting and following, memories of guardianship and of dependence, of fond, trustful love for some being greater than he. They mixed with memories of his own past life, his childhood, his adolescence, his priesting, his labor, his home, and his wife—at first without sequence or order, then slowly arranging themselves in orderly design.

At the same time he was conscious of a definitely physical sensation. He was becoming aware of his surroundings, though not, he knew, as he was normally aware of them. After a time he recognized his awareness as being through the sense of smell. He smelled the salt air and the salt sea, and the turf on the summit of the rock of Galtic, and the rank smell of the gulls' plumage—all very much as he had smelled them when he first came into the Animal Kingdom, but this time without any shrinkings of horror or forebodings of doom. For the sense of smell seemed to be linked on to other and higher sensual capacities, to be in a line of ascent. . . .

Then suddenly he understood. He was on his

way back—back to the Kingdom of Men, back
to the thoughts and ways of those whose citizenship is in heaven, with whom God walks in the
cool of the evening, when the long day's labor
is done and the supper is laid. He was about
to escape from the Animal Kingdom—by some
unseen way deliverance was coming. The second power of his soul had revived.

He wondered what had happened, by what
process he had been reached. Then he knew—
his dog had come to him. It was his dog's
memories, full of himself and of his love, which
had revived his own. Swaddy must be with
him now—he thought he could distinguish his
smell among the many that rushed in and out
of his nostrils.

The next moment he saw him. The sense of
sight returned, and he seemed to see the spaniel
standing on a rock a great way off, where long
ago he had thought he saw a child. The vision
of the dog did not remain, and he guessed that
this was not Swaddy in the flesh, but at the same
time he noticed a reviving of his sense of touch.

[449]

He was conscious of the gentle sharpness of the air, of the softness of the turf, and the hardness of the rock on which he lay. Then for a moment he seemed to feel the spaniel's silken coat under his fingers. Veils were being lifted off the world. The roar of the sea broke in upon his delivered senses, and once more he heard the cry of the gulls, though this time without his first recoils of fear and degradation.

He felt himself trembling. He was not free yet. He was still upon the rock of Galtic, still in the Animal Kingdom—merely smelling, seeing, feeling, his way out. Something lacked yet for his deliverance, something which he carried in his own heart, but which was too foul to use. The dog had been able to re-attach him to his own lost manhood before it had decayed, but in his heart still lay his soiled and misused will.

After all, was he worthy of deliverance? He had gone into the Animal Kingdom, not of compulsion, but of desire. He had sought a refuge there from the ways of the Kingdom of Men, deliberately turning his back on his own priesthood and on the ways of God. Had he any right to go back to what he had spurned? He felt that he had no right. Only mercy could befriend him; of justice he was condemned to remain in the exile he had chosen—and he had no right to mercy.

He became conscious now that the dog's soul was no longer with him. His deliverer had gone, and suddenly he found himself upon his knees, acknowledging that this was right.

"Thy Will be done," he prayed, for the first time speaking to God out of his prison, "not my will, but Thine be done. I have sinned before heaven and before Thee. Thy will be done on earth as it is in heaven."

Then immediately the third power of his soul revived. His will returned to him. Again he saw the process in an image. He saw his will as a dead coal lying in the chill brazier of his heart, and suddenly the Will of God came like a live coal, and touched it, and it kindled, and a mighty flame arose and warmed the whole house. And at the same time the voice which had been for so long silent was lifted once more, and the great cry of Law and Judgment went up to heaven from earth, while the world's heart beat in unity with the Heart of God.

"I call with my whole heart: hear me, O Lord, I will keep thy STATUTES.

"Yea, even unto thee do I call: help me and I shall keep thy TESTIMONIES."

The rhythmic pulse and throb was once more swaying on the air, but this time it seemed louder, and in a strange way universal. Tones began to mingle with it, ascending and descending notes. Then he knew that he was joining with those who throughout the world were performing the Work of God. He was with monks and nuns singing their Office in choir, he was with contemplatives reciting it in their cells, he was with busy priests reading it in trains and omnibuses, as he himself had often read it, he was with humble parish clergymen at evensong in village churches . . . all were together in the unity of that great heart of prayer, all were as one in the performance of the *Opus Dei.*

[452]

Then he knew that he was in union with more than these. These were merely the officers and organizers of the Work. Beyond them was the multitude of those who pray, whether with words or with groanings that cannot be uttered —children kneeling by their beds at night, mothers praying for their sons and sons for their mothers, husbands and wives praying together, beggars praying for those who had taken pity on them, boys and girls praying on the threshold of life, old folk praying on the threshold of death—old men and maidens, young men and children, lovers, workers, sufferers, wayfarers, adventurers, seekers, finders, losers, a great multitude which no man can number, all joined in the great work of prayer throughout the world.

It was as if one veil after another was being lifted, for beyond this great praying multitude was a still greater—souls purifying themselves by prayer in the worlds beyond death—holy souls offering holy prayers, more pure than those which can ever be on mortal lips. And beyond these, triumphant souls, offering triumphant prayers—martyrs, confessors, virgins, patriarchs, prophets, all saints, whose prayers roll as clouds of incense to the foot of the throne where stands the Intercessor. . . .

He felt that he could bear no more. Yet there was more. He could look no higher, but there upon the frontiers of the Animal Kingdom he seemed to hear voices behind him, the voices of those whom the Three Holy Children heard praise the Lord when they walked in the Furnace of Fire. *Benedicite Omnia Opera*. Winter and summer, ice and snow, heat and cold, stars of heaven, beasts and cattle, birds of the air, fishes of the sea, water, trees, green things upon the earth, all had their share in the Work of God, all groaned and travailed together in prayer for the redemption of the earth.

He was standing upright now upon the rock, giddy with it all, deaf with the million voices which were as one. Then suddenly he seemed to hear one voice above the rest, detaching itself from the others, becoming individual and separate. It was his own voice, the voice that he had throughout these three terrible days heard reciting the Divine Office as if a great way off. Now at last it was close to him, a part of himself. With a triumphing effort he united himself with it again. The last of his senses had returned—the power of speech.

"Seven times a day do I praise thee: because of thy righteous JUDGEMENTS.

"Lord, I have looked for thy saving health: and done after thy COMMANDMENTS."

The world around him seemed to disappear, the skies to heel over, the rocks to melt. He was no longer on the rock of Galtic, but he did not know where he was. The voices were dying away, they were no more than a distant accompaniment to his own liberated voice:

"My lips shall speak of thy praise: when thou hast taught me thy STATUTES.

"Yea, my tongue shall sing of thy WORD: for all thy COMMANDMENTS are righteous.

[455]

"Let thy hand help me: for I have chosen thy COMMANDMENTS.

"I have longed for thy saving health, O Lord: and in thy LAW is my delight."

The voices had died away now. He could hear none but his own.

"O let my soul live, and it shall praise thee: and thy JUDGEMENTS shall help me."

A great sigh, the sigh of the sea, rose and mingled with the last words of the psalm.

"I have gone astray like a sheep that is lost: O seek thy servant, for I do not forget thy COMMANDMENTS."

He was standing on the shore of the sea, in the bay, looking out toward the rock of Galtic. By his side stood his wife, clasping his hand to her breast; at his feet lay the spaniel, dead.

IX

AT FIRST he could only gaze—from his wife to the dog, from the dog to the changed vision of the sea. He felt bewildered and shaken, like a man waking out of a dream. The eternity of the past three days seemed to shrink and recede—it now appeared no longer than the recitation of the One Hundred and Nineteenth Psalm.

His wife spoke to him, but he did not understand, and scarcely heard her. Then suddenly he became aware of others besides themselves. The last of the sunset lay upon the sea, streaming across it in a red glory, and on the crimson path of the dipping ray stood two huge dim figures, one vested as a bishop in cope and miter, one clad in a primitive armor of steel and sheepskin, with a strange glowing wound in his forehead.

"Oh, blessed Saints!" cried his wife. "Look, dear one, and give thanks. These are your deliverers."

"Nay," said Olaf and Magnus, speaking as one, "say rather these are your intercessors. Your deliverer—he who put the divine mercy into deed—lies at your feet."

The clergyman looked down at the spaniel, who lay motionless in death, silken and scarcely cold, but still as only the dead know stillness.

"I remember now that I saw him on the rock. But is it really true that he saved me?"

"Yes, it was he who brought to your starving soul the food of human love and human memory."

"And died in the deed?"

"He died of your repentance. When your soul turned to God, and saw its sin, his animal soul could not endure. Remember that his soul was naked with yours. Neither of you had dust to veil you from each other. The animal soul knows love and sorrow, but it does not—cannot —know repentance, which is a supernatural

[458]

grace. When your soul turned to God in peni-
tence the dog's soul was flung naked into the
Supernatural, and died as a man dies of a stroke
of lightning."

"He gave his life for me."

"As many a dog has done for man by virtue
of the grace that man has given him."

The clergyman bowed his head.

"I am amazed—I cannot understand. All
this that has happened to me has been like a
dreadful dream. I have been in hell. To
live with the beasts is hell. How is it that a
beast came to me like an angel of light?"

The two saints looked on him sternly.

"You are wrong," they cried. "To live with
the beasts as a beast is not hell—it is to live with
them as a man which is hell indeed. For a man
to turn back from the WAY and seek refuge in
paths beneath is to break the LAW and to defy
the COMMANDMENT, and undoubtedly on such a
soul JUDGMENT shall fall. The Animal Kingdom is good, and has been a part of the Kingdom of God from the days when Noah gave the

[459]

animals their places in the Ark. But you entered the Animal Kingdom as renegade and apostate man. You were even as the children of Israel who said: 'We will be as the heathen,' and to whom the word of the Lord came thus: 'Say not, we will be as the heathen, for I say unto you *Ye cannot be as the heathen.*' You, to whom it is given to see the dust in terms of life, and the acorn in terms of the oak, the beasts in terms of mankind, chose instead to see mankind as the beasts, the oak as acorn and life as dust. You violated the Law of Ascent, by virtue of which a man may never turn back even to goodness past. The beasts are good, their instincts are good, their ways are good and pleasing to God; but for a man to go back and live according to their instincts and their ways is for that man sin and hell. You would have been in hell without hope of escape, but for the prayers of the living and the dead, and the sacrifice of this animal soul which laid down its life for your help."

[460]

The clergyman looked down at the dead dog at his feet.

"But surely his soul lives!" he cried. "Surely, having done this, he did not die as a dog dies."

"There is no other way for a dog to die. Even the grace that comes to a beast from man is not enough to remake his soul in the image of God, by virtue of which alone it is immortal spirit. Your dog's soul is not a separate soul like yours, but a part of the animal soul, to which after death it returns. For a short while it may live on in the ultra violet rays, but it is bound soon to disintegrate and return to the group soul from which it came."

"But his goodness—his self-sacrifice . . . I cannot believe that they are lost."

"No good thing is ever lost," said Magnus the Earl; "the dog's good deed is gathered into the world's treasury. His love and sacrifice are added to the sum of the earth's ransom. Their value brings creation so much nearer the new heavens and the new earth. For do not think that the Animal Kingdom has no share in the glory that shall be, even though separate members of it cannot claim their portion and the hope is not for the individual but for the race. In the great day when God shall make all things new, earth too shall be decked with light and beauty, earth too shall be saved from the Adversary's hand and shall forget the days of her exile and her thrall. When Adam fell, he sinned not only against heaven, but against earth; earth lost her mediator, and it was not till mankind was redeemed through the Incarnation of the Son of God that earth could hope again. O let the earth bless the Lord! Yea, let it praise him and magnify him for ever."

"And you, O man," cried Olaf the Bishop, terribly, "never dare to forget what you have learned in these three days of the sun's standing still. Never again dare to think of the oak in terms of the acorn, nor of the universe in terms of dust. Look not back to nature, to the fount of your human joys and sorrows, but forward to supernature which is their end. Let nature look forward through your eyes to supernature which is also, through you, her end. *Benedicite Omnia Opera!*"

Then the two saints moved off together down the dying sun's last ray, singing—"All ye works of the Lord, bless ye the Lord, praise him and magnify him for ever." Their voices echoed for some time across the sea, then were lost in the sighing of the night wind that had sprung up.

That night the clergyman dreamed about his dead dog. He dreamed that he saw him in some strange, happy place, where woods were massed dark against a sky full of big stars, and where the air was full of shifting, fugitive smells, dear to the heart of a hunter. He saw his dog run up tired and happy with the chase, his mouth grinning, his tongue hanging. Then he saw him lay himself down and curl himself up for sleep, pleasantly weary. He laid himself down happily and slept, and as he slept he was gone—his soul returned to the animal soul,

[463]

which now no longer showed strange and terrible, but as a mother receiving back her child.

The next morning the clergyman told his wife his dream, and they turned together to the business of restoring his body and mind, so that when his time of rest was over he could go back hopefully to his work for God. This happened in due course, and his diocesan superiors as well as his poor folk remarked how much good his holiday had done him. They noticed, however, one or two things that seemed changed about him—he had acquired a special devotion to the saints of Scotland, especially to two Norsemen whom no one had heard of in the South; and he never said the One Hundred and Nineteenth Psalm except on his knees.